HIDDEN HERO

BOOK THREE OF THE ANCIENT COURT TRILOGY

AMY PATRICK

OXFORD SOUTH PRESS

Oxford South Press/November 2017

Cover design by Cover Your Dreams

For all my incredible readers - the Hidden world lives because of you

CONTENTS

WES

Immunity.

According to my online dictionary, the word had several meanings. It could refer to exemption from criminal prosecution or liability. It might reference a condition that permits resistance to disease. One of the definitions of the word was "special privilege."

I certainly didn't have many of those in my life.

At least I eat well. Turning off the blue flame underneath it, I slid the heavy iron skillet off to one side and reached for a dinner plate. Saliva spiked in my mouth as I spooned the fragrant chicken and vegetable mixture onto the rice already on my plate, and my stomach let out a hearty growl of anticipation.

A pile of sugar cubes to one side of the dish completed the culinary tableau. It looked good. Too bad I was the only one who'd see it.

I let out a heavy sigh as a hollow ache unrelated to hunger permeated my body. Lifting the plate with one hand, I grabbed a full mug off the counter with the other and headed for the back door.

I had precious few pleasures in this life, but I *did* have plenty of food and ale here in my "fortress of solitude." Weekly deliveries from the village market kept me stocked up on fresh ingredients, and one of my chief entertainments was trying to surprise myself with different flavors and new combinations to satisfy my appetite.

Of course a guy had *other* appetites, but as I lived alone at the edge of an island whose population totaled less than a hundred people, there was no point in thinking about *that.* Using my elbow to depress the handle, I nudged the door open with one hip.

Whoa. The wind is brisk tonight. Storm coming, I think.

I used the bottom of my boot to close the door behind me before beginning my trek downhill to the barn. Reaching it, I looked back up the hill to An Sgurr—or The Notch—a four hundred meter tall sheer rock mountain that rose from the center of the island and overshadowed my house and property.

Sure enough, dark clouds boiled over the top of it. I'd have to keep my dinner "date" on the short side tonight.

Stepping inside the old wood and stone stable, I set my plate on the flat top of a tall wood barrel to one side of the doorway and reached for the gas lantern hanging from the rafter above it. Within seconds, warm, golden light filled the cozy space. Four sets of equine eyes stared back at me when I turned around.

"Hello all. What are the chances you have a table for one available this evening?"

The horses offered their usual greeting, nodding their long snouts and nickering softly, anticipating their favorite treat.

"Hold on now, let me get settled."

Moving my dinner plate to the small, rickety round table in the corner next to my chair, I took a long draught from the mug before placing it beside the plate. A few stomps joined the chorus of whickers behind me, and a grin crossed my face.

"All right, all right. I know what *you* want. I'm not sure whether you lot are horses... or hogs."

I plucked a sugar cube from my plate and approached the closest stall, holding it out in the flat of my hand to Scarlett, a roan mare who looked a bit rough around the edges but acted more like a lapdog than a horse.

She nibbled the treat, her velvety lips grazing my hand as I lowered my forehead to the white patch between her huge brown eyes. "Tell the truth... you only love me because I'm your sugar supplier, don't you?"

Lifting my hands to her neck, I patted and rubbed then moved down to the next stall.

"Hello Atticus, old boy. Aren't you a patient one?" I offered him a sugar lump, laughing when the highland pony contradicted the praise I'd just given him by snatching it instantly from my hand.

I moved down the row of stalls, greeting and treating each of the horses in similar fashion. "Hello Owain. Hello Clovis."

Last—but far too large and intimidating to ever be least—was Sebastian. He stood, tall and silent in the fifth stall, choosing to remain at the back in his enclosure like a dark shadow instead of hanging his nose out of the opening like the other horses.

"Okay, my friend. You win. I'll come to you."

I stretched my arm toward the enormous, black thoroughbred. At three years old, he was far younger than the other horses and the only one with anything resembling good bloodlines. He lifted his head and turned it to one side, eying me with a baleful glare, as if I offered him a bit of bitter ragwort instead of an enticing sugar lump.

I laughed. "Are we to go through this every time, then? It's a good thing you're a challenging ride—you cost twice as much to feed as any of the others, and you've got the personality of a bee-stung boar."

The wary beast edged forward, his eyes staying on me rather than on the treat. Finally reaching me, he plucked it from my outstretched hand without even making contact with my skin then back-stepped into the dark corner again. The spark of hope that had bloomed in my chest fizzled out.

"Fine," I said casually. "Suit yourself. The others and I are going to enjoy a romantic dinner and some good conversation. Join in when you're ready."

Chuckling to myself, I settled into my chair and pulled the plate onto my lap.

After a few bites, I said, "You won't believe what I found today. There's a cluster of DNA fingerprints from a remote village in the Peruvian Andes that closely resembles the Black Death of the fourteenth century. Can you imagine? The ECDC is completely baffled. I've had more emails and phone calls today than I've had in the past two years. I'm supposed to speak with someone from the American Centers for Disease Control in Atlanta in a few hours when they get into the office."

The horses stared at me, jaws working steadily, offering no comment on my daily job report—as usual. Their appetites awakened by the sugar, they had each started nosing into their hay buckets, and their rhythmic chewing was the only sound other than the wind outside the stable.

"Well, maybe *you* disagree, but I find life as a microbiologist is never boring. There's always an outbreak somewhere. If there wasn't, I'd be out of a job—and *you'd* be out of oats and hay."

Thanks to my medical condition, I no longer worked in a lab as I had throughout university. Not only was it hazardous for me to be around specimens of infectious disease, my immunodeficiency prevented me from working *anywhere* in close proximity to other people.

But my current job as a data analyst for the European Centers for Disease Control allowed me to continue using my expertise in the fields of epidemic intelligence and public health, tracking patterns of sickness all over the European Union and even around the globe.

The hours could be long, but I had nothing if not time, and the mental stimulation kept me from going crazy in my forced isolation.

The work was my life. That, and the horses. I finished up the last few bites of my dinner and went to give them each a goodnight pat. "So long, Owain. I'll be back in the morning to let you out for a run. Good night, Scarlett girl."

Clovis, a twenty-five year old Clydesdale plow horse, whinnied at me and nudged my arm with his substantial nose, making it clear he was ready for desert.

"No, no more sugar for now, old fellow. I'll see you in the morning. Then I'll turn you out so I can muck the stalls, and you can have a nice snack of fresh grass."

Not one of the beasts was worth a pence. Quite the opposite, they were all cast-offs, aging rejects from the few other farms on the island, or in Sebastian's case, an expensive but unsuitable mount who was headed for the rendering factory if I hadn't offered to take him in. He was my most recent acquisition.

After my first couple of "adoptions," word had traveled quickly around the isle of Eigg's meager population that there was a sucker—I mean, *horse lover*—now in residence at the old Easterly estate. As it was far cheaper than ferrying the creatures to the mainland or continuing to feed them themselves, the owners of these no-longer-useful animals were more than happy to send them my way for pence on the pound.

"So long everyone," I said to my dinner companions. "Good talk as always. Sleep tight."

As I went to extinguish the gas lantern, a flash of white lit the bit of sky showing through the windows high in the stable walls.

"Fantastic. I'm going to get soaked." I opened the door, bracing myself for what could turn out to be a wet run up the steep hill to the house.

Sure enough, the second I stepped out onto the heather-dotted lawn, the dark sky opened, and cold rain beat down on my head. The wind had turned ferocious, whipping the surf at the base of the sloping backyard into a frenzy and flinging stinging raindrops against my face as I sprinted uphill.

"Next time, bring a mackintosh, genius," I muttered to myself.

Pumping my arms and legs harder, I squinted against the onslaught and kept my gaze trained on the large, warmly-lit windows of my kitchen and study, which occupied the first floor rooms facing the ocean. When I got there, I'd have a nice, thawing glass of brandy and strip off my wet clothes in front of the fireplace before making that call to the States.

The idea of discussing an infectious disease outbreak with a stuffy American colleague while stark naked made me snicker and lifted my spirits a bit. Doing contract work from home *did* have its advantages.

And then I was down, my knees barking hard against the cold, wet ground, just barely getting my hands in front of me in time to save myself from a full on face-plant. The empty plate and mug had been discarded in favor of self-preservation and now lay scattered somewhere on the grass.

Momentarily stunned, I stayed on the ground, looking around. What had I tripped on?

I knew this land like the back of my hand, every rocky outcropping, every stone wall left behind from the ruins of the old sheepherders' village that used to stand here. I had traversed the sloping lawn between the house and stable more times than I could count, and there were no obstacles along this path. Usually.

Something was definitely under my shins and ankles now —something large, like a branch or log, but that was impossible because there were no sizable trees on the oceanfront estate—I had to have my firewood shipped from the mainland to the harbor village of Galmisdale and delivered to a collection box at the end of my driveway.

Pushing back onto my haunches, I squatted and peered through the rain-soaked darkness at the tripping hazard, trying to make out the odd, lumpy shape of it. Then I put my hands out in front of me to investigate. My fingers encountered something soft and plush and then... skin.

I leapt back, landing on the balls of my feet with my arms stretched out in a defensive blocking pose. There was a body on my land. A *body.* Adrenaline exploded through my veins. My heartbeat roared in my ears.

What the hell? Think. Think.

Remembering it had been pliable and not stiff, I edited my earlier assessment—not a body. A person. Apparently an unconscious one, since the body—person—hadn't moved throughout the process of my tripping and falling and then poking at it—him. Was he bleeding, perhaps dying?

Shock morphed into urgent concern, my sprinting pulse slowing a tic and allowing my brain to resume normal functions. I turned back and ran for the stable, wiping my fingers on my wet jeans.

It was just a second—incidental contact, I assured myself. *And*

7

his skin was wet, washed clean by the storm. No need to panic. You can scrub up when you get to the house.

I retrieved the lantern from the stable and hurried back to the dark, outstretched shape. Sinking to my knees, I held the lantern aloft over the unconscious man. And gasped. It wasn't a man.

It was a woman—a beautiful one.

What. The. Bloody. Hell.

Who was she? And what on earth was she doing *here?* No one visited my estate. No one. Ever. The entire island had a population of only eighty-seven people, give or take a few. They all knew my story.

This woman had to be a tourist, a hiker who'd gotten lost somehow on the twelve square mile island—I supposed it could happen if you lost sight of the main road. Which would be hard to do. But *something* had gone wrong, obviously, because here she was.

And she's lying unconscious on the cold earth in a driving rainstorm.

I searched the sky, taking a direct hit in the eyeball from a particularly large raindrop. There hadn't been a second flash of lightning, but it stood to reason another was soon to come. The weather here on the exposed island could be extreme. This bare hillside wasn't a safe place for either of us to stay.

I shook her shoulder, careful to avoid the bare skin of her arm this time. "Hello. Can you hear me, miss? I say, can you move?"

Nothing. No response from her. Not even an eyelid flicker. *She might actually be seriously hurt.* Perhaps she'd fallen while hiking and hit her head on a rock—she could have a concussion. At the very least, she was probably hypothermic.

There was only one thing to do. Sliding my hands beneath her, I rolled her limp body onto my forearms and then stood, holding her securely against my chest as I ran toward the house. She wasn't heavy, but she wasn't holding onto me at all, and the dead weight was a bit awkward to manage.

In spite of the slippery footing, I made it to the back porch without spilling us both back down the hillside. I righted the woman and clenched her to me with one arm around her waist so I could get the door open and do it without letting her fall.

Her head lolled back, and her face pressed into my neck. Instinctively, I held my breath and turned my nose and mouth away from hers as I turned the handle and kneed the door wide.

Scooping her up again, I rushed to the sofa and laid her on it. Then I shambled back, finally allowing myself to breathe.

Wow.

My breath caught, and my knees felt as if someone had turned a screwdriver and loosened the joints. For a moment, I just stood and stared, taking in the sight of her now that there was proper lighting from the floor lamp and nearby fireplace.

She was tall, slender, shapely. Her skin was an olive-tone and exceptionally smooth and clear. Long, dark hair streamed over one shoulder and hung down over the side of the sofa until it grazed the floor. Thick black lashes rested on the tops of high cheekbones, and her nose and lips could not have been more perfectly formed.

It had been a while since I'd seen a woman in real life, but if memory served, they didn't usually look like *this*. She resembled the models I'd sometimes get distracted by online when I was supposed to be working.

Who is *she?*

She wasn't even wearing hiking-type clothes. Her

clothing looked rather posh. She had on a pair of high-heeled leather boots and a high-necked wine-colored sweater dress that at the moment had ridden up to expose nearly the full length of her legs. *Spectacular legs.*

I blinked a few times and shook my head, coming back to reality. *Right, then.* Whoever she was, there were things I needed to do. I went to my desk where the phone receiver flashed to let me know I had a message. I looked at the readout on the screen. Mum.

Well, she'd have to wait. I had to call someone from the village to come and get the girl—then I'd carry her up to the main road to meet them and let them arrange for medical care.

Mobile signals only being available in the center of Eigg, I used a landline as almost everyone in the outlying areas of the island did. I checked my directory of island numbers and began pressing digits. My finger froze in mid-air over the keypad.

Even after two years here, I sometimes forgot the reality of where I lived. There *was* no resident doctor on Eigg. Instead, a visiting doctor from Small Isles Medical Practice traveled to the island every Tuesday, weather permitting. This was Saturday night. *Fantastic.*

The unconscious girl would need to be transported to hospital on the mainland, but no boats made the trip at night. Even an emergency services helicopter wasn't an option with a storm raging outside. I spun around to look at her again.

Sorry, darlin'. Looks like I'm your best bet.

I had an advanced degree in microbiology, but that didn't make me a clinical doctor. Still, I was probably the most qualified person available at the moment, considering the innkeepers, and crofters, and artists who mostly populated the island's tiny villages.

Retrieving a dry dishtowel from one of the kitchen

drawers, I tied it around my lower face as a sort of make-do surgical mask. Then I went back to the woman—girl? Now that I could see her better, I realized she was young, maybe nineteen or twenty—it was hard to tell with women sometimes. In any case, she looked a few years younger than me.

I laid two fingers on the pulse point in her neck and counted silently. Her pulse was fast but steady. She was breathing normally. There were no obvious wounds on her extremities, but she was still unconscious. She didn't seem to be in any pain. And her skin was chilled.

I took a moment to place a fresh log on the fire, then ran up the stairs to the second floor where I took a bath towel from the linen closet. Grabbing the quilt off the bed in the first bedroom I came to, I went back down and laid it over the lower half of her body. Then I knelt beside the sofa and used the towel on her hair, moving the terrycloth over the length of it, squeezing in sections to dry it.

The dark hair curled as it dried, showing itself to be a rich, dark brown rather than black. A tendril fell across her face, and I lifted it, brushing it back with my fingers to tuck the escaped strands behind her ear. Such a pretty little ear—small and delicate-looking—

The girl moved, causing my breath to catch and my hand to stop mid-motion. She made a small noise and turned her head to one side, sort of nestling into the sofa cushion beneath her, and then she went still again, except for shivering, which had just begun.

That got my heart going again. Shivering was a good sign —when hypothermia progressed, a person would *stop* shivering. She must have been warming up.

I lifted one of her arms and used both my hands to rub it vigorously, trying to restore blood flow. It was more human physical contact than I'd had since... well, since I could even remember. I might pay for it later, but for now, I didn't see what choice I had.

As I began rubbing the other hand and arm, the girl stirred again. Her face at first contracted into a pout, which made me think the brisk massage was bothering her. But then her lips smoothed out into a dreamy closed-mouth smile, and she hummed the way people do when they taste something particularly delicious.

Or feel something pleasurable. The girl's body shifted on the sofa, her knees drawing up and her back arching, which had the effect of pushing her chest toward me.

I scrambled back from the sofa, falling into the armchair behind me, my veins pulsating like the gale force winds I could now hear bellowing outside. I wasn't sure if the girl's skin had warmed, but mine was flash-broiling. I worked to get my rapid breathing back under control.

Not cool, buddy. Not cool.

The girl was half-frozen, possibly concussed, and I was getting turned on? And what if she were to wake to find me mouth-breathing and touching her? I decided my efforts to this point would have to be enough. Her color looked better, less pale. She obviously didn't have brain damage—she responded to touch. *And boy how she responded.*

I got up, pulled the blanket up to her shoulders, and went to the kitchen to do the surgical hand-and-arm scrub I should have done the instant I got into the house. I would have if my own health had been the night's top priority.

Beginning the procedure I'd done countless times in my life, I turned the kitchen sink tap to warm and first washed my hands with a sterile brush and antimicrobial soap, scrubbing each side of every finger, between my fingers, and the backs and fronts of my hands for two minutes. Then, keeping my hands higher than my arms, I scrubbed each side of my arms for one minute.

After that, I dried using a sterile towel and used packaged anti-microbial wipes to disinfect the sink handles and the back door knob.

Okay then. It was the best I could do. It might have already been too late, but what was done was done.

I peeked back into the study. Assured the girl was still resting comfortably, I made myself a cup of coffee and carried it in to sit in the fireside chair opposite the sofa. The crisis seemed to be over. In the morning, I'd turn her over to the villagers to deal with. But for tonight, I figured I should keep an eye on her. For a long while I sat watching her, looking for any signs of consciousness, but she slept steadily.

So I lifted the book from the table beside my chair, opening it to the old envelope I'd used for a bookmark. As it happened, it was a publication on the legends of Eigg, from the true—such as the MacLeod-MacDonald massacre of 1577, to the fantastical—the reports that the beheading of Christian pilgrim St Donnan and the slaying of his fellow monks in 16 AD was carried out by fierce female warriors who lived atop An Sgurr, the mile-long pitchstone ridge that dominated the skyline of the isle of Eigg.

There was even a chapter on mermaids, which were purported to hang out on the shoreline at the Singing Sands.

I glanced over the top of my book at the unconscious girl who had pushed the quilt back down to her waist, obviously feeling warmer now. She was certainly beautiful enough to be a mythical creature.

"Are you a mermaid?" I murmured to her with a huff of a laugh. "Or maybe you're a selkie, eh?"

My mind flashed back to an Irish film I'd seen where a lonely fisherman caught a beautiful unconscious woman in his nets. When she awoke, she had no memory, and he had to keep her and care for her until she recovered it. The man had come to believe the stunning girl he'd captured was actually a selkie, half-woman, half-seal, with an otherworldly singing voice and the power to bring good luck. Or bad.

This time I laughed out loud. "Wes, my friend, you've been alone far too long."

I had been. And I'd watched too many movies, read too many books, spent *far* too much time thinking and fantasizing. A man couldn't work *every* waking hour, though sometimes I tried.

I closed the book again and studied the stranger on my sofa, trying to imagine who she was and where she'd come from. Amnesia was probably too much to hope for—this was real life after all, not the movies—but maybe she'd *want* to stick around for a while. Maybe, like the mysterious woman in the movie, she'd been running away from something and needed a safe place to stay.

Of course, all I'd be able to do would be talk to her—and at a distance. But at the moment, that seemed like a grand thing. I wanted to know everything about this girl, what her story was, and how she came to be lying on my lawn in the middle of nowhere.

It occurred to me as I listened to the sound of her soft breathing, smelled the scent of night air still clinging to her hair and clothing, that this was the first time someone other than Mum or Nanna had been in my house—at least since I'd moved into it. The house itself was very old.

When I'd come to Eigg two years ago, I'd regretfully informed the locals I would not be a hospitable addition to their tiny island community. I explained I'd been born with primary immunodeficiency, a congenital and incurable antibody deficiency. In short—the immunoglobulin proteins generated by my blood plasma cells didn't function properly, meaning I had no natural defenses against pathogens— bacteria or viruses that caused disease. Even shaking hands with someone could make me deathly ill.

That was why the remote, sparsely populated island had been the perfect choice for me to live. And because Eigg generated its own power and had a strong broadband system, working remotely via computer was no problem.

It wasn't lost on me, by the way, that I spent all my time trying to protect the world against disease outbreaks while myself hiding from every little germ.

When I was younger, my mother and grandmother had been able to manage my frequent infections using their folk remedies and healing skills, but eventually my failing immune system had outstripped their ability to keep up, and the doctors were at a loss. Bemoaning the fact they didn't have more powerful elixir ingredients at their disposal, my family vowed to keep searching for a way to cure me while I faced reality and moved myself to one of the most remote locations in the UK.

From behind me, the phone rang, making me jump.

"Oh, bollocks—the American CDC." With all the excitement, I'd forgotten about the call I was supposed to place to the States tonight.

I jumped out of my chair and went round to the desk, quickly gathering the notes I needed to discuss with my overseas colleague. When I went to answer the phone, though, the digital readout on the handset did not say Georgia, United States. The call was coming from Bristol, UK. It was my mother again.

Letting out an irritated sigh, I answered, prepared to get rid of her quickly so I could make the overdue work call. "Hey Mum. Listen, I can't talk right now, I need to—"

"Weston," she interrupted, her tone patient but abiding no argument. "Have you found the girl?"

My heart slammed the inside of my sternum then ceased beating for a few seconds. I had a hard time finding my voice. "What... girl?"

"The Italian." Mum's voice was clipped, irritated. "She should have shown up on your estate tonight. Don't tell me she's woken up and is wandering around the island. I need her."

"No. I... found her." *I think.* She had to be talking about the unconscious dark-haired beauty I'd found.

"Oh. Good," Mum said, her voice calming. "I'm sorry I couldn't warn you ahead of time, but I did try to call just after we transposed her. You didn't answer."

"I didn't hear the phone. I was... with the horses."

I spoke as if in a daze. Maybe I was actually in one. What did my mother and grandmother have to do with this beautiful stranger? The girl must have somehow run afoul of my family's powerful magic. Or maybe Mum was sending her to *me* for some reason?

It's not even my birthday.

"Well, at least you've located her," Mum said. "You should immediately lock her up in one of the outbuildings—*before* she regains lucidity. And do *not* let her leave—she could be the key to something incredibly important to our coven and the Earth-wives as a whole. You must guard her until we can get there."

"You're coming here?"

"Of course. We'll leave straight away. Now, you know Nanna and I don't drive. We'll have to take the train to Mallaig tomorrow. The earliest leaves Bristol at half past twelve, and it's a thirteen hour trip, so it'll be Monday before we can get to you."

"Right." My mind was a scramble of confusion. "Why do I need to guard her? Does she need protection?"

There was a harrumph from the other end of the line. "Her? No—the world needs protection *from* her."

"Why? What has she done?"

"It's not what she's done. It's what she *can* do." Mum paused. "She's Elven."

A jolt of shock was followed quickly by a surge of delight. Elves didn't carry human pathogens. Possibility unfurled like the purple heather blooms that covered the moorland in summer. Touching this girl would not pose the kind of risk to me that touching another human did.

Of course there were other kinds of risk.

I'd been warned about the evil of Elves my entire life. I hadn't actually met any, but the women in my grandmother's coven had told me scary stories and warned me to keep my distance if I ever happened to encounter one. They'd even warded me and my baby sister against Elven Sway, just in case.

As a child, I had never been entirely sure whether their tales were based in tradition and fancy or in reality. As an adult and a scientist, I had come to doubt the existence of Elves at all.

Yes, Earth-wives like my mum and grandmum were real, but they were human. Elves were... not. But here was this inhumanly beautiful woman who'd appeared out of nowhere. My mind was opening to all kinds of new ideas.

I shot a quick glance at sleeping beauty. She didn't *look* dangerous. She looked helpless. In spite of her height, she didn't appear to be particularly strong. Her bone structure was delicate, her hands so much smaller than my own. I dwarfed her in every way, in fact. Was it *really* necessary to lock her up?

"Wes?" Mum's voice snapped me back to attention. "You remember the things I've told you about them, don't you? They are powerful, dangerous, and above all, cunning. They have glamours you can't even imagine. Don't listen to anything she says. Best not to even have a conversation with her. And whatever you do... *don't* let her get close to you."

My heart stuttered. "I don't understand. Elves don't acquire or transmit human diseases. And you've already given me protection against the Sway."

Mum's voice was quiet and deadly serious. "Wes... if you've ever listened to your mother in your whole life, listen to me now. Do. Not. Trust. Her. She may be beautiful to the eye, but she is like an apple that's red and pretty on the outside while beneath the peel, there is nothing but black rot."

"You know her?"

It was an honest question, but my voice came out sounding defiant for some reason. Mum picked up on it instantly.

"They're *all* like that—it's the very reason they are so beautiful—because they're so treacherous," she snapped. "This is Earth-wives business. The less you know, the better. Just let it suffice to say she's poisonous. And we lock poisons away somewhere safe, so they cannot harm the innocent."

Fingers shaking and skin prickling all over, I gave my mother my agreement then hung up, staring at the sleeping woman on my sofa through a new lens.

I had to remember no matter how sweet she might appear, this girl was lethal.

2

MACY

"Will you be having more tea then, love?" The pub waitress pushed a frizzy pouf of orange-ish hair back behind her ear and offered a friendly but harried smile. "Or another pint for you, sir?"

Nic shook his head in answer. "No thank you. Everything was delicious. Just the check please."

A morning train ride through the highlands had brought us from Inverness, where our plane had landed, to Mallaig, a quaint harbor town on Scotland's west coast. It was the best place to catch a ferry to the Scottish small isles.

There were four main islands—Canna, Rum, Eigg, and Muck. Most were only ten or fifteen miles off the mainland and very sparsely populated—at least as far as humans were concerned. Could one of them hold a nymph sanctuary? That was what we were here to discover.

We didn't have much to go on—a letter written by my mother before she'd abandoned me at a Missouri hospital shortly after giving birth, the handwritten notes of a nurse on my hospital record describing my mother as young, very small of build and stature, and speaking with an Irish or

Scottish lilt, and a suggestion from our friend Asher's Scottish grandfather that we try the small isles because there were residents there who reportedly had "the look" of my people, which I shared.

After leaving the pub, Nic and I walked the village streets, stopping into shops and coffeehouses, hoping to find some information that might point us to the right island—and my biological family.

Of course, we had to be more subtle about it than I really wanted to be. We couldn't exactly walk up to the locals and ask, "Would you kindly direct me to the nymphs?" Humans didn't know nymphs existed. Elves either.

They were certainly eying my tall, handsome Elven fiancé, though. Everywhere we went in the village, people stared. Maybe a few recognized him as the former FIFA world player of the year and the French national team's all-time top goal scorer, but I had a feeling for most of them— the women at least—it had more to do with his tall, athletic build, otherworldly bone structure, and incredible wavy, black hair than his soccer career.

We stopped into a likely-looking shop. The windows were stocked with collectibles and antiques. Maybe there would be some artifact inside that bore markings similar to the one my mother had drawn on her farewell note next to her initial—the only clue I had as to her name.

A high-pitched bell jingled as we entered, and a man with white hair and red cheeks greeted us. "Hello there. Let me know if I can help with anything."

"Thank you, we'll look around," I told him, knowing better than to jump right into questioning him. Nic had tried that at the first couple of shops, and the shopkeepers had acted as if we were asking for the combination to their home safes.

Nic and I both perused the wares—pretty, handmade

frames and heavy old furniture, tea sets, and silver flatware, and all sorts of decorative objects. In a glass case near the register, antique jewelry was displayed. That seemed deserving of close study, and I spent several minutes looking over each piece, hoping to see the mysterious distinguishing mark.

The shopkeeper came to stand opposite me over the counter. "Would you like me to take something out, lass? Are you and the young man shopping for a wedding ring, perhaps?"

I glanced up at his smile. "No—he's done a good job with that one already."

I held my left hand out for the man to see. Tiny, glittering diamonds were set into the gold band in an ancient Elven pattern. Affixed to the top, a large radiant-cut diamond caught the light as I tilted my hand toward him.

The shopkeeper leaned down for a closer look. "I'll say. This is beautiful work. You don't often see a pattern like this. Custom?" His faded gray eyes went to Nic, who'd come to stand beside me.

Nic gave him a terse nod and an answer that wasn't entirely truthful. "Yes. I'm into architecture. I like to draw. It's my design."

The man nodded slowly. "I see."

Then he got back to business, quickly pulling other items from the case and laying them on the counter. No one else was in the shop. I imagined it was slow here in the winter months. The weather had been dreadful since we'd landed in the country, overcast and cold, though not raining at least.

"A bracelet perhaps, then," he suggested eagerly. "Or some ear bobs? You've got wee little ears, haven't you miss? I think I have just the pair for you."

"Oh, no thank you," I started to protest, but Nic cut me off.

"Yes. Take them out, if you would."

I slid Nic a chastising side-eyed glance and hissed, "I don't need anything."

He only smiled and paid close attention to the selection of earrings the old shopkeeper produced. Pointing to a pair of diamonds set in antique sterling, he said, "We'll take those."

"Well, I havna even told you what they cost now, laddie." The man gave Nic an amused glance.

"We'll take them," Nic repeated.

The shopkeeper smiled and scooped up the pricey-looking earrings and turned to get a small black box from the shelf behind him.

Nic nudged me and tossed his chin toward the man's back. *Now*, he mouthed.

I nodded, finally catching on. My smart boyfriend had warmed up the "audience" for my questions with his purchase.

"How long have you had this shop?" I asked the man.

He answered while he boxed and bagged my jewelry and opened the cash register to deposit the stack of bills Nic had handed him.

"Going on forty years now. I took it over from my da, and his da ran it before him. This shop has stood right on this spot for some eight decades now."

"You must have met a lot of people over the years."

He chuckled and nodded. "Oh yes—of every sort from every country you can think of. Most of them wander in and look and wander back out again," he added with a wink. "*This is a good day.*"

"I wonder if you might have ever met any of my family," I said. "I'm told my ancestors came from this area—possibly the small isles. Do you get many customers from there?"

"Aye," he confirmed. "We do see quite a bit of the

islanders. The ferry runs six days a week. In summers it's full of tourists, but we get the locals coming here year round for supplies and such. There's not much shopping on the islands. So what's your family name then, lass?"

And this was where the lack of information about my heritage hurt our chances of success.

"Well, I'm not entirely sure. It might begin with an F. I know it's not much to go on, but I'm told I have the "look" of people from this region. Maybe you notice a family resemblance between me and some local residents you might have seen?"

I felt silly asking, but it was worth a shot. Maybe the nymphs were like Nic's people—hiding in plain sight. Since the humans didn't know of their existence, their secret was safe as long as they wanted to keep it. Of course, *his* people didn't *want* to keep hiding.

He was from the Ancient Court. Most of its members were in favor of eradicating the human race, or at least dominating it, so they could stop living in secrecy and rule the Earth as they had in the days before our history books were written.

The man stopped for a second and studied my face. "Can't say as I do. Sorry, lass. You should try one of those genealogy services, perhaps. Or maybe a book with some of the local history. There's a free library in town and a bookstore down the street."

"Are you sure she doesn't look familiar?" Nic said, his voice falling hard from high over my shoulder.

The way the old man responded, I could tell Nic was using his Sway.

"Er… yes, well I *might* have seen some folks of around her size in the village from time to time. Didn't talk to them. Don't know them. I wish I could help you more."

Feeling sorry for the old man, who looked a bit spooked, I

elbowed Nic and spoke quickly, "The library's a good idea. We'll do that. Thank you for your help. Have a good day."

I pulled my towering fiancé out of the shop. Out on the sidewalk I turned to him. "Did you have to do that? Did you read some sort of bad intentions in him or something?"

"No. I could just tell his greatest desire was to get us out of his shop. That seemed strange to me for someone who said his business had been slow. I thought it called for a few questions."

"Maybe he was hungry and wanted to close up so he could get home to his dinner," I said. "Or maybe he was afraid we'd change our mind about the purchase."

Nic shrugged. "At least we found out he has seen people around town who might have some of your family traits."

"*Might.* And I'm not sure that teensy bit of information was worth a three hundred dollar pair of earrings."

"*You're* worth a three hundred dollar pair of earrings." He lifted my hand to his mouth and kissed the back of it. "And so much more than that. I can't wait until all of this is over and we can live where we want the way we want—as a married couple. I'm going to buy you everything you could desire."

I felt my face flush at his adoring expression and laced my fingers with his as we resumed our stroll down the main street. The sky was already darkening. Some of the shops were beginning to put out "Closed" signs. Others—pubs mostly—were turning on their sidewalk lamps. It looked like our search would go into day two because today had been a total bust.

"All I really want is for my family and friends to be safe. That's worth more to me than any material thing could ever be. If we can't stop the Plague, Nic, I don't know how I'll live without—"

24

"We *will* stop it," Nic interrupted, squeezing my hand inside his larger and warmer one.

I gave him a grateful smile. His strength had gotten me through a lot. "You know, if we do run into a villager with information, they might not be too eager to share it with someone who looks like you," I told him.

"You mean they'll be intimidated by my dashing good looks?" he teased in that appealing French-Italian accent of his.

I laughed. "No, I mean, if they *do* know anything about nymphs, they might know something about Elves as well—namely that your people are the natural predators of my people. It would be like giving a prowling lion the name and address of the nearest lame antelope."

He leaned down and gave my ear a playful nip, growling with a predatory grin. "I don't bite. Much."

A shiver worked its way through me, my body warming at his nearness and the sultry sound of his voice.

Taking my hand, Nic continued in a more serious tone. "It doesn't matter. I'm not letting you do this alone. I'm not letting you do anything alone—ever again. Alessia is still out there somewhere, and the witches may not have given up hope of using you for their own purposes. We must stop the Plague, but your life is the one that matters to me most. We'll do this together."

For centuries, nymph blood was highly prized as a cure for illness and injury, as well as a treatment to enhance male potency. My ancestors had been hunted to extinction—or that's what everyone had believed until the horrible Dr. Schmitt had discovered my heritage. That had started a whole new nymph hunt—with me as the prey.

Even after Dr. Schmitt died, Nic's former betrothed, Alessia, carried on his work with the Plague and his pursuit of me, chasing me down in England to Olly's house. As far as the Dark Elves in the Ancient Court knew, my blood was the only thing capable of stopping the Plague, and she apparently had no intention of letting that happen.

Unfortunately my blood wasn't enough. There literally wasn't enough of me to go around. That was why we had to find my biological family. By the end of the day, it was feeling like an impossible task.

Pulling my hand from Nic's, I dropped onto an inviting sidewalk bench. I was weary from spending all day on my feet.

"I think we should call it a night. Where is that inn of ours located?" I drew my phone from my purse and looked up the address, intending to find a walking map.

Nic sat beside me. "A couple streets over, I think. Do you remember if it serves dinner or do we need to pick one of these places? I'm hungry again."

"Of course you are." I laughed and leaned my head against his chest, rubbing a palm over his flat belly. "You should weigh four hundred pounds with the way you eat."

He chuckled. "The Elven metabolism has its advantages—and disadvantages. I'm not kidding. If we don't eat soon, I'm going to get cranky."

Thoroughly amused, I sat up, shifting so I could see his face straight on. The word "cranky" said in his beautiful accent was hilarious.

"Cranky? Well, we can't have that now, can we?" I teased.

I was leaning forward and stretching up to kiss him when something in the store window just over his shoulder caught my eye. It was a book—an old one. My insides vibrated with a current of excitement. Etched into its cover beside the illegible Gaelic title was a symbol.

I leapt off the bench, gaping at it. "Give me the letter."

Wearing a confused expression, Nic got to his feet as well

and drew the envelope from his jacket's inner pocket, offering it to me. "What is it?"

"The symbol… there on the book. See it?"

Pulling a small rectangle of paper from the envelope, I held it up and scanned to the bottom of the short handwritten note. Then I walked to the storefront and pressed the paper flat against the large, cold pane of glass that displayed some new books and some very old-looking ones.

"See? Look at this. Don't they look similar?"

Nic's gaze bounced from my mother's letter to the antique book and then back again. "Not similar—I'd say they're identical. Come on."

3

WES

Elven. It was hard to believe that after all these years, the scary stories from my childhood might actually have been true.

As I carried her sleeping form to the stable, I studied the beguiling woman in my arms. It was a struggle to make the mental image I'd always held of Elves—steely-eyed, Teflon-coated giants who cackled maniacally and schemed against my race and especially my family—match the disconcerting reality of her, a soft, warm, living, breathing person who could be injured and rendered unconscious, who could feel pleasure and pain.

The storm had been a typical one, passing quickly, so the rain had stopped. It made transporting her down the grassy hillside much easier.

Once inside the stable, I took her upstairs to the living quarters in the loft. I'd bought the estate from a horse breeder and trainer, and the tiny apartment had served as lodging for his stable hand. It wasn't fancy. In fact, it was a bit shabby now that I really looked at it. I'd have to spruce it up a bit if the girl was going to stay here more than a couple of days.

Laying her on the small single bed, I noted that some thicker blankets should be the first order of business. It was cold, and I couldn't have the prisoner freezing to death before my mum and Nanna arrived to deal with her.

I turned in a circle, cataloging the room's meager accommodations—a bedside table, lamp, a chair, an empty set of shelves. I'd have to bring some books down from the house to fill them. Since I would not be allowed to speak to her or let her out, she'd need something to do during her captivity. Did Elves read? Or were they too busy hatching plans for world domination?

The bathroom was clean except for a few spider webs, which I knocked down with a hand towel. Making another mental note to replace it, I ticked off the other necessities I'd need to stock—more towels from the house, soap, toothpaste and a toothbrush. Did I have an extra? I'd have to check.

Glancing back first to make sure she was still out, I left the room and locked the old, heavy door behind me. Unless her glamour was teleportation, it would hold her. That was an interesting thought. What *was* her glamour exactly?

I'd been told Elves could have exceptional physical gifts, even powers of illusion and mind control. That was clearly what my mum was afraid of.

Some of them, though, had glamours of a more subtle and gentle nature, those that enhanced artistic or musical ability or made them especially sensitive to the feelings of others. That seemed more likely in this case. I was having a hard time believing the exquisite creature I'd found could be truly diabolical.

Just in case, I'd have to be extra careful when bringing her food in the morning not to let her touch me or even make eye contact. Her Sway wouldn't work on me, but if her glamour *was* some other sort of mind control, I couldn't take any chances. Mum and Nanna rarely, if ever, involved me or Pop in Earth-wives matters, and I didn't want to muck this up.

After gathering the books and supplies from the house, I returned to the stable and stocked the upstairs apartment. Just as I was finishing arranging the bookshelves, the girl began to stir on the bed nearby.

Heart rocketing, I jumped to my feet and darted for the door, stopping and turning back only when I'd reached it and was halfway out of the room. She was still sleeping. She'd turned onto her side in the fetal position and tucked her hands under her cheek.

I knew I should back the rest of the way out of the doorway and turn the lock, but I couldn't help but stay a few more minutes and watch her dream. This was probably my last opportunity to actually look at her. And I liked looking at her.

Evil though she might have been, she was captivating. Everything about her appealed to my eyes, as if she'd been designed and created on a 3D printer just to my specifications.

Of course, looks weren't everything. If I'd met her when she was actually awake, I probably would have disliked her instantly. She no doubt would have attacked me or at least spewed venomous threats. I might even be dead by now.

But as things had happened, my first feelings toward this mysterious girl had been pity, and concern, and fear for her life—mixed with a hearty helping of attraction. It was hard to change courses so quickly.

Planning to return early in the morning with a breakfast tray, I closed the door and locked it, descended the old wooden stairs, and left the stable, starting my trek back to the house. There might still be time for that phone call to the

CDC, and then I needed to get in a few hours of sleep before tomorrow's workday.

A faint creaking noise broke the silence of the night. At first I thought the windmill had caught the ocean breeze and was beginning to turn, but then I realized the sound had come from behind me.

I spun around to face the stable and saw the small upstairs window opening by gradual increments. I broke into a run, not wanting the girl to spot me.

And then I heard it—a voice that stopped me in my tracks.

"Help! Help me. I've been kidnapped. I'm being held here against my will—upstairs over the stable. Somebody help me."

The English words were followed by a steady stream of speech in Italian, French, Spanish, and several other languages I had a hard time pinpointing. The girl was a prolific language expert. And she sounded scared. Truly frightened. Her voice was enchanting—melodic, almost. I might have been right about that musical glamour. Or did all Elves have alluring voices?

It was a good thing my estate was so remote because anyone hearing her plaintive cries would be inspired to heroic acts. Hell, it was a good thing I knew who she was and what she was capable of, or I'd have run back down the hill and rescued her myself. I stood for a few moments, listening. Inside my abdomen, a chaos of hot and cold sensation twisted and roared. I turned and trudged back to the house, unable to stand hearing the piteous pleas any longer.

Somehow, even though the doors and windows were closed, I could still hear her shouts for help from inside. Maybe the wind off the ocean carried them up to my bedroom window. Maybe she had a voice with a remarkable ability to project. I couldn't say. All I knew was she kept it up for a good two hours before the night finally went quiet.

By that time I'd given up on sleep altogether. I got up, dressed, and went back downstairs to work. Thirty minutes before dawn, I went to the kitchen and started the coffeemaker then set about preparing a breakfast tray.

What do Elves eat?

She dressed like a human, so finally I decided to feed her like one. I cooked some bacon and popped two bread rolls in the oven to warm, then I made some cream of wheat—one of my favorite breakfast foods since childhood. When the rolls were ready, I arranged them on a plate with the bacon, added a ripe pear, and placed the bowl of hot cereal beside it. The final touches were a small, lidded coffee pot, cup and saucer, and small containers of cream and sugar.

Feeling a bit silly, I trekked down the hill once more, holding the tray in front of me like a butler who'd lost his way to the morning room. Easing the door of the stable open, I stood on the first floor, listening. There were no sounds from up above. She was still sleeping—either that or lying in wait to attack me.

Later, I'd have to devise some method of food delivery that didn't risk my life, but for now, I'd have to take a chance on opening the door and just be prepared to battle a furious Elf-woman if I happened to find her awake inside. The alternative was letting her go hungry. I quickly dismissed that option. Mum said this girl was important for some reason, so it made sense she should have proper care. Besides, I really didn't have it in me to be inhumane.

Ha. Good one, Wes. She's not even human.

My heartbeat thumping in my ears, I slid the key into the lock and eased the door open, thankful its hinges didn't creak. The room was dark and still. The girl's long, slender form was stretched out on the bed, buried under blankets.

She must have gotten chilly during the night. I made a mental note to put more wood in the stove downstairs.

I didn't dally this time but set the tray on the floor and quickly left the room, locking the door once more and leaving the stables. The horses were asleep as well. Later, I'd return and turn them out to graze a bit while I mucked out their stalls.

As for right now, the sleepless night had caught up to me. I was dead on my feet. Mum and Nanna would arrive in a couple of days. I had a lot of work to get done before then, which meant I needed to get at least a few hours of sleep right now.

I hadn't seen my family in nearly a year, and they wouldn't be understanding about my working while they were here, even though they were coming on "business" of their own. Perhaps they'd even bring Olly along. She was at about the right age for induction into the Earth-wives society—maybe she had been already and would take part in whatever plans they had for my "guest."

The thought of seeing my little sister cheered me as I made my way back to the house, climbed the stairs to my bedroom, and fell into bed fully clothed. My last thought before slipping into black oblivion was it was a good thing the storm had passed and their travel here would be uneventful.

* * *

BY THE TIME I WOKE, the sun was high in the winter sky. I bolted out of bed, grabbing the jacket from my bedpost before heading downstairs.

The horses would be pacing their stalls by now, and my email inbox was no doubt bursting at this point from colleagues all over Europe wanting my input on their data, wondering why the hell I wasn't answering.

Usually I was a slave to the job—I had nothing better to do—but the arrival of the female Elf had thrown my staid, predictable life into disarray. And she'd only been here one day.

Entering the stable, I looked up at the rough boarded roof over the stalls. Then I laughed at myself. What? Did I expect to be able to see her through her floor with my X-ray vision?

That would be nice, but glamour was *her* department. I had no special powers. I didn't even have the skills of the Earth-wives. They were inherited through maternal lines— only by the girls. My father and I were just regular guys. Regular guys surrounded by witches.

Chuckling to myself again, I opened Clovis's stall first and let him out into the pasture to graze. He didn't always enjoy the friskiness of some of the younger horses— especially Sebastian, who was a total self-serving bully—so I always gave my senior resident a head start. Chatting companionably with the others, I set about the task of mucking Clovis's stall.

"I know you're down there."

The words carried down the wooden stairwell, snaking around my spine and sending shivers from my scalp to my heels. Though it sounded even more melodious up close than it had from outside the barn, the Elven female's voice was laced with menace.

"You *need* to let me out," she threatened. "This is kidnapping, and you are going to be in a *lot* of trouble."

I stopped my work and listened.

"Do you know who I am? I am a *princess*. My father is very rich and powerful, and you cannot even imagine what he'll do to you when he finds out what you've done."

Her voice was even sterner this time. Insistent. *Imperious.*

I didn't know if she was making up the thing about being a princess, but she sure sounded like one. I smirked and finished the stall, then turned out the rest of the horses, one by one.

Sebastian was stand-offish as usual, edging by me before bolting out the door. As they reached the wide-open field, the horses galloped and trotted joyfully, nipping at each other and running circles before settling in to nibble on the grass and heather.

I moved on to the other stalls, trying not to think about the silence above me. What was she doing up there? What was she thinking?

What color eyes does she have? Wow, that was a random thought.

From what I'd heard so far, this Elven girl was everything her kind had been advertised to be—malevolent, spoiled, aggressive. But the next time she spoke, the difference in her tone surprised me. It was less demanding and more cajoling.

"You know... even if you're only working for them, you'll be held responsible." A pause was followed by an almost desperate-sounding, "Do you hear me?"

I shook my head and smiled to myself, continuing to work. I knew what she was up to. I'd been warned. Her attempts to be persuasive had about as much value to me as the stuff I was shoveling off the stable floor. And just who did she think I was "working" for?

"Please—if you can hear me... please tell me what's going on. I'm frightened. I have no idea where I am and no idea how I got here."

This time I stopped shoveling. In spite of my mother's warning, the tremulous quality of the girl's voice caused an unpleasant twisting in my midsection. I'd seen her when she "landed" on the island, for lack of a better word.

She *didn't* know where she was or what was happening to

her. She'd been shivering and pale, hypothermic and near frostbitten. If I hadn't found her when I did, she could have died.

And there was genuine fear in her voice now. Maybe the earlier rancor was all a bluff. I'd certainly be afraid if I'd woken up in a strange place and found myself locked in.

"My head aches horribly from whatever they did to me," she continued. "And it's rather cold in this room. I was freezing last night."

I knew it. I should have come back during the night to re-stock the wood stove. Especially considering how cold she'd been when I'd first found her. My head dropped back onto my shoulders, and I breathed slowly in and out as an internal battle waged. Guilt. Duty. Worry.

Finally I leaned the shovel handle against the barn wall and climbed the stairs. I'd keep it short and to the point, find out if she was in medical distress. I wouldn't allow anything she might say to affect me.

Stopping right outside the door, I contemplated how to begin this bizarre conversation. I'd never been a jailer before, and I'd certainly never chatted with an Elf. Before I could speak, she did. Her voice was much quieter—she must have heard me walking up the stairs and knew I was right outside the door.

"Please let me out of here. Or at least tell me where I am. I'm confused and afraid. Also... I don't really care for cream of wheat."

I laughed. I couldn't help it. Her pitiful pleas had actually gotten to me—much to my shame. And now she was complaining about the food? The girl was fine. Her health wasn't in danger—just her *refined* culinary palate. Oh, this was going to be amusing, as long as it didn't last too long.

"Nic? Is that you? Nic, are you out there?"

Her voice this time sounded truly shaken. Whoever this

Nic was, he must have meant something to her. In spite of all common sense and reason, something that felt very much like jealousy took a sneaky jab at me.

"Who's Nic?" I said.

There was a long pause. I began to think she wasn't going to respond, but then she bombarded me with a barrage of panicky sounding questions.

"Where am I? Why am I here? Who are you?"

Laughing to myself again, I decided to answer. There was no harm in it. She was in there, and I was out here, and that was how it would stay until my family arrived to deal with this pampered brat.

"You are a guest at my home. You're here because apparently you got on the bad side of some pretty dangerous witches."

I paused. Should I tell her my name? Well, she had to call me something, I supposed. And for some inscrutable reason, I wanted to know *her* name.

"My name is Wes. You might as well settle down and relax, *princess*, because you're going to be here for a long, long time."

There was a loud crashing sound, and the door quivered just in front of my face, as if she'd hurled herself at the solid wood.

Ah, back to her charming true self.

Leaning against the door, I spoke into the tiny crack between the door and frame. "You might want to take care not to dislocate your shoulder or break your foot. I can give you an aspirin for the headache if you like, but that's about it. I'm not a doctor."

"No—you're just a stupid *human*," she responded. "You're a kidnapper, and you work for *witches* which means you're even stupider than the rest of your ridiculous race."

"And *you*—are rude. A shining example of *your* race." I had agreed to guard her and keep her alive, but I didn't sign up for verbal abuse.

"Okay then." I rapped two knuckles lightly against the door before turning to descend the stairs. "I'll be back in a few hours with your lunch. But for both our sakes, I suggest we keep the conversation to a minimum. Have a good day."

"Wait? What am I supposed to do in here... locked up in this... this... hovel?" she griped.

"Read a book," I called back over my shoulder. "You might learn something, even though they're written by *mere humans.*"

As my boot reached the bottom step, something hard thwacked against the door behind me, making me flinch. A nice, thick book, no doubt—flung across the room in a fit of rage.

I can't believe I ever wished she'd stay.

My mother couldn't get here and rid me of this screeching banshee soon enough.

4

MACY

Nic bounded ahead of me to open the bookshop door, then held it and stood back, waiting for me to enter. Once inside, I nearly collided with a woman who was walking rapidly toward the entrance.

She stopped in place, holding her hand to her chest. She was short and stocky with a thick mane of straight, dark hair that might have been a wig.

"Oh dear, you nearly gave me a heart attack. I was just on my way to turn the sign and lock the door. We're closing, dearie."

"Oh no. Could I just get one thing quickly? Please. I spotted it in the window, and I have to have it."

She stood contemplating my request for a moment before letting out a breath. Pencil-thin brows pulled together over a rounded nose. "Very well then, which is it? I'll fetch it for you."

I pointed to the front window display. "The book on top of that stack—the one with the cover facing the window."

She gave me a strange look. "Read ancient Gaelic, do you?"

"No, actually. Do you? Or do you know someone who does?"

"I don't, but mayhaps I know a body or two who does around here." She leaned over a stack of books to pluck the one I wanted from the window display and started walking toward the cash register. "What are you then—university students? Or are you just collecting souvenirs?"

"Actually, I'm interested in the symbol on the cover. It looks like something from some papers I've been studying. I think maybe it's part of an archaic language, or maybe a family crest."

She glanced up from the register and quickly back down to it. "Really? I know a lot of the families around here— grew up here, you ken. I've never seen this symbol anywhere else. But perhaps I can ask around for you. I know a history buff who lives nearby. She might be able to help you."

My heart soared with new hope. "Would you? That would be fantastic. I'd like to meet her myself, if I could."

"She's a bit reclusive. Papers, did you say?" the woman asked as she slid the book into a flat, brown paper bag. "If you'd like to leave them with me, I'd be happy to take them to my friend."

I slid the letter into my pocket, pressing it tightly against my outer thigh. "No. No, I couldn't do that. They're old and fragile, and they're of great importance to me personally." On impulse I added, "And I don't have them with me anyway."

She nodded sagely. "I see. So you're an archeologist then —a researcher? Or... perhaps a treasure hunter?"

"Treasure? No." I gestured to Nic. "My fiancé and I are here on holiday. We were just window-shopping when I saw the book. It's really not that big of a deal. Just a hobby."

"Your fiancé?" Her expression was so surprised it surprised me, but then her smile fell back into place. "Well, enjoy your romantic holiday then. Where are you lodging? I can suggest a place if you haven't one yet."

"Oh, no thank you. We're at the Moorings Guest House tonight."

She smiled and started walking toward the shop's front door to escort us out. "Oh, that's a lovely place. I know the owner well. They'll take good care of you. I'll check with my historian friend and tell her you'd like to meet with her. If she's willing, I can contact you at the inn. What are your names?"

"Macy Moreno and Nicolo Buonoccorsi. Thank you so much. Tell her we'd be happy to pay her for her time."

The shopkeeper smiled as we stepped out of the store onto the sidewalk again. "I'll do that. Have a good night then, dearies." And she shut the door.

"I think she has a crush on you," I said with a giggle. "Did you see the way she reacted when I told her we're engaged?"

"I didn't notice," Nic said.

"She looked shocked. I wonder how many women I'll have to fight off in this village—young *and* old. I'd better marry you quick," I teased.

"I'd marry you this minute if I could."

Nic gave me a hungry look that was not related to food. My belly flipped, and goose bumps rose on my skin. I had to look away and fight to regain control of my thoughts and uneven breathing. Unfortunately *that* was not the appetite we'd be feeding tonight. We hadn't slept together and would not be doing so until we found my family and stopped the Plague.

He took my hand, and we started walking toward the nearest pub, its warm lights and tempting smells like a beacon in the deepening darkness. Supper would wait no longer. Everything else would *have* to.

Later that night at the inn, Nic lay in bed as I sat in an

overstuffed chair under the lamp, paging through the old book. I'd tried using an online translator to decipher some of it but without much luck. The lady in the shop had said it was in Gaelic, and the title, *Coiseachd*, meant "sanctuary" as far as I could tell. But the text inside appeared to be written in an archaic form of the ancestral Scottish language. Some of the letters weren't even represented on the keypad of my phone.

"Maybe the shopkeeper's friend will be able to read it," Nic offered, his voice rough and sleepy-sounding. "We'll stop in there again tomorrow if you want. Put it away now and come keep me warm."

He stretched an arm in invitation. A bare arm. Attached to a bare shoulder, chest, and torso—all of it so tan and touchable I found it hard to breathe when I looked at him for too long.

"You are always warm," I said. "You just want to make *me* warm, and *that* is dangerous."

His lips quirked in a rascally grin. "Guilty as charged. But I promise to be good. Come on to bed. It's late, and I need to hold you."

Though the biological imperative to bond was growing stronger every day for Nic—and it wasn't exactly easy for *me* to resist either—we both knew we could not act on our desire for each other.

According to Elven lore, only the blood of virgin nymphs was useful for healing. I didn't know any nymphs who could verify or disprove that, and we couldn't take the chance of ruining the only source of Plague cure we had at this point—me. My blood wasn't enough to save the entire population of the world, but it was better than nothing. If our mission here failed, I would donate all I could and save as many human lives as possible.

With that in mind, I'd bought some very conservative

pajamas today in one of the shops. They were soft and comfortable and *far* from revealing. I climbed into bed, and Nic pulled me to his side, running his hands over the fabric of the long-sleeved top then down over my hip and thigh, which were covered by the ankle-length pajama pants.

His voice held a hint of a pout. "I prefer the sassy little panties with cartoons of farm animals and witty sayings."

"I *know* what you prefer. That's why I'm not *wearing* the sassy panties to bed."

He let out an irritated growl, gripping the fabric at my back. "I hope we find your family soon."

Laughing, I kissed the spot where his neck met his bare chest. The skin was smooth and hot and smelled fantastic. "That makes two of us. Now let's get some sleep."

"Not so fast, *piccola*. I want my goodnight kiss first."

I eyed him suspiciously. "*One* kiss."

My tone of voice warned him, but my body was already warming and tingling, responding to Nic the way it always did. My brain might be cautious and wise, but the same couldn't be said of the rest of me.

"One is all I'll need," he said with a wicked grin.

Our lips met gently. And it was a *singular* kiss, lush, and languid, and relentless in its unhurried seduction. He tasted me slowly, caressing my lips and tongue and the inside of my mouth again and again with deliberate strokes that made me feel heavy and weak and simmering.

I was no longer sleepy, and neither was Nic apparently. As the kiss stretched out into several *more* drugging kisses, his arm went around my back, his hand dropping to my pajama bottoms and urging me against a solid bank of muscle.

As if on autopilot, I slid my knee up the outside of his thigh, letting him guide me into an alignment so perfect I nearly melted from the surge of volcanic heat it produced between us.

Attuned to my responses as always, Nic was breathing hard and fast. He released my hip and brought his hand to the front of my pajamas, beginning to unfasten the buttons from the top down. We were entering dangerous territory now. He could feel how much I wanted him—and I didn't need glamour to feel how much he wanted me.

As his hand slid inside the now-open pj top, I was simultaneously feverish and shivering with need. My breath hissed between my teeth. The desire was almost painful.

"Nic," I gasped. "I don't think I can take much more."

Suddenly Nic pulled away. He didn't just break contact with my mouth—he got out of bed entirely and paced toward the door, grabbing a robe from the post of the bed's footboard.

I sat up, a little light-headed since there wasn't much of a blood supply circulating in my brain at the moment. "Where are you going?"

"To the shower," he responded without turning around.

"You already showered—right after supper."

Now he turned to face me, his hand on the doorknob. My eyes dropped below his waist, and I suddenly understood. Liquid heat suffused my face as well as some other key parts of my anatomy.

"Yes, *piccola*, but the water in that shower was warm. This time is not for the sake of cleanliness. Go to sleep. I'll be back soon."

"I won't be able to sleep without you."

"Try," he said with a slightly pained smile and slipped from the room.

Apparently I did drift off because I was awakened sometime later by a jolt to the bed and a shout. At first I thought Nic was having a nightmare. Eyes still closed, I patted his side of the bed, trying to comfort him. It was empty.

Another muffled shout was followed by the unmistakable sounds of a struggle, a piece of furniture being knocked over, grunts and growls. I bolted upright in the dark room, my hearing nearly obliterated by the sudden, rapid rush of blood in my ears.

"Nic? Nic, where are you? Are you okay?"

My hands shook from an instantaneous injection of adrenaline as I fumbled to turn on the bedside lamp. After a few tries, I found the switch. Light flooded the room, illuminating a living nightmare.

Two men dressed in dark clothing and wearing masks had Nic pinned to the floor with his arms pulled behind his back. Nic struggled ferociously, but one of the men kneeled on his back, and the other was tying his hands.

They were short, but muscular, and no doubt they had caught him by surprise, either sleeping or on his way back from the shower.

"Stop," I screamed. "Get off of him. Who are you? What are you doing?"

The man holding Nic down glanced up at me, then his eyes shifted to something behind me, and he nodded. Before I could turn to see what he was looking at, a large cloth covered my eyes, nose, and mouth. Someone held it in place while wrapping a thick, strong arm around me to restrain my movement. A voice whispered against my ear.

"We will not hurt you. You are safe now."

The fabric smelled sweet and strange. Instinct told me not to breathe, but with my heart working so hard, I couldn't help it. My lungs emptied and refilled, taking in the honeyed air. Thrashing and struggling to free my arms, I managed to dislodge the material blocking my vision. What I saw made me cry out and fight even harder.

Nic was no longer struggling but unconscious and limp. The men had lifted him and were carrying him out of our room.

My heart pummeled my ribcage. My flailing became even more desperate. Screaming through the cloying scent of the cloth, I made one last effort to throw off my captor. It was no use, and as my lungs worked to replace the air I'd expelled while crying out, I inhaled another huge draught of the unfamiliar essence.

My muscles went weak. My eyelids collapsed. My last thought as consciousness drifted into darkness was not of our failure to find a cure for the Plague, or of the mysterious book we'd found, but of Nic—and how I wished we had continued what we'd started tonight and bonded at long last.

It might have been our last chance.

5

ALESSIA

It was impossible to determine the time with the lack of sun and the indigo-hued sky, but I guessed it was around noon, based on the emptiness of my stomach.

I stood at the small window of my prison cell, as I'd come to think of my shabby living quarters, watching a storm roll out to sea. It was an odd sight.

Back home on my father's seaside estate in Positano, it seemed storms always came *in* from the ocean, not the other way around. But these dark clouds cascaded down the hillside toward the constantly shifting water from some point behind the shingled house where my human captor apparently lived.

He'd be returning before long with more food—if I hadn't infuriated him too much. I probably shouldn't have spoken to him so harshly. No doubt he was a servant or a hired hand. It would probably have been smart to be sweet and docile, to gain his sympathy and then trick him into letting me out. But I'd always had difficulty controlling my tongue, and I'd always been terrible with men.

Wes. With his rumbly, low voice and his mocking

laughter. Acid blistered my insides. I *hated* him—hated all of them, Elven and human alike. Not a one of them had any honor, any decency.

First Culley Rune had broken our betrothal without ever meeting me, humiliating me by choosing to bond with a human girl instead of the princess of the Italian Dark Court.

Then Nic had lied to me, promising to marry me, when all he wanted was to be with his nymph lover. And this *human*—well, he wasn't even worth wasting my breath on. He'd suggested keeping the conversation to a minimum. *Fine.* I wouldn't speak to him at all. And I certainly wouldn't read his stupid books.

I only hoped he'd come back at some point with lunch. The growling in my stomach was becoming more insistent with each passing hour. If worse came to worst, I could drink from the vial of saol water I carried in my jacket pocket, doling it out in small increments.

My parents had urged me to keep it with me at all times, in case I inadvertently made someone sick and my glamour was in jeopardy of being revealed. A few drops of the healing elixir in their drink would alleviate suspicion while I got away as quickly as possible. I didn't want to waste it on mere hunger, but who knew how long this would go on—or if he'd ever return.

I flopped onto my bed, facing *away* from the bookshelf, and listened to the lash of rain on the barn roof. If I focused on the sound, maybe I could nap. Maybe I could just sleep away this entire nightmare—at least until whoever was coming to "deal" with me arrived.

I'll deal with them. I smiled in spite of my hunger pangs. For the first time in my life, I was grateful for my secondary glamour. I couldn't wait to use it on Wes and whoever else came along. Anticipation quickened my pulse and took my mind off my empty belly.

When he returned—he'd have to return, wouldn't he? When he returned, he'd open the door to deliver my food, and I'd use my superior speed and strength to surprise him. I'd touch him somewhere, anywhere there was exposed skin, and *then* he'd be sorry.

While he writhed on the floor in agony and developed some horrendous disease—whatever he was most prone to— I'd step casually over his weak, pitiful human body and be on my way.

With that happy thought in mind, I did manage to drift off into dreams of horseback riding, my happy place. I was jumping a one and a half meter fence on Nic's estate on Corsica, in fact, when the sound of boots ascending the stairs awakened me. I leapt from the bed, nerves singing with sharp impatience as I readied myself to attack and overcome him.

But there was no sound of a key turning in the old iron lock, no scrape of the heavy wooden door opening. Instead, there was a buzzing noise, a high whine that obliterated all other sound and had me pressing my palms to my ears. What was happening?

And then I smelled it—a sharp, pleasant fragrance, like burning wood. A minute later, the tip of a small, silver blade peeked out from underneath the door. A saw.

The tip retreated then reappeared minutes later, about twenty-four inches away from the first cut. Sawdust pooled beneath the door as the blade turned and followed a parallel path from one of the upward slits toward the other. He was cutting a narrow rectangle in the center of the door's bottom. It wiggled and then fell as the freshly sawed lines met. Then all was quiet again.

A tray, barely narrower than the new opening, slid through it into my room. It held a napkin, silverware, a plate of sliced mixed fruits, and a sandwich.

"You know, if you'd been a little nicer to me that could

49

have been a double-decker sandwich." My captor's voice held humor and a touch of reproach. "But as you are *not* a model prisoner, I've got to keep the opening small and your food flat."

Refusing to acknowledge his irritating words but too hungry to refuse the food, I marched over to the tray and snatched it up, carrying it to the bed, where I sat and began wolfing down the meal.

"I'm afraid there'll be no more coffee. You'll have to make do with water from the sink—it tastes pretty good here on the island."

The island? I was on an island. But which one? There were so many in the UK. Again, I did not answer him. There was no need for me to humor this human puppet who allowed himself to be directed by witches. He acted so friendly, but he was definitely not my friend. The friend of my enemy was my enemy, and the witches had pitted themselves against my kind for centuries.

Even if they'd *forced* the feeble-brained fool to play the part of my guard, I had no use for him.

The food was another story. I ate quickly—not only was I starving, but the meal was exceptionally good. The fruit was enhanced with some kind of sauce, and even the sandwich had a special flavor I couldn't pinpoint. I had eaten at many fine restaurants, but rarely had I tasted anything so delicious.

Of course my enjoyment of the meal was tempered by the fact I was trapped here, with no choice but to eat whatever was shoved at me under the door, good or bad. I was helpless. I *hated* that.

When the food was finished, I slid the empty tray underneath the door again, expecting Wes had left already and would collect it later. But he spoke.

"How was it? I spread lemon-basil aioli on the sandwich and used a balsamic reduction drizzle on the fruit."

Suddenly angry again at my helpless state, I broke my own rule about staying silent and lashed out. "It was edible."

"Edible?" he laughed.

"Yes. For an amateur chef, it was adequate."

His voice still sounded amused. "Wow. You are a piece of work, lady. All I know is Elven men must have a high tolerance for hostile women."

The remark stung. If I hadn't endured two broken betrothals, maybe it wouldn't have bothered me so much. As it was, there was an annoying sting in my tear ducts—which made me even angrier.

"I don't *want* a man," I snapped. "Elven or otherwise."

"Really? I thought your people were all about bonding—one person for life and all that stuff—that's what my grandmother told me anyway."

"How would your grandmother know?" I snarled.

"She grew up in a small village out in the country—there were lots of legends and superstition."

"Well, she was wrong. Not *all* of us bond. I don't need a man in my life. There is nothing a man can do for me I can't do for myself."

A low, knowing chuckle preceded his answer. "Nothing? You sure about that?"

"Positive."

"I don't know. I can think of a thing or two that might come in handy on a long, cold night."

I was thankful he couldn't see through the door as a hot blush spread from my forehead to my chest. I was not adept at sexual banter. I recognized the tone in his voice, though, and it stirred up uncomfortable feelings throughout my body.

My first impulse was to go silent again, refuse to speak with him any further. But I didn't want to give him the satisfaction of knowing he'd rattled me. That would just lead to more teasing remarks and knowing tones.

"I have no interest in physical relationships," I informed him coolly.

"Everybody's interested in that."

"Not me. I don't like to be touched."

There was a long pause. I supposed he was contemplating his next snide comment as I'd successfully shut down this line of conversation. Or maybe he didn't believe me. But I didn't really care. It was the truth.

With my glamour, I couldn't be close to anyone—not unless I *wanted* them to fall ill. Sex would be virtually impossible, and so over the years, I had basically put it out of my mind. If such thoughts ever occurred to me, I disciplined myself to put the weakness aside, focus on other things, and the urge went away.

Whether a result of instinct or something else, no one felt compelled to touch me—it was like I was covered in jagged glass. And that was a good thing. It made everything easier as I didn't have to be bothered with warning people away from myself or making excuses for not responding to a man's advances.

"You know, princess," Wes said, startling me out of my private thoughts. "I always say, 'Don't knock it till you've tried it.'"

His gentle tone of voice and insinuation that I was sexually inexperienced—which was entirely accurate—lit a flame under my highly flammable temper.

I raised my voice and used my most brittle tone—the one I reserved for the servants when they failed to perform their duties adequately. "And *I* always say humans are the ugliest, most idiotic, worthless race on the planet. I cannot *wait* until you are all eradicated."

On the other side of the door there was rustling and

scraping as if he'd been sitting on the floor and was getting to his feet.

"Okay, you win, sweetheart. I won't expose you to my ugly, idiotic, worthless company any longer. With any luck, this storm will let up tonight, and we can both be rid of each other."

I heard the now-familiar sound of Wes's feet clomping down the stairs and across the stable floor. Struck by a sudden burst of curiosity, I crossed the room to my small window and peered down at the grassy lawn outside.

Through the drizzle I spotted a large form loping up the hill, and the breath whooshed out of me. I couldn't have been more wrong in my earlier prediction of stepping over his "weak, pathetic," human body. There was nothing pathetic or weak about this human.

He was as tall as any Elven man, with wide shoulders and long legs. It was almost mesmerizing to watch the rhythm of his gait, the long, lazy stretch of his legs as they carried him away. He had on a hooded raincoat, so I could not catch even a glimpse of his face. What did it look like?

What does it matter?

Whirling away, I sat on the bed and stared at the wall above the bookshelf. *His face.* If I could get this human man face-to-face, I could sway him and be free of this place, long gone by the time the witches arrived. In spite of my tough talk, I really *didn't* want to see them again. The last time had been painful.

Like it or not, this annoying guy was probably my best chance of escape and survival. Yes, *that* was the reason I wanted to see his face—the *only* reason.

But how to persuade him? I had little experience with humans up-close and even less with men. I had no idea how to flirt or be seductive. I'd never even tried, since it was pointless. An arranged marriage had been my only hope of ever really connecting with someone. But I had to find a way to connect with *this* guy long enough to get him to open the door.

My gaze dropped to the books neatly arranged with their spines facing me. There had to be at least fifteen of them. As I read the titles one-by-one, a plan formed in my mind.

My heart fluttering with excitement, I went to the case and pulled a likely-looking title from the top shelf. I'd never had any interest before in something a human had created, so I'd never been a big reader.

But I was about to be.

6

WES

The weather on Eigg could be temperamental to be sure, but this was remarkable.

The storm had come on suddenly, to the bafflement of the weather presenters on the telly. Unlike the usual squall, it refused to subside. Day after day it went on, drenching the land and keeping the sky above gray and gloomy.

Normally, I wouldn't have minded too much. I rarely left home anyway. And as my house had a landline and an excellent broadband connection, I'd been able to maintain communication with the outside world. I could still do my job.

But it wasn't just the islands that were affected. The violent weather cell was focused around the west coast of the mainland. The winds were treacherously strong, churning the waves and making the fifteen-mile stretch of ocean between Mallaig's ferry port and the small isles impassable. Which meant my mother and grandmother were stuck in the village there. They were growing more frustrated with each passing day, and I had to hear about it.

"Remember—don't let her get to you," Mum warned

when I'd spoken to her this morning by phone. "There is no end to their tricks and lies."

"Why did you even send her *here?*" I'd asked. "If she's such trouble, why didn't you use the transposition spell to send her to Timbuktu or something?"

Her answer was cryptic but intriguing. "As I said, I need her. We may have found a way to cure your condition—for good this time."

"What? How?" And what did the girl have to do with a cure? "Does she have healing powers or something?"

"No," Mum barked definitively. "She's nothing but destructive. But we believe she can *lead* us to a cure. She tracked someone to our house in Bristol—someone very special."

"Who?"

"I'll explain when we get there, love. There are too many interested ears about here. Just keep her from escaping—and do *not* trust her."

Here on the island, the rain stayed steady, making my thrice-daily food runs to the stable cold, wet, and miserable. Considering the Elven girl's sharp tongue and lack of appreciation, I wondered why I even bothered.

I should just shove a week's worth of protein bars under the door and call it good.

But I couldn't actually do that. I was cooking for myself anyway, and each mealtime I seemed to always prepare enough for two. She never complimented the food, of course. In fact, we hadn't spoken at all since Monday, but the plates came back empty each time. My prisoner must have been enjoying my cooking more than she let on, which pleased me for some reason. In a weird way, it was nice to have someone else to cook for.

Today, I delivered her lunch tray then went down to muck the stables and turn out the horses. When I went back upstairs to collect the tray of empty dishes, the girl surprised me by speaking to me for the first time in days.

"Why do you think Arwen chose to give up her immortal life and be with Aragorn?"

"What?"

"It seems to me the advantages of an eternal life are much more valuable than a paltry few years of keeping company with a mortal man, no matter how pleasant those years might be. I don't understand."

Her question was clearly in reference to The Lord of the Rings, one of my favorite book series ever. Well, they were all favorites, as I didn't hang onto books I didn't love. I ordered new ones regularly, and if one didn't suit my fancy, I donated it to the island's library system.

I was baffled by her sudden interest in conversation after all these days of silence, but I answered. "Well... you make a good point, but I don't see it exactly like that. I think a life lived with passion—and true love—even if it *is* shorter, is worth more than endless years of apathy and indifference."

"But what about peace? And constancy? Passion, as you call it, brings with it the likelihood of great pain and suffering. It seems better to me to have a life one can manage and predict. The risk of emotional distress is far less."

Despite our philosophical differences, a balmy sense of pleasure invaded my chest. She'd read the books. And it was delightful to discuss something I'd read and loved with another person face-to-face—well, almost face-to-face. Her take on it was fascinating.

"I think it's worth the risk. Maybe we'll have to agree to disagree on that. I'm glad you found it interesting."

"It was. But I really preferred the newer fantasy book. You only gave me the first two in the series, though. Don't you have the others?"

I felt a smile spreading across my face. George R. R.

Martin was my new favorite author, and I was also chomping at the bit for the sequel to arrive in the post.

"It's on order. It should have been here yesterday, but the storm is preventing the ferry from crossing between the mainland and the islands so there's been no mail delivery. Maybe you could read one of the others until it comes in."

"I did."

"Did what?"

"Read the other books."

"You mean you've read them already, before you came here?" The first Martin book alone was nearly seven hundred pages long. It was impossible she'd read every book I'd left for her.

"No. I read them these past few days."

"All of them?" I was stunned. She'd read fifteen books in three days. Were Elves speed readers as well as strong and powerful?

"All but one. I don't like the one with the brown cover."

That made me smile. "How do you know?"

"It's ugly. Why would they make a book so ugly? It cannot be good."

"Oh now… haven't you ever heard the saying, 'Don't judge a book by its cover?' I happen to *know* that is an excellent book—one of my all-time favorites, in fact."

Her tone was unconvinced. Obstinate. "I'm sure I won't like it. I'd rather read the fantasy sequel."

"You and me both. Unfortunately, you'll be gone by the time it arrives."

Was it unfortunate? I'd been frustrated by my family's delayed arrival, eager to rid myself of this unwanted responsibility and interruption to my life. But now… I was surprised how good it was to hear another person's voice, up close and present and alive, how nice it was to exchange ideas and opinions that had nothing to do with communicable diseases and epidemiological science.

"Well, what am I to do in here then?" Her tone was saturated with frustration. "My mind is going to turn to mush with nothing to do and the rain falling day and night— I can barely even see anything out the window."

A blade of guilt lanced my chest. Which was silly. She was a prisoner, not a house guest. But still...

"I'll bring you some new books tonight—I have more at the house." Turning to go, I paused and turned back. "Is there anything else you need? Still have plenty of towels and toothpaste?"

"Yes, but well... there is one thing I'd very much appreciate."

"What is it?"

"Do you have another set of clothes around I could wear? I couldn't exactly bring along luggage. Maybe your wife has some I could borrow? Or your daughter?"

I laughed at the thought, but of course, she didn't know anything about me. She'd only heard my voice through a door. As far as she knew I was a squat old man with white hair and ten grandchildren.

"I'm too young to have a daughter," I told her. "And I'm not married. Not a stitch of women's clothes for miles around, I'm afraid. But I could bring you a few of my shirts and maybe some joggers. They'll be way too long on you, but they have a drawstring waist and you could roll up the legs."

"That would be acceptable. And since you asked, may I request one more thing?"

I was chuckling again. As hard as the girl tried to sound humble, it was obvious she was used to bossing people around. Maybe she really *was* a princess.

"I'm all ears."

"Well, I like your bathtub very much, but I could really use a shaver. And some bubble bath if you have it."

And then my ears were completely forgotten. Other body parts were perking up, though, as my mind was hijacked by the image of her soaking in a hot, steamy bath, her bare shoulders peeking above a cloud of fragrant foam, her delicate hand drawing a razor up the length of one long, lovely leg.

"Er... I uh... sure, I have a plastic travel razor I can lend you. No bubble bath, though, I'm afraid."

Of course, I *was* due for a delivery from the island market today. I contemplated calling and asking if they had any in stock. *That should be interesting.* The island's residents probably already considered me weird and wondered what I did holed up here by myself all the time. They'd assume I'd taken to long soaks in a flower-scented bath.

"Perhaps I could have a different kind of soap then?" she asked. "This one is very drying to the skin. Maybe the kind you use?"

My head quirked to the side as I smiled at the door panel. "How do you know what kind of soap I use?"

"I don't exactly. I just like the scent. You always smell good."

And there went those other body parts again, now even more awake and alert. Body parts that had *clearly* been neglected for far too long if a simple comment from a girl I didn't even like could get them riled up. *How pathetic.*

It had to be the solitude. It wasn't good for a man. Had I actually considered buying her *bubble bath*?

I gave her a gruff reply. "Fine. I'll... see if I have a bar to spare."

"Thank you," the girl said.

The girl. I was tired of thinking of her as "the girl," "the Elf," or "my prisoner." The last one especially bothered me.

She must have been thinking along the same lines because she said, "My name is Alessia, by the way."

Alessia. A beautiful, feminine name for a beautiful female. A beautiful female who thought I smelled nice, and liked my favorite author, and was planning to take a bath with my soap and sleep in my shirt. My body parts might never recover.

Get it together, Wes.

There was a long pause before I answered, "All right then, Alessia. I'll be back at suppertime. Talk to you then—unless your mind has turned to mush."

If I didn't know better, I'd have sworn I heard a soft giggle.

After getting some work done, I went to the cellar of my house, which I'd converted into a home gym. I lifted free weights and followed that with a turn on the exercise bike then a hard twenty minutes on the rowing machine. Daily exercise was my practice, as my job could be rather sedentary, and staying in top physical condition was something I could actually control about my health.

Pulling off my damp t-shirt and using it to mop my chest, neck, and face, I climbed the two sets of stairs to my bedroom and attached bath. Though the temperature in the house was cool, I was sweaty and in need of a good, long shower. The workout had tired me, but I felt good, my muscles pumped and tingling pleasantly with increased blood flow.

I opened the shower door and turned the water to scalding. One look at the bar of soap on the small ledge inside, and my mind heated up as well, going right back to the small stable room and clawfoot bathtub.

As I dropped the rest of my clothing and started to step into the shower, my gaze snagged on my reflection in the large bathroom mirror. I ran a hand through my overgrown hair and over my beard. I'd seen myself in this mirror every day for years and never really paid any attention to my appearance.

Living apart from everyone else as I did, it had ceased to matter. It had been a long time since I'd actually thought about what I looked like—or what I smelled like.

You always smell good. A lilting female voice curled through my mind.

Now suddenly, I found myself wondering what Alessia would think if she were to see me like *this*. Of course, I could never let her see me, dressed or undressed—it was too dangerous.

And her opinion didn't matter anyway. She'd be gone in a matter of days. But I couldn't help but wonder how I stacked up against the Elven men she was used to.

The old women told tales of Earth-wives who'd fallen victim to Elven males in ancient days, so mesmerized by their supernatural beauty they couldn't remember their spells or even have the desire to use them until it was too late. It wasn't fair... for them all to look so good, especially if their race was as evil as I'd been led to believe.

The memory of Alessia's sleeping face crossed through my mind as I stepped under the steaming spray, soaping up my hair and body. She was so stunning, she *had* to be highly sought after among the males of her own kind, not to mention all the human men who looked at her and forgot their own names.

It was hard to accept, actually, that she was one of them. I mean, other than her unusual height and extreme beauty, she seemed normal. She liked bubble baths. She had food aversions. She had interesting opinions on literature.

No. Stop it. Do not go there.

I turned off the water and grabbed my towel from its hook, rubbing it over my head more vigorously than was necessary to dry my hair. *Idiot.* This was exactly what my mother had warned me about. I couldn't let anything she said get to me. I couldn't let myself think about her seeing me naked. I couldn't think about me seeing *her* naked.

Oh, damn. I was thinking about seeing her naked.

Well, maybe thoughts couldn't be controlled, but I *was* the master of my own actions. No matter what happened, I would not open that door and let her out. I would *not* encounter her face to face.

But it wouldn't hurt to shave.

7

ALESSIA

I looked at the hideous brown-covered book for the thousandth time.

Having already practiced my yoga and bathed, there was nothing left to do. It would be hours before Wes was back with my supper. An afternoon nap wasn't appealing, as I got more sleep than a two year old these days.

It was either obsess about what Wes's face looked like, mentally re-live and regret all the bad decisions that had led me to this point in life, or read the book.

With a huff, I slid from the bedspread and grabbed the homely thing off the shelf. Carrying it over to the chair in the corner, I switched on the lamp and sat down. Title page, acknowledgments, prologue. I hated books that began with a prologue. *Oh Dio.* I snorted. *Get to the story already.*

Two paragraphs later, I was hooked. I devoured the words so eagerly, my eyes could hardly move fast enough. I was beginning the final chapter when I heard a *shooshing* sound. Looking up, I was startled to see the food tray sliding beneath the door. The sky outside my window was pitch dark. Was it suppertime already?

Though I was hungry, I didn't want to stop reading. I stayed in place, poring over the pages even faster, my heart racing to the conclusion along with the heroine's.

"Alessia? You okay in there?" Wes called out a couple minutes later.

"Yes. I'm fine."

"Why aren't you getting your food? You're not sick, are you?"

If I'd been smart, I would have said, "Yes." It might have been the perfect ploy to make my human captor open the door and give me the chance to sway him. But I was too enrapt in the book's final pages.

"I'm fine. I'm just... busy. Give me a few minutes."

"Oh." There was a long pause. "What are you doing?"

Call it distraction—or maybe it was the influence of the novel's sassy heroine—but I answered him with a coy, "Wouldn't *you* like to know?"

"Oh... okay," Wes stammered, sounding flustered. "I'll uh... give you some privacy—some time—some... space... and go feed the horses. Let me know when you've finished... eating."

His boots set a quick, loud pace down the steps.

When I finished the book about ten minutes later, I closed it and held it to my chest, leaning back in the chair and breathing deeply. Wes had been so right. The cover might have been hideous, but it was in no way an indicator of what lay beneath. The story was sublime.

Suddenly it occurred to me—maybe there was a good reason he refused to let me see him—something that went beyond security protocol. Maybe there was a reason he'd been so defensive of the ugly book. My mind flashed to the one human story I had loved throughout my childhood —*Beauty and the Beast*. I only knew it because the animated movie had been shown at one of my cousins' birthday parties.

While the other girls all pulled for Belle to escape the clutches of the evil Beast, I remembered secretly sympathizing with the isolated creature. Lonely and hurt by the fear and disdain of all the so-called "normal" villagers, he was so desperate for companionship, he'd held the girl against her will. I understood him.

Was *Wes* embarrassed by *his* appearance? Maybe that was why he lived alone, far away from other people. Maybe he was horribly scarred... or perhaps in spite of his height and powerful build, he had not been as blessed when it came to bone structure and facial features. I was terribly curious now to know what he looked like.

I crossed the room and retrieved my dinner tray, quickly eating the fish and potatoes and vegetables he'd prepared. The food was still warm, and as always, it was delicious. As always, when he returned, he asked me how I'd enjoyed it. This time I was ready for him.

"It was tolerable," I said, making it obvious with my tone I was teasing him.

"Tolerable? Oh, you're feeling generous tonight. Whatever it was you were doing in there earlier, it put you in a good mood."

"I was reading," I admitted.

"Oh. *Re*-reading?"

"No. I read the ugly book."

"I see. And?"

"You were right. It was wonderful. Though of course the love story was completely unrealistic."

I could almost feel his smile through the thick door. I could certainly hear it in his response. "Why do you say that?"

"Well, for one thing, the insta-love."

"Insta-love?"

"You know—the whole *wow you're the most beautiful person I've ever seen let's be together forever* thing. That never happens in real life."

He took a few seconds to answer. "Whatever you say."

"And the ending. No one could truly forgive someone who'd been so horrible."

"Oh, I don't know about that. We all have reasons for the decisions we make—even some of our worst ones. Sometimes you have to get to know a person before you can understand why they do what they do. And understanding leads to forgiveness."

The remark struck me like a bolt of lightning, searing my heart and frazzling my brain. I'd never heard anyone say such a thing. It took me a moment to gather myself enough to respond.

"You don't think some people are just born bad?"

"No. Not at all. I think our actions and choices are largely determined by our upbringing, what we're taught by our families and the community and environment around us. Take my thoroughbred, Sebastian, for instance. He was once owned by royalty—lived on a large, fine estate. But his master was cruel. Sebastian was never shown gentleness, so he never learned gentleness. He's ornery, and overly sensitive, and he's a nightmare to ride."

"So why did you take him in? Should he not have been put down?"

"Well *that* approach leaves little room for improvement."

"My family's stable master used to say, 'Once a bad mount, always a bad mount.'" *Ooops.* I'd let another personal detail slip. How did he keep managing to draw me out?

"Ah—a horsewoman. I should have known from your *commanding* attitude that you were a rider."

I had no idea how to respond to his assessment of me, but he continued without pausing. "Myself, I believe no one is all bad or good. We each have the potential to lean one way or the other. Which way we go depends on which part of us is nurtured."

Suddenly tired of this thread of conversation, I responded in a disdainful tone. "Is that what your human parents taught you?"

"Actually, no. They have some rather inflexible opinions about certain things and certain... people. But I've... chosen to make up my own mind."

He cleared his throat, and the heavy boots shuffled on the wooden floor. "Listen, I've got to get back to the house and get some work done before bed. I know I said I'd bring you some new books, but it was raining so hard. I couldn't keep them and the food dry at the same time. I'll bring them in the morning."

"That would be nice. Thank you."

I stood close to the door. Naturally I couldn't see Wes, but I could hear the sound of his breathing, which made me think he was standing close as well. He didn't say anything, but neither did he move away. For some reason, my own breathing shallowed, and my pulse sped as if I had been running uphill.

Finally, he spoke again. "Well, if you don't need anything else..." The boots started moving away.

Wait. I did need something. I didn't want him to leave. I had learned to get along quite well in my life without companionship, but the thought of the long night stretching out ahead of me with the storm raging outside and no new books to get lost in had me feeling an uncharacteristic sense of loneliness.

In this moment, any company—even that of a human—seemed preferable to being alone.

"Wes—"

The footsteps stopped. "Yeah?"

"What do you look like?"

There was a delay before he answered. "Why does it matter?"

"It doesn't. Not really. I mean, whatever you look like, it's fine. I'm just… curious. You've seen me, but I've never seen you. Only heard your voice. And tasted your cooking."

"My *tolerable* cooking."

"Right." I couldn't help but grin, absurdly pleased he remembered my earlier joke. "Your very mediocre, passable cooking. It just feels odd after all these days of talking to have no idea what you look like—except that you're tall."

"How do you know that?"

"Your shirt. It's very large. And I saw you through the window yesterday walking back to the house. But you had a raincoat on. I couldn't see your face or even what your hair color is."

"It's brown. Dark brown—like yours."

"That's right." I was pleasantly surprised. "Most people say my hair is black. Of course, most people don't look at me closely enough to detect the difference."

"Yeah, right." The words were muttered, almost as if he hadn't meant to say them aloud. I blinked several times and drew back from the door. Did that mean he *liked* the way I looked? The pulse point in my neck gave a short, hard throb.

I leaned my shoulder against the door and rested the side of my head on it. "What color eyes do you have?"

The door shifted slightly as he leaned against it from the other side. "You tell me first."

"You want me to guess your eye color?"

"No. I mean *your* eyes. I didn't see them. They were closed earlier when I brought you into the room. It's only fair if you're asking about me that I can ask about you as well."

A strange, pleasurable heat bubbled up inside me.

"They're blue. Light blue. When I was very young, Babbo used to call me sky-eyes."

"Who's Babbo?"

"My father. That's the name I call him. It's very common in Italy. But you haven't answered my question."

"Which one?"

"About your *eyes*."

"They're blue as well. But not light blue. Darker than that."

"Deep blue." I smiled, picturing the evening skies above Positano or maybe the waters of Lake Como, one of my favorite getaway spots. "They must be beautiful. I should like to see them."

There was no response—nothing—for nearly a full minute. His words, when they came, were terse and stilted. "It's late. I should be getting back. Good night, Alessia."

Merda. I spun away from the door, fighting hard not to stomp the floor. I'd scared him off. I was no better with men than I'd ever been. And I'd completely forgotten about my plan to win his trust and persuade him to open the door.

He'd probably refuse to even speak to me from now on. The storm would end, the witches would arrive to take me away, and I'd never get to read the book sequel or see those blue eyes for myself. Somehow, that seemed like the worst part.

* * *

THE NEXT MORNING I was startled awake by the slide of several new books under the door followed by my breakfast tray. Instead of the rapid retreat of his boots, I heard Wes's cheerful voice.

"Good morning. Did you sleep well?"

I sprinted from the bed to the door. "Yes, I just got up, as a matter of fact."

"I slept later than usual, too. This storm has been waking me up during the night. You?"

His tone was pleasant, but a bit impersonal. It reminded me of the way my nanny used to speak to me—polite and respectful while holding me at a distance. I hated it.

I answered his question, eager now to keep him talking so I could read his tone of voice further. Maybe I was imagining things.

"At times. But I've actually slept better here than I have almost anywhere else. It must be the ocean air."

"That—or maybe you needed a break from your stressful life."

"How do you know my life was stressful?"

"I don't. But in general when you find yourself on the other end of a witches' spell, it's not an indicator of a peaceful and harmonious existence."

Ah, the witches. After our conversation last night, I was more convinced than ever Wes was just an innocent pawn of theirs. Contrary to my lifelong beliefs, there *were* decent humans. Based on his treatment of me and his general demeanor, he was one of them. I couldn't imagine how a nice, ordinary human could have become involved with a vengeful sect of fanatics like the Earth-wives.

"How did you come to work for them?"

He hesitated before answering. "I... don't really think we should get into that. Let's just say, sometimes you find yourself in a place in life you never planned on being, you know? Some things we don't ask for—they just happen."

Now the real Wes was back—the warm, genuine tone. The honesty. My ears drank it in, and my soul responded to the sincerity. An agreeable warmth bloomed in my midsection.

"I understand what you mean." Did I *ever*.

I wondered what else we might have in common. Instead of continuing the conversation and giving me the opportunity to find out, he started to walk away.

"Breakfast looks and smells delicious," I said, raising my voice to be heard over the sound of his boots.

"Good. I hope you enjoy it," he said, continuing his retreat.

"I'm sure I will. Are you going back to the house already?" I cringed at the needy sound of my own voice.

He stopped in place. "Not yet. I'm going to turn out the horses for a while. Thanks to this storm they've spent far too much time inside. It's still bad out, but if I leave them cooped up much longer, they'll never forgive me."

"That's what I like about horses," I blurted. "They *don't* judge you when you make mistakes. They love you no matter what."

Instantly, I was embarrassed. I was supposed to be drawing him out, not sharing information about myself. Somehow he managed to keep turning the tables on me.

The sound of footsteps drew near again, stopping just outside my door.

Wes's tone was low. Patient. "Why are you here, Alessia? You might as well tell me what happened. Who knows? Maybe I can help you out with the witches—put in a good word, you know?"

The air left my lungs in a rush. Once again he'd shocked me. I truly didn't know what to say. Actually, I didn't intend to say anything, but my mouth opened, and what came out was total honesty.

"It won't matter. There is nothing anyone can say or do. Their kind has hated mine since long before either of us was born. And perhaps they should. I have done something... unforgiveable."

"Nothing is unforgiveable."

His voice was full of conviction. He truly believed it. How nice it must have been to grow up a regular person with average, caring parents, to live a simple life far from the pressures and traditions of the Ancient Court. To believe good triumphed over evil and that unconditional love was there for the asking.

This naïve human could not even conceive of the realities of my life, of what it was like to know you were born unlovable, untouchable, and destined for rejection. To know you'd always be alone. To know you might very well be responsible for the elimination of the entire human race.

Though he meant well, I couldn't prevent a frisson of irritation from leaking into my voice. "Never mind. You couldn't possibly understand, tucked away here on your safe little island, far from the world. Probably the worst thing you've ever done was letting the neighbor's sheep out of their pen when you were a boy."

"I haven't always lived here. I've seen plenty of the world. And you might be surprised. I'm capable of understanding a *lot* of crazy stuff."

"Not this."

"Ah, I get it now," he said as if he'd just solved a mystery ten pages before the end of a twisty suspense novel.

"What do you get?"

"You're a porcupine."

"What?"

"A porcupine. It's a rodent with pointed quills. Common in North America and—"

"I *know* what it is. I just have no idea what you're talking about."

"At first I thought you were just rude and stuck-up. But now I see that your prickly exterior is a defense mechanism. You're afraid. I'll bet you hold everyone at a distance. You probably have very few friends and trust almost no one because you're afraid they're going to let you down or hurt you. "

His words had the effect of a hard slap to the cheek. My eyes burned, and my chest felt like a weight had been dropped on it. I had never been more offended. The thing was—he was absolutely right. At least about the "no friends" part. But I wasn't going to admit that to him.

"You don't know me at *all*," I snarled.

"I think I'm right. You've got a definite ice queen vibe going, but I bet inside you're as warm and gooey as baked brie."

"That is ridiculous. You are way off base—not to mention in possession of a *colossal* ego. How *dare* you diagnose me."

"You wouldn't be so angry if I hadn't hit pretty close to the truth."

I spit out the next words. "Well... if I'm a—a *porcupine*, then you're... you're an opossum. A dirty, rat-faced, squirmy-tailed opossum. You hide away here all alone and play dead while you're still alive. What kind of life is that?"

He had the audacity to laugh. "Fair enough. But which would you rather hug—a cute little furry opossum or a hard, prickly porcupine?"

"Just... just go away. I can't abide your stupidity any longer. Don't you need to go turn out the horses?"

"That I do. I'll check on you at lunchtime."

"Don't bother. I *won't* be hungry."

"I don't know... you've got a pretty good appetite on you. See you later Princess Porky."

Letting out a growl of rage, I kicked the door. On the other side, a low laugh was followed by the heavy tread of Wes's boots on the stairs.

I grabbed the breakfast tray and carried it to my bed, steaming with fury. I was even angrier when I lifted the fork to my lips and found my Eggs Benedict had gone cold. What was *wrong* with me—wasting my time and energy on meaningless conversations with a human? And allowing him to upset me? It was unacceptable.

I needed to toughen up, get my mind back in the game. My *only* focus should be on getting out of here before the witches arrived. The storm couldn't last forever, and when it ended, it could spell the end of me. I was through being distracted by this surprisingly distracting human.

The next time I talked to him, I would be the ice queen he'd accused me of being—*without* the warm and gooey center.

8

MACY

My white noise machine was extra loud this morning. The sound of waves seemed like it was coming from just beside my ears instead of across the room where I kept the sleep therapy device.

My alarm clock hadn't gone off yet, but I felt great, fully rested and ready to get up, which was rare for me—*not* a morning person. I yawned and stretched. *Tried* to stretch. Something was wrong with my arms.

My eyelids opened. No, actually, I wasn't awake. Couldn't be. Because clearly this was a dream. A weird one, too.

I was on my back, lying on pillows or some other kind of soft surface, and I couldn't separate my hands. Bringing them in front of my face to see what was holding them, I discovered my wrists were bound. The muscles of my arms and shoulders contracted, tugging against the thin, golden threads. Nothing. They looked no more substantial than dental floss, but they held tight.

There was the watery sound again, a rhythmic swish and swirl. It wasn't waves. It sounded more like... rowing. I struggled to sit up and sucked in a huge breath. I was in a boat—not a big one—something more along the lines of a gondola. Long and narrow, it appeared to be made of polished wood, and the inside where I was sitting was indeed lined with soft cushions. The fabric covering them felt like silk, and either they or something else smelled like flowers.

The vessel was moving, propelled along by two girls with long paddles. One stood at the front of the boat while the other stood closer to me in the back. They wore Halloween costumes. At least I thought that's what they were. Sparkly and a tad on the too-short side, their dresses reminded me of the fairy princess costumes I'd worn as a kid several years in a row.

What a bizarre dream.

The girl closest to me turned to look back at me. Oh—not a girl—a woman. She was so small, I'd thought—

That's when the memory of last night's struggle at the inn came back to me. I wasn't dreaming.

I'd been kidnapped. Panic flooded my veins and boiled over, stealing my breath.

"Where is Nic?" I wheezed, struggling against my bonds.

The woman turned back toward the boat's bow, gave her companion a pointed glance, and pushed her long paddle through the water without even acknowledging my question.

"Who are you? Where are you taking me?"

The women ignored those questions as well, facing straight ahead and continuing to navigate the boat down a narrow, twisting, crystal clear river. Glancing around did nothing to help me ground myself because I'd never seen anything like this place before. Everything was incredibly green, like a tropical rainforest. Clearly I was no longer in Scotland—or at least, not in March.

Oh God. I hope I haven't been asleep for months.

It was possible. We *were* dealing with the Fae here. Or at least I was pretty sure that was who these small, beautiful women were. They had to be nymphs. Nic and I had found the book with the symbol matching the one drawn by my mother, and now—I was here.

And where was that exactly?

The riverbank rose high on both sides, and the bend in the river obscured any view of what was ahead. It reminded me of a rafting trip I'd taken with Mom and Dad and Lily years ago in Colorado. We'd floated down the Arkansas River, right through the massive Royal Gorge, feeling miniaturized by the sheer size of the rocky walls rising high around us.

This was different, though. Instead of unyielding stone and scrub brush, these banks were covered in vegetation, twisting green vines, flowers of every color and variety I'd ever seen—and quite a few I hadn't. There was a strange quality to the light here that made the flowers glow as if it were sunset and dawn at the same time. Their reflection turned the river into a canvas of multi-colored ripples, like a watercolor painting come to life.

As I looked up to see what was causing the strange light, all the breath left my body in a gasp. Buildings were engineered into the cliffs on either side of the river. I wasn't sure if they were homes or what, but there were lights within and figures moving beyond the shaded windows.

Between the structures, bridges crossed the chasm, staggered at intervals and various heights, some of them reaching nearly all the way to the top of the cavern. Because that was what we were in—some kind of very long, very deep cavern with a river running through it. It made me think of Altum, the home base of the Light Elves in America, with its beautiful subterranean river. That one had been much wider, though, and I'd never seen any boats on it during my visit there. It was much lighter and brighter here, too. Altum had been lit by glowing phosphorescent stones while this place had an opening overhead that let in daylight.

We passed under one of the lowest bridges. Like the riverbanks, it was covered in greenery—moss, ferns, vines, flowers—with small trees growing on the sides and forming a sort of arbor of branches and vines over it. Lamps hung from the center of the natural arbor, spaced a few feet apart and casting a glow on the people passing back and forth beneath them.

This bridge was busy. The pedestrians didn't even bother to look down at the small boat floating beneath. *They* were busy, obviously, with places to go and things to do. They had lives—lives that were apparently lived within this long, rock-walled enclosure.

Where could we be? It felt tropical in here. Though I still wore my nightgown, I wasn't cold. All the people I saw were dressed in light clothing as well. Most of the women wore outfits similar to those of the women in the boat. The men wore a bit more—belted, knee-length tunics of varying shades with tall leather boots.

"Where are we going?" I asked my escorts again, not really expecting an answer this time. They might not have even understood me.

And then the boat rounded a bend, and I didn't have to wonder anymore. Our destination was obvious.

In front of us, still about a quarter mile in the distance and just inside the end of the cavern stood the capital city. I knew it was the capital because an awe-inspiring vision like this couldn't be anything else.

It stretched from the bottom of the cavern to nearly the top, its graduated layers building on one another, rising toward the light like the grandest wedding cake ever imagined or constructed. Now that I could see how high it reached, I was convinced we were inside a mountain—maybe a volcano?

Around the city's wide base near the river rose a straight, high wall of sheer, smooth rock. At the top of that were structures like multi-story buildings with windows and roofs, towers and turrets. They joined and intersected at various intervals, some receding, some jutting out from the continuous facade. But that was only the beginning.

Behind them and farther up was another wall—this one taller and more imposing than the first. From its top borders, spaced at even intervals, hung long banners made of red silk or some other iridescent fabric. Emblazoned on each of them was the symbol I carried in my pocket on my birth mother's letter.

My belly flipped with excitement. There could be no more doubt about it. This was the nymph sanctuary. Although, "sanctuary" now seemed like a rather docile word, implying fragile, timid creatures, cowering in fear. Seeing this place, the word "fortress" seemed more appropriate, and the race of my biological parents now seemed rather... intimidating.

The layers of the fantastical city kept climbing, comprised of towers and spires and domes. At the very top stood a palace. It appeared to have been hewn entirely of white stone. I wondered who lived there. I wondered if I'd ever find out.

It was possible I'd never make it farther than the lowest levels of this place—the dungeons, if they had those here. My curiosity about the nymph symbol had obviously caught the attention of someone—and they were unhappy enough about it to snatch us from our room in the middle of the night.

Was Nic in this place somewhere? Was this city where they'd taken him? He was obviously Elven in appearance. If the legends were true, a city full of nymphs wouldn't exactly welcome his presence. Maybe our attackers hadn't even brought him here. It was possible they'd killed him outright.

Cold, sharp pain clutched my heart. *No.* I wouldn't go there. Not yet. I couldn't. Not until I saw where this mysterious boat ride led.

I wondered how we'd enter the city with that imposing stone wall wrapping its base, but the boat circled to its far side, and I saw the entrance. A set of stone stairs led directly from the river to a huge doorway made of two carved-metal panels. One of them opened as our boat floated toward the lowest step, causing small waves to lap at the stone.

One of my escorts took my arm and pulled me to standing while the other used her long oar to direct the boat to the stairs. With the help of my guard, I stepped out of the boat and onto the lowest dry step, gazing up in wonder at the tall marble statues flanking the city entrance.

Inside the open door, glowing light silhouetted a figure and emphasized the massive height of the doorway. My guard kept hold of my arm and was joined on my other side by the second woman, both of them leading me toward the opening.

Once we were inside, the enormous door closed behind us with an echoing clang. The person who'd been waiting inside had disappeared, and my escorts led me through a wide, empty hall. It was spooky, shadowed and much cooler in here than it had been outside on the river. I was getting a definite dungeon vibe.

But the women led me to a lift. As we boarded, an equally uncommunicative operator pressed a button marked by a strange symbol, and the lift began to rise. The trip continued for some time. So long, in fact, I began to wonder if we were headed for the palace itself. *At least it's not the dungeon.*

When the ascent finally ended, the lift doors opened, and we stepped out into a wide hallway lined with marble columns and what looked like gas torches burning all along its length. The gleaming polished stone floors were so pristine they looked like they'd never been walked on.

The palace.

At the end of it we came to a grand double staircase, the two sides of it bowing out and curving upward to meet at the next level. The columns, both on this floor and the next, were covered in elaborate scrollwork, the designs foreign and beautiful. The ceilings were also fascinating, decorated with raised plasterwork swirls and flowers and leaves and shells. I nearly tripped several times from looking up while walking.

Finally we reached what appeared to be our destination, a set of tall golden doors, rounded at the top to form an arch. My nerves simmered as the doors soundlessly swung open. When we stepped inside, I gasped.

It was like being inside a domed kaleidoscope or maybe a soap bubble colored in iridescent prisms by the sun. The floor seemed to be made of a mirror-like material, and the entire ceiling and three of the walls were made of glass.

Outside on the other side of the myriad tiny windows were plants and flowers of such vivid color their reflection on the mirrored floor created a watery rainbow of color underfoot.

My escorts had either been here so many times before they didn't notice the spectacular surroundings, or they were more focused on something else, because they dragged me forward. And then I spotted where their attention was directed.

At the end of the room a pair of gigantic statues stood on either side of a set of clear glass stairs. The sculptures were beautiful, like angels without wings, wearing flowing robes and reaching out toward each other, their hands nearly touching. Beneath them, at the top of the stairs, was a chair made entirely of gold in the shape of an open flower—a rose or maybe a tulip.

A woman sat in the center of the chair. A very small, very beautiful woman. She wore an elaborate long gown. The top of it around her torso and arms was deep green fabric, made to look like individual leaves sewn together. From the bodice down, the dress was variegated shades of deep pinks and purples.

She wore matching flowers around her neck in the style of a choker, and on her head was a tall, willowy crown studded with tiny, colored jewels.

Oh, not a chair. A *throne.* This was a throne room—had to be. And that would make this woman—

"My queen," said one of my guards.

I did a double take. "You speak English?"

The woman ignored me completely, bowing low before the queen, just as the other guard was doing. Belatedly getting with the program, I bent at the waist and dipped my head as well.

I wasn't sure what their intentions were for me, but my goal was to live long enough to find out what had happened to Nic and ask these people to help the human race survive the Plague. I figured showing a little respect couldn't *hurt* my situation.

"You may rise," said the queen.

I did as instructed then launched into an introduction. "Hello your... Majesty. I'm—"

"I did not say you may speak."

I stopped talking and just stood there as she looked me over.

"Who are you? Who are your family?" she said then added, "You may speak now."

"Oh. I'm Macy Moreno. I'm from Missouri—in the U.S., you know. My parents are Joel and Natalie Moreno."

Her nose wrinkled. "Missouri? Moreno? You lie."

"No. I'm not lying. I guess I should add the Morenos adopted me. That's why I'm here—I mean, that's why I was in Scotland—to look for my birth family."

Now she nodded as if more satisfied with my second answer. "You were with an Elven man. Was he holding you hostage? Forcing you to look for your people?"

"Nic? No. He would never... Nic is my boyfriend—fiancé I mean. We just got engaged."

Her eyes widened at this news. "Engaged? To an Elf." She sounded incredulous.

"Yes. When we met, I had no idea he was Elven. And he thought I was human. He didn't know I was... what I was."

"And what is that?" Her tone told me she already knew the answer—she just wanted to find out if I did.

"A... nymph."

She nodded again then her ultra-smooth forehead creased. "Still an odd pairing, even if he believed you to be human."

"Maybe," I conceded. "But he loves me. And I love him. He's protected me and helped me in more ways than I can even explain. Is he here?"

Her interest in Nic had me feeling suddenly hopeful. She didn't answer my question, though, only offered another of her own.

"You purchased a book in the village. You told the shopkeeper you had... papers."

Did this woman have spies in Mallaig then? I couldn't imagine why, but then, I couldn't begin to understand a *lot* of what was going on here.

"Yes. Nic and I spotted the book in the shop window. We went in to ask about it because of the symbol on the front. I thought it might have some information in it that would lead me to my family. You see..."

I went to put my hand in my pocket to pull out my mother's note but realized I was wearing my pj's. "Oh no. The letter. It's back at the inn, in my room."

"All of your belongings have been brought here. Your letter is with them."

"Oh." So she knew about the letter already. Why had she asked me about my papers then? "Did you read it?"

"Who wrote that letter to you?"

"My birth mother. I don't know her name. I never got to meet her. She left me at the hospital a few hours after giving birth to me. All I have is that symbol and the initial F."

"Fallon," she said. There was no doubt in her voice. "You look like her."

I blinked in astonishment. A frothy sense of lightness lifted my hopes. "You know her?"

"I *did*. She was a citizen of Sidhe Innis." She lifted her hands to either side, indicating that Sidhe Innis was the name of this incredible place.

"Do you have any idea why she would have traveled to Missouri... and left me at the hospital instead of having me here?"

"Fallon left us without explanation many years ago. She was betrothed to a nobleman here, but there were rumors of a handsome young warrior... of a possible pregnancy. I suspect you may be the confirmation of that rumor as fact. What is your age?"

"Nineteen."

"Yes. The resemblance is uncanny. When you first entered the room, I thought..." She let the sentence drift without finishing it, studying me closer.

"So the symbol... from my letter and on that book cover... I saw it on the banners outside on the city walls," I said. "It represents Sidhe Innis? Maybe my mother gave it to me so I could find my way here someday."

The queen's expression faltered. "Perhaps."

"Why was it on the book, though? Was that why we were abducted—because I bought the book?"

As was apparently her habit, she answered my question with one of her own. This one was asked in a harsher tone. "Were you *followed* to Mallaig?"

Followed? Was Alessia on our trail again? Icy fear crept over me until I looked around at my surroundings. It was unlikely *anyone* could find us here, even Alessia, who'd been creepily good at staying close at our heels.

"Not that I know of. I guess it's possible though," I admitted. "There's an Elven woman from the Dark Court in Italy who was pursuing us before."

She shook her head, and her hand brushed the air in irritation. "Not an Elf. A pair of Earth-wives arrived in the village shortly after you did. They were asking *questions.*"

The witches. Could she mean Olly's mother and grandmother? I really had no idea if the women had somehow followed us from Bristol and told her so.

"Well. It's of no importance. I've stirred up a slight... *weather disturbance* that should slow them down quite nicely."

Wait, what? "You created—" My head was spinning.

The queen interrupted. "That will be all for now. My Queensguard will see you out." With a sweep of her hand, she dismissed us all, and my guards took my arms once more to guide me from the room.

"Wait. What about Nic?" I called back over my shoulder. Panic made my voice shrill and my knees nearly too stiff to walk. "Where is he? Is he okay? Is he alive?"

The queen did not respond, and the golden doors closed behind us with a decisive clang.

9

ALESSIA

I lay on my bed staring at the ceiling for the next few hours, plotting my next move and girding my strength for my next encounter with Wes.

I reminded myself again and again of the betrayals I'd endured at the hands of men—starting with my own father. No one cared, *no one* had my best interest at heart, except for me. I had to do whatever it took to save myself, up to and including overpowering Wes. I might not kill him as I'd originally intended, but I would not let any softness into my heart where he was concerned.

When he knocked at the door and slid my luncheon tray underneath, I walked over and picked it up without comment.

"Read anything good while I was gone?" he asked.

"No."

"I see. Been busy thinking of how to get back at me for what I said earlier? I'm sorry, by the way. It was presumptuous of me and really none of my business."

"I don't even remember what you said earlier," I lied.

Then I added in my best dismissive tone, "Thank you for lunch. That will be all."

"Oh." He chuckled. "Well, enjoy it then, princess."

I carried the tray to my bedside table and reached for the fork. Beneath it was a large, white paper napkin, and on it, a drawing made in pen. Moving the fork aside, I leaned closer to examine the image. It was a porcupine. Not a bad likeness either. Wes was a talented cartoonist—was that his job? His work had to be something he could do remotely from an island. An artist made sense.

The animal's arms were curled in front of it. Boxing gloves covered its paws. And it wasn't alone. Lying on the ground in front of it was an opossum. The marsupial's eyes were closed, but one of its arms was extended skyward, holding a flower as if making a peace offering to the combative porcupine.

Hmmph. It would take more than a comical drawing to make me think well of him. I wasn't even sure why he cared enough to try to entertain me. We weren't friends. He was my jailer, and I, his prisoner.

Using the fork, I started cutting into the chicken breast he'd prepared. It was drenched with a lemony-butter sauce but a bit too firm to cut easily with the fork. Too hungry to deal with the challenge, I moved on to the pasta and broccoli side dishes.

When those were consumed, I renewed my attack on the chicken breast. Wes was right about my appetite—I was ravenous. I'd pick up the chicken and eat it with my fingers if it came to it, but the sauce pooling around it on the plate would make that a messy venture.

Instead, I used the side of my fork, which slid through the filet, but I splashed sauce on my hand in the process.

Irritated, I grabbed the napkin to clean up. The first thing I noticed was the sprig of flowers lying beneath it. Deep purple in color, they were greenhouse orchids, the long stem covered in tiny, delicate petals that smelled of chocolate and vanilla. Automatically, I lifted the flowers to my nose. And that was when I saw the knife.

My heart contracted in a painful, sweet squeeze and then galloped in excitement. Wes had given me flowers. And a knife.

Of course, it wasn't sharp—just a butter knife, suitable for cutting tender chicken and not much else. If he was ever foolish enough to open the door, it had no chance of piercing his skin. My mind immediately recoiled at the thought of stabbing him. It wouldn't be necessary anyway. I had better weapons at my disposal.

Lifting the silver cutlery, I studied its fine tip. Then I looked across the room at the keyhole in the door. *Perfect.* As soon as Wes left the stable, I'd pick the lock and be on my way.

First I wolfed down my lunch—who knew when I'd find my next source of food? Then I went to the window and surveyed the weather. Ugh. Still windy and raining. No matter. This was my chance to get away, and I was going to take it.

If I could time it right, there would be no need to even confront Wes. After the flowers and the apology comic, those blue eyes were the last thing I wanted to see.

When I heard him climbing the stairs, my heart started racing. What if he checked the tray and noticed the knife was missing? I had to think quickly.

He rapped on the door. "Alessia? Finished with lunch?"

Using my haughtiest tone, I said, "I told you I wouldn't be hungry. I haven't eaten it yet."

"Well... push the tray back out here then. I'll eat it."

"No," I blurted then hurriedly recovered my calm. "I'll eat

it later, perhaps at supper. That way you won't have to return tonight."

There was an audible sigh. "Guess you didn't like the drawing, huh? The chicken piccata will be cold and disgusting by suppertime. I'll bring you something fresh to eat then—I don't mind."

"I *said* I'll eat this later—when I'm ready. You may go now. I'm sure you have much work to do."

I heard no retreating footsteps. There was a delay before Wes spoke again. "Listen... I spend a *lot* of time alone, and I don't always have the best people skills. I'm sorry if I hurt your feelings."

I felt an unwilling twinge of commiseration. My own people skills were not the best. His apology took some of the fight out of me, but it didn't dampen my determination to escape. I had to. It was a matter of life and death.

"You didn't hurt my feelings. I'm just... tired of talking to a door. As you've said repeatedly, hopefully this storm will end soon. You can get back to your life, and I can stop waiting and go ahead and face my fate."

He sighed again. "Okay then. I'll see you this evening."

Lifting the knife, I ran my fingers over its hard, cold, smoothness.

Not if I can help it.

10

WES

I had a hard time concentrating on work. My mind kept drifting back down the hill to the stable where Alessia was apparently determined to conduct a hunger strike.

Her last words had my guts twisted in a knot. *I can stop waiting and go ahead and face my fate.*

What *was* going to happen to her? Whereas before I'd been eager for the storm to end, now I found myself wishing it would go on a while longer. I needed more time to figure out exactly what Alessia had done—and what Mum and Nanna had planned for her.

I was convinced she wasn't the monster my mother had portrayed her to be. Elves might be capable of Sway and deception, but I'd heard real pain in Alessia's voice, recognized genuine remorse. No one was *that* good a liar.

And I wasn't in a hurry to get back to my "life," if anyone could call this solitary existence *living*. Strange though it was to interact through a slab of wood, I had found myself looking forward to mealtimes in a way I hadn't in years.

It wasn't just having another person to talk to—it was Alessia herself. She was interesting. She was smart. She was funny when she wanted to be. The more I talked to her, the more intrigued I grew.

Did Mum even know anything about her—or had she just passed a blanket judgment on Alessia because she was Elven? The thought festered as it sat in my brain.

By the time my mother called late that afternoon, I was feeling testy and combative.

"Hello darling. How are things?" she said when I hit the answer button.

"By 'things' do you mean my health, my work, or are you perhaps referring to the *girl* I have locked in a *barn* like a farm animal?"

"Oh my, you are in a foul temper. You spoke to her, didn't you?"

"Yes. As a matter of fact, I did. And I believe I'm ready for a full explanation. Why *exactly* am I holding her here? I'm going to need something more specific than 'you need her because she could be important.' Unless there is some critical reason, I'm not comfortable keeping this girl prisoner any longer. Not only is it highly illegal, but it's starting to feel just plain wrong."

"Now don't you start feeling sorry for her. That she-Elf made a threat against your sister—and your grandmother and me."

That gave me a moment's pause. "She could have been bluffing because she was afraid."

"What if she *wasn't*? From what she said, we gathered there is a new plague coming. She suggested she had the power to trigger it and sicken everyone in our entire county with a single touch. That is why we sent her to the island, where there are so few humans."

Apparently worried by my stunned silence, Mum said, "Are you quite all right, son? Have I frightened you?"

"No, I'm fine," I lied.

"Try not to worry. Just keep her locked away. We'll be there to take her off your hands as soon as this storm lets up."

"Okay. Good. Yes. See you soon."

I hung up the phone, shaken to the core. *A new plague.* Could Alessia's threats have anything to do with the strange new outbreak I'd been tracking? Was *that* what she'd meant when she said she'd done something unforgiveable?

As she was not human, she couldn't be a disease carrier herself, but I supposed it was possible her glamour could have been involved somehow. No wonder she was so morose. I thought of her spending day after day alone in that small room with nothing but her thoughts and regrets to keep her company, and my first impulse was not fear, but pity.

Now *that* frightened me. Why was I more concerned about her feelings than what she might have done to humanity? What was wrong with me? Was it possible she had swayed me through a solid wood door—in spite of my mother's protective wards?

Or maybe Sway and glamour had nothing to do with how I felt. Maybe Alessia herself had *already* triggered something. Something inside of *me*—something more dangerous than physical illness.

Angry with my mother, Alessia, and myself and planning to demand some answers, I grabbed my mack, pulled on my Wellies, and threw open the back door, storming down the slippery-wet hill. Like it or not, *Princess* Alessia was going to talk to me—even if it meant me opening the door and shaking the words out of her.

Why were the Earth-wives so determined to get to her? What, if anything, did she have to do with the outbreak in Peru? And how could she possibly be instrumental in curing my incurable condition?

I'd almost reached the barn when I realized the door to

the stable was open. Had I been so distracted I'd forgotten to secure it on my last visit here? Had the wind somehow blown it free?

Breaking into a run, I reached it but then fell back in a scramble for self-preservation as Sebastian's huge form filled the doorway. He shot out of the stable at a dead run. Atop his back, riding with no saddle, was Alessia.

"No! Stop," I yelled after her. "He's too dangerous. No one can ride him." *Except for me.*

Alessia turned back and looked over her shoulder, her dark hair whipping in the wind. "I can," she called, her laughter carrying on the breeze. "Farewell, Mr. Opossum. I shall miss our chats."

Then she turned and leaned over Sebastian's neck, digging the heels of her boots into his sides, growing smaller and smaller as the nightmare horse gained speed.

Oh dear Lord. She was going to die. It would have been foolish to ride Sebastian on a balmy, clear day in a training ring. But the weather conditions were horrid, and the island's terrain was treacherous—especially after dark.

On my own property alone there were boulders and jagged rocks jutting from the ground, remnants of ancient stone walls constructed by the island's earliest settlers, not to mention cliffs that dropped off into the ocean or onto bone-splitting rocks far below. Alessia had no idea where she was, much less where she was going.

Heart pounding like thunder, I ran into the stable and yanked a saddle off the wall. I had to stop her—not because my mother would be infuriated over my losing her—for her own safety. Opening Scarlett's stall door, I saddled her as quickly as I could and mounted.

"You're not going to like this, girl, but we're going for a cold, wet ride."

The mare did actually balk a bit at the stable door when

the rain slapped her in the face, but at my urging, she trotted out into the pasture and then broke into a gallop when I prodded her again.

"Let's find your boyfriend Sebastian, shall we?"

Unlike Alessia, I knew the grounds of my estate as well as the bordering properties. I guided Scarlett around the danger zones, urging her to keep as fast a pace as was safe to maintain. Thanks to the home field advantage, we soon closed the distance with my runaway prisoner. As soon as I thought she might hear my voice over the storm, I called out to her.

"Alessia! Listen to me. Turn back—please. It's very dangerous out here. And Sebastian isn't suitable to ride—he's only half-tamed."

Her head whipped back to face me. "Then we're a perfect match." She turned back around and kicked the horse into a faster pace as I should have known she'd do.

Damn it. Scarlett was in better condition than the rest of the horses back at the stable, but there was no way she could compete with the thoroughbred. Sebastian had been bred to race, and he loved nothing better than running wild.

What chance did we stand? I allowed Scarlett to slow to a trot, contemplating turning back. And then I realized what was up ahead. Something Alessia knew nothing about, something that could kill her. Dread slid down my backbone like a wintry chill.

The terrain she currently traversed was among the smoothest in the area—deceptively smooth. What looked like a wide-open field ended abruptly in a drop-off just on the other side of the bend. If she kept urging Sebastian on a straight path, they'd run right over it.

Actually, no. Sebastian and I had ridden near the precipice many times. He wouldn't gallop off the cliff. Rather, he'd stop short just at the edge of it, throwing his stirrup-less rider over his head and right over the edge onto the boulders and jagged rocks far below.

I had to warn her. Pushing Scarlett harder, I managed to close the distance again, enough to yell, "Alessia—stop now, before it's too late. There's danger ahead."

Once more she turned back without slowing her horse. "Let me go, Wes. I don't want to hurt you."

The pair of dark beauties stretched the space between us once more, racing toward disaster. What could I do? I couldn't let this happen. But how to stop them?

Looking up the rocky hill, I spotted an area where we could gain advantage. The land down here swept out into a wide arc as the precipice at the northeast corner of the island approached. If I took Scarlett uphill, we could cut off some of the curve and then charge down again, hopefully making up the difference and apprehending Alessia and Sebastian.

The stubborn girl obviously wasn't going to listen to me —but maybe the stubborn horse would if I could get close enough to command him. My breath quickened, my jaw clenching with new determination and a bit of anger as well.

Turning Scarlett uphill, I urged the mare to climb. This was a risk. We'd move slower on this sloping path, but hopefully the ground we'd gain would be worth it. It was the only thing I could think to do.

As we climbed, the rain seemed to pound harder, if that was even possible, making it necessary for me to swipe at my eyes every few seconds. I could tell Scarlett was nervous about the conditions as well as the uneven terrain.

I patted her neck. "You are in for a whole box of sugar cubes, my love. Just a few more minutes. Good girl."

Reaching the top of the summit, I guided Scarlett across the narrow hilltop and around to the other side. The ominous cliff lay directly below us. Alessia and Sebastian were about to round the corner, still running hard directly toward it.

"Okay Scarlett, love, let's do this."

I gave my horse the go-ahead, and we began our descent, gaining speed as we tore down the hillside. Alessia had not turned her head, did not see us coming, and I was beginning to believe my reckless plan would work when Scarlett lost her footing on the slippery slope.

Rearing back in terror, the horse fought to regain her balance while I leaned forward, keeping my weight centered on her back and dropping one of the reins. The last thing I wanted to do was pull on them involuntarily, forcing her head back farther and causing her to fall.

Everything slowed until I felt like I was in an action film. Scarlett's panicked screams, the sting of rain pelting my cheeks, the smell of horse sweat and churned up earth—all of it claimed a shard of my attention.

But foremost in my mind was the vision of Alessia astride Sebastian, the two of them silhouetted against the backdrop of open ocean. She'd apparently spotted me on my collision path and pulled him about-face to run the opposite direction.

The first sensation to assail me was relief—they were no longer headed for the cliff. The second was fear.

Losing her battle for balance, Scarlett slipped sideways. She was going down. I had to jump free of her—for her sake and for mine. The mare wasn't as large as Sebastian, but she still weighed a good five hundred kilograms. Plenty enough to cause damage.

Using my full strength and a whole lot of adrenaline, I pushed away and made the leap. Scarlett did fall onto her side, but without my extra weight, quickly righted herself again, getting to her feet with no apparent injury.

I didn't fare so well.

I heard the bone pop before the physical sensation hit me.

When it did, the pain wiped everything from my mind. In my effort to prevent being crushed by the horse, I'd thrown myself into a large rock. The sole of one foot had struck it first, and the speed and pressure had been too much.

My leg below the knee was bent at an unnatural, sickening angle. It was supposed to be exceedingly difficult to break your tibia, but this was, without question, a compound fracture.

I immediately retched from the overwhelming pain. Lying back on the ground with the rain pelting my face, I fought for rational thought. *Think. Think.* I needed immediate medical intervention. It was possible an artery had been severed by the broken bone. Even if that wasn't the case, I was losing a lot of blood and had no time to waste. Soon I'd go into shock and be unable to help myself.

Help. I needed help. Lifting my head, I looked around for Alessia. There she was—off in the distance—far beyond earshot, her figure on horseback growing smaller as she succeeded in her escape. There would be no help from that direction.

Horseback. Right. *God, I was getting groggy already.* Scarlett could carry me back to the house.

"Scarlett. Girl?"

The sound of her answering snort was like a symphony. Stepping closer, she nosed my face, and I lifted my hand to her harness.

"I should have known *you* wouldn't leave me. Some women are reliable. Good girl. Okay, let's see if I can manage this."

Gripping her neck I pulled, attempting to get upright. A blast of searing pain sent me back to the ground with a shout. Scarlett took a few nervous steps backward. Her fall had no doubt unnerved her, and seeing me like this wasn't helping.

Sweating now in spite of the cold and rain, I sat on the ground, breathing hard and staring at my mangled leg. There was no use denying it—this was bad.

I couldn't stand, much less walk. I was far from the house with no phone. There was no chance of anyone happening by—I lived on the least inhabited end of the island, and the storm no doubt had most everyone housebound. Even if someone *were* close by, the rain and increasingly regular thunder would drown out my cries for help.

I had to get myself on that horse—even a belly flop over the saddle would do. I would not—*would not* lie out here in the mud and die.

"Come here, girl. I need you," I coaxed the skittish horse, fighting to keep my voice calm though I was in agony. "Yeah, that's right. Ready to head on home? Me, too. Let's just get mounted and be on our way."

Lowering her head once more, Scarlett allowed me to encircle her neck with my arms. I locked the fingers of one hand around the wrist of the other then gave her a command I prayed she'd understand.

"Okay, up."

Just as the horse began to raise her head and draw my body up with it, a flash of brilliant lightning coincided with a deafening crack of thunder. The storm was directly over us now. The terrified horse reared, breaking my grip on her neck. I dropped to the ground with a blast of blinding pain.

The sound of hooves stampeding away was broken by another loud boom and eerie brightness. The craggy profile of the Sgurr stood out in stark contrast to the electrical show in the night sky.

I must have lost consciousness for a moment because the next thing I remember was opening my eyes and turning my head side to side. Scarlett was nowhere in sight.

It's over. I'm going to die.

An eerie sense of peace settled over me. I'd always known I'd die young, but I'd assumed it would be from an illness. With my condition, even a common cold could take me out. Maybe this was a better way to go—surrounded by the desolate beauty and wildness of the island I'd come to love, lying in the shadow of the majestic An Sgurr, giving my life in an attempt to do the right thing, at least.

The thought of Alessia was followed quickly by an image of my family searching for me and coming across my cold, stiff body out here. It would devastate my mother and grandmother, and poor little Olly would never be the same. The peace evaporated.

Knowing there was no way I could drag myself all the way home, I pushed onto my stomach nonetheless and dug my fingers into the soggy turf. Using just my arms and shoulders, I strained to pull forward, actually achieving some movement.

I paid for it in a shriek of pain through my injured leg, which dragged the rough ground. No doubt the movement would speed up the bleeding out, but maybe that was a good thing.

The next time I dragged my body forward, my broken leg struck a stone protruding from the earth, and a scream ripped from my throat. My head swam, and though the heavens were enshrouded by storm clouds, I saw stars.

My forehead dropped to the cold earth in defeat. I didn't speak aloud, for there was no one to hear me, but inside I said my goodbyes to my family. I said goodbye to the island, the work I'd devoted my life to, and to my beloved horses.

I prayed my co-workers would wonder why I hadn't been online for a day or two and send someone from the villages out to check on me. Finding me dead, surely they'd arrange for someone new to feed and care for the horses.

I mouthed their names one by one in farewell. *Clovis, Atticus, Owain, Scarlett, and Sebastian.*

Dear, damaged Sebastian, as frightened as he was fierce. His combination of ferocity and vulnerability had won my heart from the moment I'd seen him. Though I'd made progress, I'd never quite managed to penetrate his defensive armor and convince him my love did not come with conditions or punishments.

Perhaps Alessia would choose to keep him, as she'd apparently been right about her ability to manage the bad-tempered beast. They were two of a kind, after all. I smiled, picturing the fiery, beautiful pair.

And as consciousness faded, I imagined I heard the heavy, rapid footfall of my challenging but exhilarating mount, cantering back to carry me into eternity.

11

ALESSIA

That Wes was a clever one. He'd almost caught me by cutting off my path from above. But just as I hadn't fallen for his deceptive warnings, I would not allow myself to be captured and made a prisoner again.

I'd chosen my horse well. There was no choice, actually—the stallion was the only animal in the stable of any quality, and he was clearly bred to run. He was temperamental, to be sure, but I was an experienced horsewoman. I'd even broken quite a few colts in my teen years when I spent nearly all my free time at the stables.

I'd spoken to the thoroughbred with the voice of authority, touched him with confidence, and he'd allowed me to mount. Once we were free of the stable, he'd been as fast and strong as I hoped. And now that Wes had apparently given up his pursuit, there was no one to stop us.

I slumped in the saddle and let out a shaky laugh, relieved. I'd meant what I said about not wanting to hurt him. Yes, he'd kept me locked away, but I was convinced it was not a situation of his making. He'd simply been a pawn of the witches, and he'd been kinder than he had to be.

The lights of Wes's estate came into view, revealing an oceanfront home much grander than what I'd pictured. Though he'd said no one else lived there, I would avoid the house and guide my mount up to the road that must lie beyond it. Wes might return at any moment—I would not take the chance of using the phone inside to call my people.

Detecting a sound rising above the wind, I turned back. His horse—approaching from a distance. *Merda!* How had the inferior roan caught up to me so quickly? Maybe the mare was faster than she looked.

Or maybe Wes was a superior rider—he'd nearly caught up to me twice tonight. I was out of practice. I'd spent so much time in recent months on a wild goose chase after Macy and Nic, I'd neglected my riding. Like everything else, it was a skill that needed regular practice to maintain.

I leaned farther over the stallion's neck and urged him on. I'd get beyond the house and then surely come to a town or at least another estate before long. Turning back for a quick glance, I was in disbelief. The red horse was about to overtake me.

And then she did. But rather than pulling in front of me and forcing my horse to slow down, the mare shot past me and kept going, running toward the stable. I sucked in a breath. She was riderless.

Where was Wes? Directing my horse to slow to a walk, I turned back and surveyed the open land behind me. The last I'd seen, Wes had been charging down the rocky hillside, shocking me with his ingenuity and his courage—not many riders would attempt terrain like that at such speed. He'd been riding like lives depended on it.

But where was he now? Had the mare thrown him? A blaze of lightning lit the landscape revealing stark, barren land as far as I could see. No sign of Wes.

Good. I turned my horse back toward the road. It served

him right to have to make his way back to the house on foot during an electrical storm. But when we reached the road beyond the house, I pulled back on the reins.

What if he's not on foot?

What if he was lying there somewhere at the bottom of the hill? Riders fell all the time. I'd been thrown myself many times over the years. Usually it resulted in a sore tailbone and a bruised ego. But once... once I'd seen a horrible injury. A shudder went through my body just remembering it.

A stable hand—a boy of about my age—had been exercising one of my father's champion horses, and a snake had crossed its path. The horse reared, and Tommaso had done exactly the wrong thing. He'd yanked back on the reins, causing the large horse to lose its balance and fall backward on top of him.

I'd never forget the sound of crunching bone as long as I lived. Without the quick thinking of our stable master and the skill of our healer, the boy could have easily died.

At the time, I'd been desperate for him to live. Both being horse lovers and the only two teenagers on the estate, Tommaso and I had spent a lot of time in the stables together and had become friends. I'd cared *so* much about his welfare, in fact, my father had ordered him sent away as soon as he'd recovered enough to be moved. Tommaso was human.

Since then, of course, my sympathy for the human race had lessened—a lot. But Wes... he didn't deserve a fate like that.

I turned the stallion around and trotted him in the direction I'd fled initially. I'd just get a look at Wes. No doubt I'd spot him trudging back toward the house, freezing cold and sopping wet. I'd laugh and be on my way. There was no chance of him catching me on foot, anyway.

But as I continued to backtrack and still did not see him, my belly began to swim with dread. Finally reaching the area where I'd seen him bolting down the hillside, I stopped the horse. And then I spotted him in the barely-there moonlight. Wes's body. Facedown. He was not moving. Without stopping to consider the consequences, I slid from the horse's back and ran toward him.

His arms were outstretched in front of him, and one of his legs was bent at a cruel angle. It was obvious what had happened. He'd either fallen from the horse or been crushed beneath it and was trying to drag himself home when he'd passed out—or died.

Heart galloping like Sebastian's strong hooves, I knelt beside him, lowering my ear to his mouth. He was breathing! He let out a piteous moan, the unexpected sound causing me to scurry backward and fall onto my backside.

I fought paralyzing fear as my mind flashed back to the gut-churning scene in the exercise yard on my father's estate, to Tommaso's mangled body. I had stayed far away from the injured boy, not wanting my terrible glamour to worsen his condition. Instead, I'd run for the mansion to alert our healer.

There was no healer here. As far as I'd seen, I was the only other person for miles around. But what use was I? If I touched Wes, it could possibly exacerbate his already serious condition.

And even if I kept our contact to a minimum and he didn't get sick, he was just going to die eventually of the Plague. While I'd been trapped here, it had been spreading unabated. Perhaps it was a mercy to let him die quickly here and now from this injury instead of preserving him only to have him die of the disease later.

I got to my feet and glanced over at the black horse, who waited impatiently, stomping and blowing, clearly eager to get out of the storm. He was easily strong enough to carry us both to the house. Once there, I could call someone to come and help Wes. I'd still have time to escape. I could take his car or a fresh horse and leave before the emergency medical personnel arrived.

On the other hand, why take chances? Delaying my escape could backfire on me in the worst way. If I left right now, the witches would have no idea where I'd gone. Wes certainly wouldn't be able to point them in the right direction. I'd be free. I'd be safe.

I'd be the monster everyone believed me to be.

So which *was* I, really? More importantly, who did I want to be? The toxic villainess who cared for nothing and no one and therefore could never be hurt again... or a girl whose heart still held a few surprisingly tender places deep beneath the hard-frozen outer layers?

There was no time for self-reflection. Looking at Wes's prone body and his broken leg, I knew I had to decide—quickly. Making my decision, I took Sebastian's reins in hand.

"Come, my friend. Let's go."

MACY

We left the palace, but instead of boarding the lift again, my guards guided me outside onto a terrace. Perched high above the capital city as we were, the river and villages far below seemed no bigger than miniatures.

As my guards led me down a long, winding walk through the mountainside city, I was again struck by the strange, almost mystical quality of the daylight here. Looking up, I noticed something I hadn't been able to see from the river valley. What had appeared to be open sky before was actually a sort of skylight—not an open space—but a clear membrane between this domain within the mountain and the world outside.

What was more, the membrane changed appearances as I moved and viewed it from different angles. It wasn't truly clear but seemed to bear a hazy image of bumpy gray rock that sort of came and went as if it was a digital photo you could manipulate with a sliding toggle button, making it fade and intensify. It was one of the weirdest things I'd ever seen.

Was the ceiling of this underworld a video screen then, upon which a semi-transparent image of stone was being projected? Or were we actually looking *through* stone, right through the summit of the mountain to the sky above?

I knew Elves had special abilities, and the witches had been powerful enough to zap Alessia to another location—or right out of existence. But I couldn't imagine the level of magic it would take to make an entire mountaintop transparent from the inside. Or to alter the weather. If the nymphs could do *that* and manipulate solid rock… what else were they capable of?

I was aware of the ability of our blood to heal, thanks to Dr. Schmitt's life-threatening attack on Nic. Speaking of that, the queen had dismissed me so abruptly I hadn't gotten a chance to ask her about helping the humans. I had to arrange another audience with her.

"Where are we going now?" I asked my guards, who could no longer pretend they didn't speak English. "Will I get to see the queen again?"

One of them actually answered me. "You should be grateful you survived *one* meeting—don't push your luck."

"We're taking you to your quarters," the other said. "There you can rest and bathe and change into some *suitable* clothing before dinner."

She sniffed at my conservative pajamas as if I was grossly underdressed. *She* was the one wearing a fairy costume. *I* was fine.

The footpath wound down two more levels before we came to a stop at the door of a charming stone house. Leafy vines outlined the doorway, and the window boxes overflowed with fragrant, colorful flowering plants.

"Who lives here?" I asked as one of the guards rapped on the door.

"You do—for now," answered the other. "Mind that you don't give the lady of the house any trouble. She is old, but she'll suffer no nonsense from you or anyone."

Well, okay then. Apparently I was to be left with only an elderly lady to watch over me. That would give me the perfect opportunity to escape and go looking for Nic, though finding him in this labyrinth of a city would be a challenge to say the least.

The door opened, and a small, lovely woman gestured for me to enter. She didn't *look* elderly. She looked like she might be in her late thirties. She had shiny, straight brown hair and wore a longish version of the other women's clothing, a dress made of several layers of filmy, shimmery material. Hers was a deep amber, matching the color of her eyes.

She acknowledged my escorts, who nodded to her then departed without another word. Then she shut the door and looked me up and down, her smile never fading.

"Well, well. Look at you. The spitting image of Fallon, just as they said. You can't always believe what you hear in the market, but this time the gossip was true. You've had quite a day, haven't you my dear—going through the portal, traveling the river, visiting the palace? Do come in and have some tea."

I was a bit thrown off by her hospitable demeanor. After being dismissed by the queen and dragged around by the guards, this woman was treating me as a guest. Warily, I moved into the cozy home, following her to a kitchen where a teakettle rattled and whispered with building steam atop a wood burning stove.

"Sit right over there." She gestured to a small round table in the corner. "Won't be a minute. Oh look at you—you're spooked as a fox-chased rabbit. Don't worry. No one's going to hurt you here. You're quite a welcome arrival, you know."

You could have fooled me. So far, I'd been treated as a criminal.

"Who are you?" I asked, half expecting her to ignore my question the way the queen had.

She lifted the kettle and poured steaming water into the two teacups waiting on the counter. That done, she turned back to me.

"I'm Mae. I was your mother's nanny. I've retired, but it's my privilege to look after you now." She beamed.

"My... mother. You knew Fallon?"

"Oh, yes. Since the day she was born. And I've missed her every day since she left. I understand you never knew her, but she was a very special girl. I can already tell you're a lot like her."

"Really? How?"

"To start, you look like her—well, you look like a blend between her and your father."

"You knew my father, too? Is he here? Can I meet him?" My heart sped with excitement.

Mae stared at her hands and the corners of her mouth turned down. "I'm sorry, dear, but no. Fallon was betrothed to a very powerful nobleman. He was a member of the court, very much in favor with Queen Ragan and much older than Fallon. She was a sweet girl, but she could be... willful at times."

She smiled as if revisiting an old memory. "She had fallen in love with a young soldier by the name of Uric. Even after her engagement was announced, she continued to sneak out and see her beau. Word found its way to Lord Hulder. He challenged Uric to a duel, and the young man was killed. Your mother ran away shortly afterward. Some people said it was because she was angry at her parents and preferred to take her chances among the humans rather than stay here, but I suspect it was for a different reason."

"What was that?"

"To protect *you*. If she'd gone through with the marriage and Lord Hulder learned she was carrying Uric's child...

well, he would never have let it stand. His wealth is only exceeded by his pride."

"So you think he would have killed her?" I felt myself go pale and my hand covered my mouth.

"No. But he might have forced her to end the pregnancy. You were the child of the man she loved. The girl I knew would never let that happen."

"It's such a sad story."

She nodded. "Made even sadder by the fact that our dear Fallon never returned—perhaps she was afraid they'd force her to tell of your whereabouts or make her marry Lord Hulder after all. Her parents never recovered from her disappearance. Her father did go out searching for her, but he had no idea where to look, and the human world is vast compared to ours. Their hope was that she'd return on her own someday. I'm sure they were astonished when the girl who returned was their grandchild instead of their daughter."

"My grandparents are still alive? When can I meet them?"

Mae turned and removed the tea bags from our cups before carrying them to the table. "Soon perhaps. They are very old and set in their ways. I think they're still processing the information of your existence. I don't know *everything*, child. But I do know some things, and I've been given leave to answer some of your questions and to… bring you up to speed so to speak."

Questions. I had a million of them, starting with what had happened to Nic.

"Do you know anything about my fiancé, Nic?" I asked eagerly. "He was with me when I was taken last night, and I haven't seen him since."

"That's something I don't know. There *was* talk that you were found with an Elven man."

"That's Nic," I said eagerly. Maybe if gossip about him had

reached the city that meant he *had* been brought here as well. "I need to find out what happened to him. I need to know if he's here and if he's okay."

"Be patient," she advised. "This is a unique situation in our society. We don't often meet outsiders—or prodigal nymphs. There's a lot of uncertainty. And if your young man has been brought here... well, that would have caused a whole different level of alarm and fear. There has never been an Elf in Sidhe Innis before—dead or alive."

"Where *are* we? I mean, where is Sidhe Innis? Is it like... a fairy realm in another dimension or something?"

She laughed. "Sidhe Innis? No. I can see how you might think that, but we are still very much on planet Earth as you know it. Our sanctuary is simply hidden from human view by a natural geological formation. It serves as a shelter both from the elements and from danger."

"You mean from Elves." I remembered what Nic had told me about how Elves in ancient times had hunted nymphs— they believed to the point of extinction, though obviously it wasn't true.

"Yes. And from others who would seek to harm us and use us for their own purposes. The Earth-wives for instance."

"The witches who followed me to Mallaig," I said more to myself than to her. "The queen said she 'slowed them down' with a weather disturbance. What does that mean? She can control the weather?"

"Not everywhere. But close by, yes. Our people have influence over the natural elements. If she wished to cause a storm over our location, she could easily do that. Just as sometimes she'll clear the skies above our mountain, while elsewhere on the island, it's overcast and chilly."

"The island. We're on an island?"

"That's what Innis means, dear. It's Gaelic. I think it's time we got you settled into your room. I'll draw you a bath and set out some clothing for dinner tonight."

"What are we having for dinner?" Suddenly my appetite had awakened, and my belly was growling furiously. The tea had been delicious, but it was not enough by a long shot.

"I have no way of knowing. But I believe the question, when you see the spread, will be what are you *not* having for dinner? You'll be dining at the palace. The full court will be there, and you'll want to look refreshed and pretty when all of *those* ostentatious busybodies get their first look at you."

"You're not going with me?" I didn't know Mae well, but she felt like an ally. As far as I could tell, the only one I had in this strange place.

"Me? Oh no. I'm in the serving class. *This* is a gathering of Sidhe high society. Come along now."

I followed her up a short, winding staircase to the second floor where she led me to an open doorway and gestured inside. The small room held a twin-sized bed, a bedside table with drawers, and a chair. My suitcase stood at the end of the bed as the queen had promised.

"I hope you'll be comfortable in here," Mae said. "There's an assortment of dresses in the closet—something there should fit you, I think. And the washroom is just here down the hall. The house has only one—I hope you won't feel too uncomfortable about sharing it. I feel like *I'm* your grandmother, in a way. I raised your mother and loved her as if she were my own."

"You don't look old enough to be *anyone's* grandmother," I told her honestly. "You look like you'd be the right age to be my mother."

"Well, I guess there's much for you to learn about your people and your heritage. When we reach full maturity at around thirty years of age, we stop developing physically."

"You mean you don't age? Like Elves?"

"Well, I suppose so. I don't know much about Elven folk, except what I've read in the scary stories."

"You have books here?"

"Well, of course we do. How else to record the histories and entertain ourselves?"

"Are any of them in English?"

She gave me a chiding glance. "Now why would we have books written in a human language?"

"But you *speak* English. And so did the guards—and the queen."

Mae narrowed her eyes, grinning as if she suspected I was joking with her. "How much of that poppy powder did you breathe in while they were rescuing you last night? Very few of us have ever even seen a human, much less bothered to learn one of their languages."

Rescuing me? Ah, that must have been what the people were told. Or maybe the nymphs really did believe I'd been taken by an Elf and they were saving me by attacking Nic.

"I don't understand. You're speaking English right now," I argued.

She laughed. "Oh no, dear. I'm speaking the one and only language I've ever known—Nymphian. And so are *you*."

I reeled back in shock. That was impossible. I'd never even met any nymphs. How could I be speaking and understanding their language? But the old woman seemed entirely sincere, and something told me she was not a liar.

I thanked her and went into the bathroom to bathe. The tub worked exactly as I would have expected one to, with hot and cold plumbing, but the soap and shampoo were different. Each was in a small lidded pot perched on the side of the tub. I sank into the hot water and pulled the curtain around it. Removing the lid of one of the pots, I sniffed its contents.

The scent was heavenly, reminding me of honeysuckle

and vanilla. I touched it and decided its consistency was more like a body scrub than shampoo, so I used that on my skin. Then I poured the syrupy substance from the other pot onto my hands and worked it into a lather through my hair.

This one smelled like jasmine and something tropical like coconut. Rinsing it out, I found I had no need for conditioner, which was good since there wasn't any. But my hair was smooth, slick, and tangle-free. Squeezing the water from it, I stood and slid the shower curtain back to reach for a towel.

My pajamas. They were gone. I'd left them piled on the bathroom floor, but Mae must have opened the door and taken them while I was bathing. Maybe she'd put them in my room. Luckily there was a robe hanging on the doorway, and I pulled it on, enjoying the plush softness of it.

I wished I could stay in this all night and burrow in this cozy house with Mae instead of going back to the palace to face Sidhe society.

But really, it *was* the best thing. I had to speak to the queen, and she was in the palace. I needed to ask her for permission to see Nic. I needed to explain to her why I'd come looking for my people in the first place, that the human world was in grave danger, and only the nymph race could help.

Of course after meeting her, I wasn't convinced the queen would even care.

Going to my room, I opened the closet to check out the clothes Mae had mentioned. Nothing but pixie dresses— exquisite, ethereal, and breathtakingly beautiful, but pixie dresses nonetheless. The longest of them would cover my upper thighs if I was lucky. *No thank you.*

I stepped back into the hallway. "Mae? Could you come here for a minute?"

She emerged from her own room. "Yes dear?"

"Um... I think the clothes in my closet are going to be a little... small. Could I maybe borrow something from you, more like what you're wearing now?"

"Oh no, my dear. You don't want to wear something like this. Only the old biddies like me wear long dresses. And it certainly wouldn't work for an occasion like tonight. The things in your closet are all very stylish and perfect for a girl your age."

"You know what? I think I'll just wear my own clothes."

I didn't have anything fancy in my suitcase, mostly jeans and sweaters, but I did have one long, black skirt I could pair with a cute top I brought in case Nic and I went to a nice restaurant.

Mae laid a reassuring hand on my shoulder and dropped her chin, looking at me from under a brow quirked in tender amusement. "I know it's not what you're used to, but trust me. Choose something from the closet, and you'll fit right in. You'll see."

Okay then. Skimpy pixie clothes it is. I sighed in resignation and went back to my room. My attitude got a little better once I tried the tiny dresses on. They felt wonderful against my skin—as soft and light as flower petals.

The colors reminded me of flowers, too. There was a sunflower yellow one, a bright pink one, and one of a lighter pink color as well as several others.

I settled on a floaty white dress trimmed with a spattering of sparkling crystals and a waist studded with deep pink jewels in the shape of roses. Affixed to the back of it between the shoulder blades were feather-light extensions of a filmy, iridescent material—*wings* was the word that came to mind.

Was this dinner a costume party as well? But then, I'd noticed some girls in the city wearing the wing-like accessories today. And a woman I'd seen crossing a footbridge during our boat ride had also worn the unusual bejeweled appendages.

On the hanger along with the dress was a matching headpiece, but I opted to go without it. It reminded me too much of a Las Vegas showgirl.

When I came downstairs, Mae turned from her food preparations. Her mouth dropped open. "Oh well now, don't you just look splendid? A perfect Sidhe princess, you are. And that dress was your mother's favorite."

"It was?"

I looked down at myself, smoothing my hands over the gossamer fabric, trying to imagine what my mother must have looked like when she was my age and wearing this dress. A warm feeling settled over me at the thought. We were the same size.

"What's with the wings on everything?" I asked Mae.

"Our people are very close to nature. Birds, butterflies, all winged creatures are very beloved and inspiring to us." Her forehead wrinkled as her gaze moved to my hair. "Where is the headdress? You must wear it—it completes the outfit."

"Um, not tonight, thanks. It's not... me."

She looked disappointed but didn't argue. "Well, it would have been nice, but you look lovely all the same. Oh—shoes. My goodness, you cannot wear... *those* with that. Let me go rummage in the attic a bit more. Wait here."

Leaning over to survey the space between my billowy white hem and the floor, I supposed I had to agree—my black lace-up ankle boots *were* a little incongruous with the diaphanous dress. But they were the only shoes I'd brought on the trip, other than fuzzy slippers.

After a few minutes, Mae returned carrying, not a pair of delicate slippers or even some nice walkable gladiator sandals, but a pair of spindly stiletto pumps that were apparently made of... plants.

I'd never seen anything like them. The heel, which had to be at least six inches tall, looked like it was formed from a green rose branch, complete with sharp thorns. The sole seemed to be comprised entirely of green rose bush leaves. The strap over the toes featured a single, perfect ruby-colored rose bloom, and the heel cup was embellished with tight red rosebuds.

They were the most beautiful shoes I'd ever seen. And there was no way I'd be able to walk a single step in them.

"Oh. Those are... lovely. But I think I might just... go with these," I said. I could easily picture myself tottering into the palace and falling flat on my face in front of the entire Sidhe court.

Mae eyed my current rugged footwear dubiously. "If you're quite sure."

"I am."

Chimes from the front door alerted us that my escorts had returned and saved me from possible foot pain and certain embarrassment. At least from *that* source. When Mae opened the door and I stepped out, the nymph women eyed me with obvious surprise.

They didn't *say*, "You sure clean up well," but their side-eye glances at each other said it all. I looked like one of them tonight. Of course, we hadn't made it to the ballroom yet.

We set off together up the hill toward the palace, and I couldn't help but feel a little like Cinderella on her way to the ball, although my handsome prince would not be waiting for me inside.

ALESSIA

Wow, he's big.

Wes was not overweight by any means, but he was tall—even taller than I'd realized when viewing him from the stable window—and his bones were apparently made of iron.

Even with my typical Elven strength and agility, hefting his dead weight onto the horse's back and then carrying him upstairs to his room took everything I had. The task was made even more difficult by the necessity of keeping my skin from contacting his.

Once he was settled on his bed, I stoked the coals in the fireplace with fresh wood and went downstairs to search for an emergency telephone number. I'd call it and leave as quickly as possible.

I had never been inside a human's home. Other than Tommaso all those years ago, the only humans I'd ever associated with were concert organizers, a few shopkeepers, and my fan pod members. Even then, I'd always kept the involvement limited to brief conversations and allowed no physical contact, for obvious reasons.

Wes had mentioned he worked from home, so I assumed

there was an office downstairs. It would have a phone, and *that* would have emergency numbers in it—hopefully. I made a quick survey of the ground floor rooms—kitchen, living room, extra bedroom, laundry.

Then I came to a room that overlooked the hillside, the stable, and the ocean beyond it. There was a large desk with an open laptop on its surface. *Aha.* Beside the computer was a telephone. I lifted the handset from its cradle and turned it on, quickly scrolling through the digital list of saved numbers.

There wasn't anything resembling a police or fire department or a hospital. At home in Italy, you could summon an ambulance by dialing 1-1-8. Elves of course would never seek medical care from humans, but I'd seen it on television. I tried that and got an error message. *Merda!* A flurry of extra heartbeats made me feel a bit dizzy. The readout on the phone blurred for a second before coming back into focus.

Slowing down and taking slow, deep breaths, I read the English words more carefully and located a promising entry —Small Isles Medical Practice. This had to be it. Dialing that number took me to the same error message. The storm must have knocked out telephone service. *Merda, merda.*

My plan had been to summon medical help for Wes and then leave this place as quickly as possible. But there *was* no medical help available—not tonight anyway. What was I going to do? He was no doubt bleeding internally thanks to the gruesome compound fracture, and when he regained consciousness, he'd be in terrific pain.

I glanced around the empty house in despair. I was all he had. Poor man. Remembering the events of that horrible day in the training ring, I was nearly overcome by a sudden urge to flee. I was no healer, quite the opposite in fact.

But I *had* watched our healer carefully as he'd dealt with

the stable hand's injuries, resetting the bones and administering pain relief. I did have *some* knowledge of the workings of human bodies thanks to all the time I'd spent in Dr. Schmitt's clinic. I supposed all of that taken together made me better than nothing. Not much better, but better.

All right then. I got up from the desk and went to the first floor bathroom. A search of the cabinets came up empty. *Upstairs then.* He must have some sort of first-aid supplies on hand—unless he was impervious to illness. Starting up the staircase, I spotted a bottle of whiskey high on the office shelf. *That* could come in handy. I went back down and grabbed it along with a short, heavy tumbler I found beside it.

Upstairs in the master bath, I had better luck. There were sterile bandages, iodine, pain reliever, and something that said it was for reducing inflammation. Better, but not great.

I dug through the vanity drawers, searching for something stronger. When I attempted to reset that broken bone, it wasn't going to be pretty. Wes would not only wake up, he'd likely shoot off the bed and straight through the roof. I wanted something that would knock him out or at least make him nonsensical.

Finally I discovered a prescription medication authorized by a dentist. Vicodin. It warned of drowsiness and potential for abuse and addiction. That seemed promising.

And of course, I did have the copper tube of saol water in my jacket pocket.

I had no idea how useful the traditional Elven drink would be in treating a human with a compound fracture, but I would certainly be putting it to the test tonight. The saol water might not heal the injury completely, but at the very least it should keep infection at bay, stem the bleeding, and relieve his pain.

With all my supplies gathered, I took a steadying breath

and went back to Wes's room. He was still out, thank the gods.

Heart spinning crazily, I approached his bed, set the glass and whiskey bottle on the bedside table, and shook two of the pills into my hand. I couldn't give him the saol water yet. That would have to wait until the bones were back in proper alignment, otherwise his tissues would start healing and the edges of the bones might knit together improperly.

I uncapped the whiskey and poured a small amount of the amber liquid into the tumbler then sat on the edge of the mattress, near the head of the bed. *Here goes nothing.*

Taking care not to make direct contact with Wes's bare skin, I slid an arm behind his head and propped his upper body. He groaned and mumbled something in protest.

"Wes. Listen to me. I need you to take these pills. Open your mouth."

He moaned again and turned his head away from me. The look of obvious pain on his face tugged at something deep inside me. Lowering my face, I spoke close to his ear, careful not to touch it with my lips.

"No. Now don't be stubborn. You need to open your mouth for me. It will help you—it will take the pain away."

I gingerly wedged one tiny pill between his lips and held the edge of the glass to them. To my great relief, Wes cooperated, opening his lips enough for me to tip the liquid into his mouth and wash the first pill down.

We repeated the process, and I went to the end of the bed where his long legs stretched to nearly the end of the king-sized mattress.

Okay... pants. I had to get them off and see exactly what I was working with fracture-wise. Going back to the bathroom, I rummaged through the drawers once more, searching for a pair of scissors. There was nothing but a tiny pair meant for trimming fingernails. That wasn't going to work.

I ran back downstairs to the office and pulled open the top desk drawer. *Yes.* There was a nice, large pair of scissors. Hopefully he hadn't let them get too dull. Cutting through denim would be much tougher than cutting paper.

Starting with the undamaged leg, I tried them. The blades made a smooth, easy cut through the hem of the jeans. Encouraged, I moved over to the affected leg. I contemplated removing the huge boot but decided to leave it in place until I knew more—and until the medication had a chance to knock him out.

"Please don't let him feel this," I said to no one in particular. I slid the scissors to the inside seam and began cutting, moving as quickly as I dared while trying to be as gentle as possible.

I wasn't sure whether Wes could feel what I was doing or if he was just waking up, but he moved a few times and flinched when the cold metal touched his inner thigh.

"Be still," I advised. "This is *not* the point where you want me to make a mistake."

Just in case, I decided to veer toward the outside, turning the scissors toward his hip and snipping quickly. Carefully, I peeled back the flap I'd created, praying Wes would lie still as I evaluated his twisted lower leg.

Mercifully he did. Maybe the whiskey and narcotics were kicking in. Maybe he'd heard and heeded my warning despite his pain-induced stupor. I didn't care. All I knew was the jeans were open, and I could get a look at his injury.

Once I did, I never wanted to look at it again. A rush of adrenaline made me lightheaded. It appeared his shin bone was broken. The very tip of it protruded from a cut on the side of one leg.

Fighting nausea, I rushed to my supply table and

retrieved the iodine. I elected not to apply it with a cloth, which would require touching the area. Instead I simply poured the bottle over the open wound.

Next, I grabbed the towel I'd brought in with me. Draping it over my hands, I gripped Wes's ankle with one hand and his calf with the other.

"Get ready. You're going to feel some pressure," I warned him. "Try not to jump or move."

Pulling his heel slightly toward me, I then guided Wes's leg back into a normal position, re-aligning the bones end to end. I hoped. The whole procedure would probably have to be re-done later by someone who actually knew what they were doing.

Unfortunately, Wes did not sleep through my manipulations as I'd hoped but rather groaned and writhed in obvious pain. He even managed to kick me with his good leg, but I succeeded in setting the break. As soon as I removed my hands, he settled again, his face covered in beads of sweat.

"Good job," I told him. "Hard part's over now. I've just got to splint it and then you can sleep."

Searching his room, I spotted a short shovel among the fireplace tools. It wasn't perfect, but it would do for now. I went to his bureau and grabbed a handful of clean, white t-shirts then went back to the bed. Sliding the shovel beneath his injured leg, I worked it until his heel rested in the scoop of the shovel and began cutting one of the t-shirts into long strips. Those I used to secure the makeshift splint to Wes's leg.

Sweating from effort and stress, I stood and surveyed my work. "That's as good as it's going to get with Dr. Adamo in the house."

I pulled the saol water from my pocket. Splashing a bit over the wound first, I lifted Wes's head and shoulders once more. "Drink this," I urged. "It's probably your best chance of living through the night."

With the edge of the vial I prodded his lower lip. When he got a taste of the sweet, simmering liquid, he opened his mouth and licked his lips. I couldn't help but chuckle despite the gravity of the situation.

"I know—it's good, isn't it? There aren't too many humans who've tasted this stuff. You're in rare company. Now open up."

I poured the entire contents of the vial into his mouth. There could be no better use for it as far as I was concerned. Anyway, I'd soon be on my way back home where I'd have access to an unlimited supply.

Knowing I'd done all I could for him, I finally collapsed into a chair by the fireplace, exhausted. I stared into the flames, letting my pulse and my thoughts settle. Then I looked around the room, studying the objects Wes had collected and chosen to display. There were maps of varying sizes and ages. A license plate from a car. A jar brimming with loose change. A small corkboard covered in postcards.

What the hell was I doing? I was in a *human's* home. I'd done everything in my power to save his life—that, after activating a plague meant to wipe *out* human life.

My gaze settled on the bed, on the man splayed out there. He was quiet now, sedated and, I hoped, comfortable. Was he chilly? I got up and went to him, touching his face as lightly and quickly as possible then retreating. He felt warm, but not overly so.

It was odd to be this close to a human. He looked different than I'd expected—well, I wasn't sure *what* I'd expected, but it wasn't this.

I'd always thought of Englishmen as these pale, pink-cheeked fellows with light hair and soft mid-sections. But of course, I'd never spent much time in the country, and I certainly wasn't checking out the male human population. When Wes and I had communicated through the closed door, my imagination of his appearance veered toward the weak and dull.

But this guy looked... rugged. And he was far from dull. With thick, dark hair and strong-features, he reminded me a bit of the English actor who played Superman in the movies. He had large hands covered with scars, and his forearms were densely muscled with a dusting of hair.

His eyes were closed, of course, but the brows above them were substantial and nearly black. His nose was long and straight but with the slightest bump at the bridge as if he'd been in a tussle or two during his life—the kind of nose you might see on an American football quarterback.

It looked like he'd recently shaved. His jaw bore just a bit of dark bristle, and his chin had a cleft in the center of it. His lips... well they were... nice.

My stomach fluttering uncomfortably, I turned away and gathered up the scraps of t-shirt and denim. *I must be hungry.* Yes, it had to be late, and I hadn't eaten in hours. That was the cause of the unfamiliar wobbly sensation in my belly.

I went downstairs to investigate the kitchen. Wes's home was interesting. Clean but charmingly cluttered with books stacked on the various tabletops and lining the shelves. His pantry and refrigerator were absolutely stuffed with food—which made sense considering the complex meals he'd made for me.

I would not be doing any gourmet cooking—I'd always lived with a kitchen staff to provide every meal. Now *I* would be the provider, for myself and for Wes, too I supposed. He would need to eat when he eventually awakened. A body that large must need frequent feedings. The fluttering returned, annoying me.

With a glance out the window, I assured myself the storm

continued. The witches would not come tonight. I wasn't sure how long Wes would be out, but my new plan was to wait until he awoke, check his pain level and his injury, and then leave him with a telephone so he could call whomever he wanted to come and take care of him.

As I prepared a plate of cheese and cold, cooked meats for myself, a draft from the kitchen window reached me. I shivered, only just now realizing I still wore the clothes I'd ridden in. They were soaked through, and my hair was wet.

After eating, I climbed the stairs again and peeked in on Wes. Still sleeping peacefully. It was likely he would be for the next few hours. I had time for a hot shower.

I opened his bureau drawer and withdrew a t-shirt, a pair of socks, and a large sweater—no doubt it would fit me like a dress—then tiptoed into the adjoining bathroom. I was excited to see it had a large, modern shower with a rainfall shower head. The house seemed old, but it had clearly been renovated in recent years.

The hot water and steam were heavenly, soothing the aches from my hard, chilly ride. I had toweled off and was just pulling the sweater over my head when a noise from the next room caused me to jump in fright. It sounded like something had fallen. My nerve endings pinged with alarm.

Wes. Was he trying to get up? There was no way he could walk—even trying could cause the newly set bones to move out of alignment and start the bleeding again.

I jerked the door open and ran into the bedroom, skidding to a stop when I saw all was calm. He was still asleep, though the crystal tumbler was on the floor beside his bed. He must have flung his arm to the side and knocked it from the bedside table.

But the incident scared me. If he was capable of flailing like that in his condition, he was also capable of rolling off the bed or even drug-induced sleepwalking. I decided to stay in the room—just until he woke up.

Strolling to the large bookcase, I selected a title at random and took it to the overstuffed chair near the fireplace. There was no way I'd be able to concentrate enough to enjoy any story right now, so it didn't really matter what the book was about. I just needed somewhere for my eyes to be while I kept up this bedside vigil.

Looking over at him, so vulnerable in his unconscious condition, I realized this was exactly how he'd found me. He could have done anything he wished to me while I was out cold, under the witches' spell. Apparently all he'd done was take care of me and then make me as comfortable as he could in my stable room.

The thought produced an odd tightness in my abdomen. *Why* had he been kind to me? It couldn't have been the witches' order.

I shook off the worry and opened the book. Perhaps it would be the perfect thing to numb my mind and maybe even allow me to drowse off in the chair.

Five hours later, I hadn't stopped turning the pages. Full of mystery and excitement, and more emotional tension than I'd ever encountered before, I had not been able to lift my eyes from the page.

In fact, the story had held my attention so powerfully I hadn't noticed at first that Wes seemed to be waking up. His body stirred in the bed, and he mumbled something.

I stood and laid the book in the chair, approaching his bed.

"Stay," he murmured. His head turned side-to-side, though his eyelids remained closed. Then more loudly, he said, "Don't leave me."

My heart crackled and sparked like the fire burning in the hearth. He was dreaming. Who was he talking to? Perhaps a woman who'd been in his life before he'd inexplicably ended up here alone.

Perhaps his parents—maybe he'd been abandoned? Perhaps he was reliving the moments after his fall from the horse when he'd seen me riding away, oblivious and focused on myself, as usual.

His eyelids began to quiver and then to flicker open. Suddenly, I was overcome by fear. What was I going to say to him? What would he think when he realized the tables were turned, and I was the one now in control? I wasn't ready to face him just yet.

Feeling like a nervous school girl, I hurried from the room. I'd go downstairs and find some food for him. *Yes. Food.*

That I could handle. I'd make him a tray, carry it upstairs, be calm and casual, make sure he was on the road to recovery, and then I'd leave this house before it was too late.

I could handle a face-to-face conversation with this human man. No problem. It wasn't like he was dangerous.

MACY

The capital city after dark was entrancing. I'd heard people speak of "fairy lights" before, but this place... it *had* to be the source of the phrase.

The front of each home and building we passed was illuminated by glowing lamps. Strings of tiny lights stretched from building to building, overhanging the walking path below and casting an alluring glow all the way to the top of the mountain city.

Up ahead, the palace itself was luminous—no longer appearing pure white as it had in the daytime but now a watercolor prism of constantly changing hues. I looked overhead at the transparent membrane separating this underground realm from the world above and realized why.

A full moon shone in the night sky. And the sheer film that comprised the cavern's ceiling was shifting through shades from magenta to emerald to sapphire to topaz, the moonlight shining through it creating the incandescent color-show for all the palace's guests tonight. The effect was as fascinating as fireworks but more serene.

As we drew near the palace, I began to see other dinner

guests walking in. The Las Vegas style headdress would not have been out of place after all. In fact, it might have been a little tame compared to some of the getups. These high society nymphs *really* liked to dress up.

Nearly all the women wore elaborate hats or head pieces, tiaras, feathers, and it seemed their tastes ran along the lines of the-bigger-the-better. They also wore pixie dresses, to my infinite relief. It was hard to tell based on their appearances, but I assumed the ones in the longer, less revealing dresses were older and the ones in the skimpier models were closer to my age.

The men didn't wear hats, but their clothes were brightly colored, most often tunics embellished with gold or silver embroidered designs and bejeweled belts as well as plentiful jewelry.

I'd spent a little time with the Light Elves in Altum. They had all been very natural and subdued—beautiful, but wearing modest styles made with fibers and colors you'd find in the woods and meadows. The nymphs of Sidhe Innis obviously believed in using the whole rainbow—and covering it with layers of bling.

Huh. Fae fashionistas. Who'd have thought it?

We fell in with the procession entering the palace. No one stared at me as I feared they might. They were all busy chatting amongst themselves as we made our way through the gleaming, elaborately decorated halls and stairways. And then we were in a ballroom filled with light and music and people. Round tables were placed throughout the room, sort of like a Fairy prom or a wedding reception on steroids, each one set with beautiful plates decorated in a floral pattern, crystal water goblets and wine glasses, and gleaming silver utensils.

In the center of each table was an enormous bouquet, overflowing with countless roses, and from the middle of the arrangement rose a small tree whose branches supported glowing lights.

Roses also encircled and wove through the numerous multi-tiered chandeliers hanging from the ceiling of the room. Illuminating each individual place setting was a floating candle. With all the flowers and warm lighting, I felt like I was in the middle of a Monet painting.

But the experience was far from two-dimensional. Incredible scents drifted through the room, the fragrance of flowers mixing with delicious food aromas. And the music was enchanting. Searching the ballroom, I located its source. An orchestra of perhaps thirty musicians played, intent on their music, ignoring the chattering crowd filtering into and through the room.

I watched as the other guests who'd arrived with us made their way to tables, taking their seats, obviously knowing exactly where to go. I felt like a transfer student on my first day at a new school. I had *no* idea where to go or what to do or even *how* things were done around here. My palms felt moist, though the ballroom temperature was perfect.

"This way," one of my guards said and led me toward the front of the room where a long rectangular table was elevated above the rest on a raised platform. It was set even more beautifully than the others, though no one was there yet.

We stopped just before the platform, at a round table where many people were already seated. While most of them where wholly uninterested in our approach, one of them, a man of about thirty, stood abruptly.

He had a mane of light blond, curly hair that draped over the shoulders of his shimmering gold evening coat. The silky white shirt beneath was only slightly paler than his skin, and a pair of coal dark eyes stood out in sharp contrast as he stared at me.

Though not a tall man, he was good looking in an aristocratic, dapper sort of way. His fine features and elaborate attire made me think of men from a bygone era as I'd seen them portrayed in movies and paintings. Compared to modern men, those finely dressed fellows in their ruffled collars and shiny, embroidered waistcoats and breeches seemed prissy and even a little effeminate.

This guy was no exception, though the look of appreciation in his eyes assured me he was *indeed* interested in the opposite sex.

"Fallon?" the man asked in a choked voice.

Shocked, I turned and looked behind me on instinct, as if he were addressing someone else. Belatedly I realized he was addressing *me*. He had taken me for my mother. I guessed I really did look like her.

"Uh... no. I'm not Fallon. I'm her daughter... Macy."

Now the others at the table turned to look at me, falling silent.

"You knew my mother, sir?" I asked.

One of my escorts said, "You are addressing Lord Hulder, a distinguished member of the court." She pulled out the empty chair next to him. "Sit down. Dinner is about to begin."

I did as she suggested, and she and the other Queensguard departed. The fancy blond man—Lord Hulder —still stared at me. *Lord Hulder.* Oh my God. This couldn't be the same man who—

"Yes," he said. "I knew her. Was very fond of her, in fact. We were to be married. But she... left us unexpectedly."

My face burned with crimson heat. It *was* the same guy my mom jilted for another and then ran away from. *Awkward.* And now he was looking at me as if I owed him an explanation—or something more. *Why* had I been seated at his table? Were the party planners unaware of the bad blood between his family and mine? Maybe they were aware and thought it would be entertaining to watch.

Not really knowing what to say, I responded with a weak, "I never knew her."

He nodded, a smile of understanding developing on his face. "I see. Well, you are welcome, Macy, daughter of Fallon. I look forward to getting to know you... as do we all."

As if a switch had been turned on, the others at the table all smiled and began introducing themselves. Servants entered the room and went from table to table, pouring a shimmering pink liquid into everyone's wine glasses. When ours were both filled, Lord Hulder picked his up and raised it toward me. "To old friends... and new."

"Old friends and new," several voices around us chorused.

Realizing he'd just made a toast, I lifted my glass as well. All our table mates followed suit, and the sound of clinking crystal circled the table. Lord Hulder was the last to tap his glass against mine and take a swallow.

"You may call me Darius," he offered in a friendly tone. "If we are to be friends, Lord Hulder is much too formal. Now— I must hear all about you. Where you grew up, how you came to this place. But first, you must drink."

"Oh right." I giggled, not because anything was funny but out of nerves.

I brought the rim of the glass to my lips and inhaled. The sparkling beverage smelled sweet, not alcoholic, but I decided to take it slowly just in case. I took a cautious sip. It was delicious, rich and surprisingly creamy-tasting for a clear liquid. It reminded me of melted ice cream, but with a bit of warmth to it. Maybe it *was* alcoholic after all. I'd definitely have to use caution.

Looking around at my place setting, I saw I had a full water glass as well. I set my toasting glass down and picked up the water glass instead, taking full swallows instead of sips. I was very thirsty all of a sudden. Definitely nerves.

Lord Hulder's smile widened. "Like our water, do you? You should—it comes from the fairy pools on the Isle of Skye. Our people used to live there before we had to go into hiding and migrated to this island."

"I've seen photos," I told him. "They're gorgeous. I'd love to read some of your history books. I don't really know anything about my birth mother's heritage."

"You don't need a book. You have me," he said.

"Oh—are you supposed to be, like, my tutor or something?"

He grinned as if I'd said something highly clever. "If you like. What I meant was… I was there, and I can give you a first-hand account of how we were driven underground by the scourge of Elves—and their partners, the Earth-wives."

I could tell by his tone I shouldn't offer to introduce him to my Elven fiancé. I almost hoped Nic *hadn't* been brought here. If all the nymphs felt that way about his race, this wasn't a safe place for him to be.

I wasn't sure how they felt about me yet. They might be treating me nicely—for now—but I had no idea how long that would continue or what the real purpose was for inviting me to the dinner tonight. And if Nic had been brought to Sidhe Innis, I doubted very much he was dressed to the nines and being served a formal multi-course dinner. Worry tunneled through my mid-section, and I glanced around, feeling unsettled.

I *had* to speak to the queen again, secure her assistance, and find out what had happened to Nic.

"That must have been a terrible time," I said to Lord Hulder, making conversation, as I surreptitiously surveyed the room looking for her.

"It wasn't pleasant," he agreed. "And I do miss the outside

world at times. But Queen Ragan has created a paradise for us here."

He gestured at the sumptuous ballroom. "We might never have come to this place without those terrible events. And here we are entirely safe from the interference of the inferior human race as well. You must be so relieved to be away from them and back with your own kind."

My own kind. These people did not feel like my own kind. I felt one hundred percent like a member of the human race—and I certainly didn't consider them inferior. I was saved from having to come up with an answer to his rude remark by a swell of music from the orchestra.

At once, all conversation in the ballroom ceased. Practically as one, the dinner guests rose from their chairs and turned toward a door at the front of the room. Scooting my chair back awkwardly, I did the same.

The doors opened, and through it glided the queen, followed closely by a man in formal wear. His long evening coat was silvery in color and covered with enough ornamentation to make Lord Hulder's jacket look plain by comparison.

He had long hair, straight and black as raven feathers. Like Nic, he had olive-toned skin, which was set off perfectly by his elegant light jacket and the snowy shirt he wore beneath it. This had to be the king—or at least, the queen's consort.

Her dress was silver as well, sheer in some parts with designs like flowers and leaves and vines winding through it in silver thread. On one shoulder, a beautiful silver bird had been embroidered, and instead of wearing a pair of wings affixed to the back, her dress featured multiple pairs of wings, the highest stretching far over her head, the lowest nearly touching the ground behind her.

The garment swept the floor as she walked. If the hem

length rule applied all around, she was very, very old. Whatever her age, she looked spectacular. A starburst crown surrounded her head in thin silver filaments that caught the light and sparkled as she moved.

Side by side, the elegant couple proceeded across the room to the raised platform and ascended the stairs to the head table. Servants pulled their chairs out for them simultaneously, and they sat.

The room came back to life with all the diners retaking their seats and servants buzzing between the tables, delivering plates full of food.

My fingers and the tips of my ears tingled with excitement. The queen was here. Maybe I would be able to talk to her, to ask her about Nic and about helping my human friends and family. Obviously not right now. I needed to watch for a while, get the lay of the land. Maybe Lord Hulder would be able to give me some advice about requesting an audience with her.

Guards stood at either side of the platform, blocking the stairs that led up to the head table. As we were seated at the table closest to theirs, I sneaked frequent glances at the royal couple throughout the meal.

They did not speak, only ate in silence, looking out over the gathering from time to time. Once, the king returned my glance, and I turned my head hurriedly, not wanting to appear as if I'd been staring.

"He's very handsome, isn't he?" the girl sitting next to me said.

She was wearing a floofy peach-colored dress with a short tutu-like skirt. She must have been young, like me. Her dress was embellished with very realistic peach and orange flowers and artificial monarch butterflies. At least I *hoped* she wasn't wearing actual dead insects as accessories. Her wide green eyes waited expectantly for me to agree.

"The king?"

She shook her head in a flurry of surprise then leaned in close and lowered her voice. "No—*Lord Hulder*. He's one of the wealthiest men in Sidhe Innis and notoriously choosy about his company. He's single, you know," she added.

"Oh. I…" I literally didn't know what to say. She seemed to be getting at something. "Did you want me to switch places with you so you can talk to him?"

Again the Tinker Bell head shake. She giggled. "No, silly. I'm mated. And he hasn't stopped talking to *you* all evening. Usually he's so bored at these gatherings. He must find you *very* interesting."

"Oh no, I—"

"What are you whispering about over there, Trina?" the object of her admiration asked. "I haven't missed some bit of juicy court gossip, have I?"

In spite of what she'd said about being mated, the girl adopted a flirty tone and batted her eyelashes. "Why Lord Hulder, we all know—you are the *source* of most of the juicy gossip. There is no way you *could* have missed it."

He smiled, obviously pleased by her reference to his playboy reputation. Turning his attention back to me, he said, "I trust you've had an audience with the queen?"

Yay. A subject I actually wanted to talk about. "Yes. Earlier today. But we didn't talk much. She asked me a few questions and then announced it was over. I'm really hoping to speak with her again tonight."

"Oh dear girl, no one will speak with her tonight. This is dinner, not open court." He laughed, his tone haughty but tinged with sympathy. "You have much to learn. I'll be happy to acquaint you with all our mores and customs."

"Oh, well, that's very nice of you, but my hostess, Mae, said she would—"

"Lord Hulder." An imperious female voice rang through the hall, overriding the music.

The man beside me bolted to his feet. "Yes, my queen?"

"Please join me for dinner."

"Yes, my queen," he said again and left the table and his plate without a backward glance.

As he hurried up the stairs to the platform, Queen Ragan and the king both looked directly at our table—at *me*, rather. I suddenly felt overheated, though the pixie outfit was like wearing nearly nothing. Had I done something wrong? Had he? Was this my opportunity to speak to her?

The queen broke eye contact with me and gestured for Lord Hulder to take the seat beside her. They immediately began conversing in low tones. The guard who'd allowed him access to the royal table snapped back into position, blocking anyone else from entering. After a minute, I sighed and turned back to my plate. Apparently this had nothing to do with me. I would have to wait my turn.

At least the food was good. I really was very hungry—more than I'd realized—and I quickly cleaned my plate. To my surprise, it was only the first of many. Servers continued to bring several more courses, removing our empty plates and replacing them with new ones bulging with further culinary delights. Eventually I had to put my fork down and throw in the towel.

Trina kept on eating. She was so tiny—I had no idea where she put it all.

"So... you *must* tell me of the human world across the ocean," she said. "Is it terribly ugly and filled with pollution and *murder*?"

Her expression and tone were all gleeful anticipation as if she was settling into her seat at a movie theater, ready for a horror show to begin.

"Oh. No, actually. I mean some places are—but it's very,

very large. There are lots of beautiful places, too—mountains, lakes, oceans, beaches, cities of every size and shape. It's really... it's really too much to describe over one dinner."

"What about the place you come from?"

"Well, I grew up in Missouri—it's a state in America, the United States. You've heard of the States?"

"Yes, a select few have traveled on missions for the queen. Once, one of our soldiers went to *Cal-ee-for-nee-ya.*"

It took me a second to interpret the strangely pronounced word as California. "Right. Okay, well, Missouri is..."

For a moment I was at a loss for words. How did I describe my home? Especially in a way that would mean something to someone who'd never even seen the outside world, who probably never would.

When it came right down to it, the natural beauty of the land probably wouldn't impress this girl. She was surrounded by perfect weather and incredible visuals every day. Finally, I decided to tell her about what really mattered —to me, anyway.

"The people there are wonderful—hardworking, neighborly, caring. I have many good friends there."

She quirked her head in surprise. "You *liked* it out there among the humans? Then why are you here?"

"I guess I wanted to know about my family."

I couldn't tell her more than that—about my mission to save the human world I loved so much. Blurting out that I was here for nymph blood might put a damper on the dinner conversation. Trina seemed satisfied with my answer, lifting her glass of pink liquid and raising it between us.

"To family," she said.

I lifted my own pink drink and tapped my glass against hers, blinking back the sudden onset of tears. "Family."

My full stomach still managed to produce a hollow ache. Now that I was forced to think of them, I felt severely homesick for Mom and Dad and Lily.

I maintained my pasted-on smile and took a drink from my own glass, letting the warmish-sweet liquid fill my mouth and run down my throat. I didn't want to overdo it, but I risked a few more sips of the tasty pink drink, making sure to pace myself. I was careful to drink several glasses of the delicious pure spring water to balance it out.

Apparently even that small amount of the pink stuff was too much—after a few minutes, I started feeling a bit light-headed. The lights and music around me seemed to soften, the colors of the ballroom blurring and swirling like a vibrant pinwheel in motion. I gulped down another glass of water, trying to counteract the effect of the obviously strong liqueur.

The sensation wasn't exactly unpleasant—the food now tasted even better. The music sounded more enchanting. The people around me grew more beautiful, and funnier, and nicer, even.

As a matter of fact, I'd really never met *anyone* I liked as well as these members of the Sidhe court. I'd certainly never been to a better party. I was saturated with a sense of serenity and well-being, truly happy for the first time since my arrival in Sidhe Innis.

When I'd been dressing after my bath, I had anticipated this night as some sort of test. But now it seemed more like I was just being folded into Sidhe society with very few questions asked. As I sat and chatted with Trina, other dinner guests made their way to our table by twos or threes and introduced themselves, smiling and welcoming me home.

Home. It *was* starting to feel rather homey, come to think of it. I'd never been among so many people who looked like *me* or who seemed so happy to have me around. Wasn't that what family was all about? Being accepted? Being part of your culture?

When Nic and I had talked about finding my birth mother, we'd discussed the possibility that my reunion with the race of my birth could go *very* badly—that they might be hostile, suspicious, unwelcoming. That they might even kick me out without listening to me.

But we'd been wrong. Here I was, in a gorgeous ballroom, seated with noblemen and ladies of the court, being wined and dined as if I was one of them. As if I belonged.

I smiled, accepting the greetings and good wishes of yet another noble couple. In one corner of my mind, there was a tickle of doubt, a whisper that something about all this seemed a little too easy. But turning my attention to the thought seemed to make it vanish like a wisp of smoke in a strong breeze, and trying to contemplate it seemed much, much less pleasant than focusing on the delightful sights and sounds around me.

"Are you enjoying yourself?"

I turned languidly and raised my gaze to the man standing beside me. Lord Hulder smiled down at me. *Wow.* I hadn't appreciated quite how attractive he was earlier.

"The dancing has begun. May I have the honor?" he said, offering one hand with a flourish.

Dancing. In spite of my gymnastics background, I wasn't very good at it. I'd spent my youth training at the gym and traveling for competitions. I hadn't actually been to any school dances. I would probably embarrass myself. But then, on the other hand, what could be more delightful than ballroom dancing in a glittering palace with a handsome, well-dressed nobleman?

"I'd love to," I told him and stood, my words only slightly slurred, letting him lead me out onto the floor where other couples already swirled and swayed.

"You'll have to teach me what to do," I said, groggily eyeing their steps as Lord Hulder placed a hand firmly on my waist and lifted the one he was already holding.

We began to move together in time to the orchestra. "Don't worry. I won't let you fall. And it will be my pleasure to teach you *everything*," he said.

He was a skilled dancer, very graceful and obviously well-practiced. That made sense. He'd told me he'd been around hundreds of years ago when the nymph race was driven into hiding. He'd probably been to *plenty* of dances.

It was a good thing. As we stepped and twirled, my head spun even more. I would have had no hope of keeping up—or even standing up—without his help.

I laughed and let the dizzying kaleidoscope of music and color and light carry me away. All my worries and concerns drained away as well. There was only this night, this incredible, carefree feeling, and the smile of my suave and graceful dance partner.

Before I even realized it, the evening had ended. The music stopped, and couples began leaving the dance floor. Lord Hulder bowed and kissed my knuckles in a chivalrous courtly gesture.

"Thank you for the pleasure of your charming company tonight, my lady. I do look forward to our next encounter."

My escorts materialized to take his place. They'd returned without my even seeing their approach. As we left the palace and traveled back down the winding road to Mae's house, I sobered slightly. I hadn't even gotten the chance to approach the queen. In fact, I'd forgotten all about her. And the Plague. And Nic. *Ugh.* What was the matter with me?

As the evening's euphoria started to wear off, a mantle of guilt settled over my shoulders, making me feel tired and a bit depressed.

"How do you go about getting an audience with the queen?" I asked the Queensguard.

"You don't," one of them said.

"Not unless she wants to speak to *you*," the other added. "If she does, you'll know about it, believe me."

"You can't just, like, call and get an appointment?"

They looked at each other and broke out into genuine laughter.

Okay then. But I wasn't going to give up so easily. Sidhe Innis was entrancing, to be sure. I'd had a far better time tonight than I'd expected to. But I wasn't here to play dress-up and go to fancy parties. I'd somehow forgotten that for a while during the dinner and dancing.

Now my focus was returning. I had a mission to accomplish. I had a fiancé who was missing. I could not let anything distract me from saving my people and getting back to the guy I loved. No more dinner parties. No more dancing. Definitely no more pink drinks.

At the guard's knock, Mae opened her door, her eyes bright with anticipation. "Did you have a delightful time, dear?"

"Yes, it was… interesting." I tripped as I stepped over the threshold, still feeling a bit woozy.

Mae's smile faded, and she closed the door, inviting me into the kitchen for a late-night cup of tea. As I flopped into a chair at her table, she surveyed me with grandmotherly concern.

"Have a wee nip tonight, did we?"

"A wee what?"

"A nip. An intoxicating drink."

I shook my head vigorously. "No. I specifically tried to be very careful with that pink stuff. I barely sipped it and stuck to water all night."

She made a sympathetic clucking noise with her tongue.

"Macy, the water from the fairy pools *is* the intoxicating beverage. The pink stuff is only for toasting. It's the food and water that make you forget your troubles and become muddled and carried away. Did you not notice all the dinner guests getting... shall we say... *looser* as the night went on?"

I folded my arms on the table and rested my head on them with a yawn. "No wonder."

Mae placed a teacup in front of me. "Here we go, love. This should help."

After a cup of tea, I felt more alert. Mae wanted to hear all about the dinner, who I'd met, and what everyone had worn. When she heard I'd been seated beside Lord Hulder, she clucked her tongue again and shook her head.

"He might have toasted to your friendship, but I'm not convinced he's your friend. Don't let your guard down with him. He was very bitter and indignant about your mother's desertion. He blustered on for years and years about how he'd been insulted and what he was *owed.*"

"I'll remember that," I vowed. "He didn't bother me, though. He was actually rather pleasant." Wait—had I actually thought Lord Hulder was *charming*? Ugh. "All of it was... lovely." I sighed.

"Then why do you seem sad, dear?"

"Well... I'm worried about my fiancé, Nic. I still don't know what happened to him or where he is. If he's still back in Mallaig, he's bound to be frantic by now, wondering where *I* am and if I'm okay. No one here will tell me anything. I wanted to ask the queen again tonight, but I couldn't get near her."

Mae's eyes darted from side to side in the small kitchen as if someone might have snuck in and hidden in a corner when we weren't looking. She leaned over the table toward me.

"I went visiting down in the villages while you were gone this evening, and one of the ladies from my sewing group said her son knows one of the soldiers who took part in your rescue. He said he brought the Elf—I mean Nic—here. She said her *son* said his *friend* said they're holding him in the gatekeeper's cottage down by the river."

Now I was fully awake, my sluggish heart springing to life and thumping hard. "Gatekeeper's cottage? Do you know where to find it?"

"Well, yes. It's just inside the portal. You didn't see it when you came through?"

"The portal? No. I'm not even sure what that is. I was unconscious when I was brought here. I woke up on a boat going down the river."

"Ah. I see. Well, the portal is at the very end of the river on the opposite side of the cavern from the capital city. It's how people travel in and out of Sidhe Innis."

Her expression turned stern. "You cannot go there, though, if *that's* what you're thinking. You are welcome to walk freely about this city and get to know the home of your people, but you're forbidden to leave the capital city. And the area around the portal is closely guarded, as will be your young man, I'm sure."

"Oh, I know. I wasn't planning to," I lied to the kindly old woman. "I'm just glad to know he's here and he's safe."

What I didn't say was that if he was in Sidhe Innis... I wasn't at all convinced Nic *was* safe.

15

WES

My leg. It throbbed, and at the same time, it felt frozen, immobilized. Though the pain was no longer agonizing, it ached from my knee down to my ankle.

Hypothermia must be setting in. Or shock. Blessed shock, it would make my death out on this cold, hard ground bearable.

But when I flexed my hands at my side, my fingers didn't encounter cold earth or even wet ground cover but something cushiony and warm. Slowly my eyelids opened.

I was in my own room. A fire burned in the hearth, and there was a glass of water and two pain relief tablets on the table beside my bed.

Someone had found me after all. They'd somehow managed to get me home, up the stairs, and into bed.

I ventured a glance down at my maimed leg, which was outside the covers, propped on several folded blankets. Whoever he was, my rescuer had also set the break. The shin was back in proper alignment, firmly splinted, and looked like a human limb again, though the skin was black and blue.

Who could have done this? And what germs were they carrying?

This could be really bad. I'd been exposed to who-knew-what pathogens. But then I supposed it was better than being left to die in a field. I really wouldn't have stood a chance out there alone.

Perhaps the visiting physician happened to be on the island off-schedule. But then... no. No one had been able to travel to and from the mainland all week because of the bizarrely persistent storm. And the splint was made from a fireplace shovel—not exactly medical-grade equipment.

I sniffed the air, detecting the distinct aroma of sizzling bacon and toasted bread. My rescuer and erstwhile paramedic was apparently cooking.

The only thing I could come up with was that Mum and Nanna had found a way around the ferry situation. As far as I knew, the transposition spell could not be used to teleport oneself—only someone or something else. But who knew what sort of solution they'd cooked up? I knew Mum had tired of being stranded in Mallaig days ago.

And then I thought of Alessia. Was she still on the island? And what was I going to tell Mum and Nanna about her? No doubt they'd checked the apartment above the stable immediately upon their arrival.

As soon as they realized I'd regained consciousness, they'd both pepper me with questions about my injuries, how their prisoner could have escaped, and where she might have gone.

The door to my room opened, and I slammed my eyelids closed again, feigning sleep. I wasn't ready to give any answers. My lungs demanded extra air and my hearing turned super-sonic as someone moved about the room—I could detect the rustling of clothing and light footsteps on the wooden floor.

Light footsteps. Perhaps Olly *had* come along after all. Slitting my eyes for a peek, all I could see against the backlighting of the fireplace was a female figure. And then I smelled the food. And the soap. *My* soap.

Alessia. I didn't say the word out loud, but she turned toward me anyway, catching me wide awake and wide-eyed.

She jumped, clearly startled, but quickly composed herself. "Oh. You're up. How are you feeling? Are you in any pain?"

My mouth opened, but for the life of me I couldn't utter a sound. What was she doing here?

Alessia crossed the room toward me, carrying the tray I'd used so many times to deliver her meals. She must have noticed me eyeing the food on it because she offered a coy smile.

"The shoe is on the other foot now, isn't it, Mr. Opossum? Only I am not as good a cook as you, so I'm afraid your pain and suffering will go beyond just a broken leg."

I shook my head, wondering whether I had actually woken up after all. This had to be some sort of delirium dream. I was still out there on the moors, dying a slow death of exposure and blood loss. That made far more sense than what I was seeing before my eyes—Alessia, serving me food and wearing—what was that? My favorite green sweater. It hung down to her knees. Below it, her long, shapely legs were bare except for a pair of my own athletic socks.

Yep, definitely hallucinating.

"I hope you don't mind me raiding your closet—my clothes were soaked to the skin. I'm sorry I had to leave your wet shirt on you. I was… busy."

Glancing down at myself, I realized I still wore the same flannel button down I'd left the house in. It wasn't soaked anymore, but it was damp and uncomfortable. A quick peek under the sheets revealed a pair of cutoff jeans. What the hell was I doing wearing Daisy Dukes?

"I had to cut your pants off," Alessia explained. "There was no way I could pull them over your leg. So how is it? I gave you something for the pain, but the break was very bad. I've never used it to treat anything worse than a cut, and of course I have no idea of your pain level because you're human."

When I didn't answer, she walked back over to the bed, standing at the foot of it. "Oh dear. Did you sustain a head injury as well? I didn't think about the fact you might have bumped it during the fall. Can you hear me? Can you speak? Do you remember me at all?"

This was no hallucination. I didn't know exactly *what* was going on, but everything about the scene—the smell of soap on her freshly washed skin, the glow of firelight on her smooth cheek, the melodious sound of her voice—it was too real to deny. Alessia really was here—in the same room.

My muscles warmed and tingled, blood rushing in a fight or flight response. Of course, in the shape I was in, I wouldn't be doing much of either.

"I remember," I croaked through a dry throat. I reached for the water glass at my bedside, drank thirstily, and tried again. "I remember you. What are you doing here? I saw you ride away."

"Yes," she said, drawing in a breath and pressing her lips into a grim line. "I did. But then your horse flew past me, and you weren't on it."

"You came back for me?"

She gave a delicate shrug and glanced away. "It's basic riding etiquette. You don't leave a fallen rider down."

"But…" I lapsed into stunned silence. None of this made sense. Why would this Elven girl care about the fate of a human man? Especially one who'd held her captive for several days.

"I'm human. From what I hear, you'd like to wipe out the lot of us. Why would you save me? Why would you *stay*?"

She stiffened and darted her eyes away again, busying herself by refilling my glass with water. Her tone was harder now. "I didn't stay for *you*. It's the storm. It's picked up. The weather was too severe to go on horseback, and the stallion had been ridden too hard already. You have no car."

The last she said as if she was informing me of a fact I might have overlooked.

"Sebastian," I said. "Where is he?"

"In the stable. I groomed him and the roan and checked their feet. They're both fine."

"He let you touch his feet?"

This was perhaps the most shocking information of all. Even I had a devil of a time checking the monstrous thoroughbred's hooves as was necessary before and after a ride.

"That horse has nearly killed people for far less."

"He didn't love it," she said, "but I think he was too tired to argue. And I told him it was for his own good."

"Is that your glamour, then? Communicating with animals?"

She let out a shocked bark of a laugh, but her expression sobered quickly. "No. That's not it." She paused unnaturally long before saying, "I am a singer."

"Oh. Wow. I thought it was something more... well, I was told..." And then it hit me. "Wait? What time is it? Did the storm clear?"

I had no idea how long I'd slept. If the storm had ended and morning had come, my mother and grandmother could be on their way here right now. Perhaps the thought should have given me relief, but I felt only a heavy weight in my stomach at the idea of them walking in and finding Alessia here like this.

"It's late—three in the morning. And no, it hasn't. Can you

not hear the wind and rain? It seems like the gale will never stop."

I let out a pent up breath. "Good." Trying to raise to a sitting position, I accidentally moved my leg and hissed in pain.

"Don't do that. You should stay as still as possible." Alessia hurried forward and grabbed an extra pillow from the foot of the bed, then jammed it behind my back to prop me up.

I stared at her, baffled. "Thank you." Then I nodded toward my splinted leg. "You did this?"

"Yes. I know it's very crude, but I've never set a bone before. I did try to call a doctor, but the phone was dead."

"Must be the storm. I don't even bother with a cell phone because there's no coverage even in good conditions. The landline's usually fairly reliable, but in weather like this, I'm not surprised. Anyway, there's no full-time doctor on this island, and even the emergency transport wouldn't be able to respond. They couldn't get a chopper or life boat over here until the storm lets up."

"Why would you live in a place with no medical care? Don't you humans need that sort of thing?"

I couldn't help but snicker at her indignant attitude. "Generally, yes. But I *can't* see a doctor, so it doesn't matter. Actually, it's a good thing you weren't able to call anyone to come out here. That probably would have ended me quicker than my injury."

She gave me a baffled glance. "What do you mean? Why can you not see a doctor?"

"I can't be around *anyone*. I have a genetic condition. I was born with almost no natural immunity against pathogens—germs that cause illness. With an open wound like the one on my leg, I would most likely have contracted some fatal infection from whoever responded to try to help me."

Alessia fell a step back—staggered would be the more accurate word. "You can't be around... anyone," she repeated.

"Yes. Thanks to my infantile immune system. So... 'crude' as your medical care was—you're literally the only person on the island whose help could've actually *helped*. Anyone else would probably have killed me. Thank you, by the way."

She appeared a bit taken aback, and her face colored, turning her cheeks pink. It was a good look for her. The rosy glow highlighted her arresting light blue eyes. I felt my own color heighten, warmth flooding my cheeks.

"It was nothing," she said. "Anyway, you would not have been in that situation if not for me."

"How'd you know what to do?" I asked. "It looks like you set the bone well and disinfected the site of the cut thoroughly."

"I saw it done once a few years ago. A stable hand was crushed under a rearing horse. The boy was human."

There was something... *different* in the way she talked about him. It piqued my curiosity. "A friend of yours?"

"Of course not," she snapped. "As I said, he was *human*."

"I see. Well, you're definitely a quick study, in any case. Most people wouldn't have even attempted this."

Examining it more closely, I was shocked the wound didn't look worse. I would have sworn most of the tissue around my broken tibia and fibula had been rended by the shattered bones. That should have meant swelling and more surface laceration. But the skin was hardly discolored now, and the cut itself was small—it actually looked like it was healing already. Which was strange.

"How *long* was I out?"

"I don't know exactly. Six hours, maybe?"

I looked at my leg again. It even felt a bit itchy inside as if the bones were already knitting back together. Which was impossible at this early stage.

I glanced back up at Alessia. "What did you *do* to me?"

The sky-blue eyes went wide, her voice betraying true horror. "Why? Did I make a mistake? Are you in terrible pain?"

"No. I'm not. That's the thing. I'm in much better shape than I should be, in fact. Are you a... that is, do you have *healing* glamour?"

Her eyes shuttered, and her expression turned bitter for some reason. She took a step back, moving toward the door. "No. I don't. I will leave you to have your food and go check on... I... need to go check on something."

Well, okay then.

She was certainly in a hurry to get out of the room. I still didn't understand what she was doing here in the first place, why she hadn't just left me in the field and escaped the estate. Or why she'd stayed once she brought me here. Unless she'd already checked the ferry schedules and knew there was no getting off the island tonight.

No doubt she was planning to take advantage of the availability of a warm, dry bed and then take off first thing in the morning. That's what I'd do in her position.

When she returned to my room—if she returned—I'd ask her to leave me a good supply of water and non-perishable food within reach before she left. I'd also need something to serve as a bedpan, I supposed, since I probably wouldn't be able to get out of bed for at least a few days.

How had she managed to get me *into* bed? Perhaps the reality of her strength should have frightened me, but at the moment, all I could manage to summon was a considerable amount of awe. The woman had lifted me. She had set a compound fracture with no assistance and stemmed my internal bleeding. She was incredible.

On second thought, I'd ask for something I could use as a crutch—the kitchen mop, maybe. I was *not* going to ask

Wonder Woman's more beautiful Elven cousin for a bedpan. At the moment, thankfully, I was too dehydrated to require one.

I finished the water in my glass and refilled it then investigated the plate of food. There were two slices of toast —overdone and bare of butter or marmalade. Beside them lay four strips of bacon, cooked to a nearly blackened crisp. I grinned, remembering what she'd said about not being able to cook. No matter. Food was food, and I ate it all, grateful to be alive to do so.

That done, I studied the room, plotting out my best route to the bathroom. Once the storm ended, my family would arrive and be able to help me out with things such as food preparation and changing clothes, but until then, I'd have to manage on my own.

Speaking of changing clothes, I was broiling. Alessia had built the fire up to such a degree the room was like a sauna. She'd already turned my jeans into jorts (shudder) but the flannel long-sleeved shirt clung to my upper body and made me feel like I was trapped in an electric blanket.

I unbuttoned it and fanned myself with the open sides, but that did little to relieve my overheated condition. I wanted it off. Now.

So I did an ab crunch, raising the top of my body off the pillows while attempting to pry the damp garment over my shoulders and down my arms without moving my injured leg. It wasn't easy. In fact, the simple act turned into an impossible feat.

I pulled the left cuff over my hand then pushed the top of the shirt off my shoulder. But when I attempted to pull it off my arm, the sleeve became stuck just above the elbow, effectively winging me and trapping me in an awkward side-leaning position.

Great. Just great. I continued to struggle with the inflexible sleeve, my abdominal muscles trembling now from the continuous sit-up I was required to maintain. My leg was beginning to throb, too, as I was involuntarily putting pressure on it in an effort to maintain my balance.

Finally I collapsed backward in defeat, my shirt half-on, half-off. I'd fix it later. At least I was a bit less overheated now, though of course, my twisted arm was starting to complain and ache. A few minutes later after I'd rested, I sat up again and began yanking my elbow upward repeatedly, trying to force it free of the fabric.

The bedroom door opened, and Alessia let out a sound of dismayed surprise.

"What are you doing, you idiot?" She rushed forward, her hands outstretched. But when she reached me she stopped, frozen in place.

I stopped moving, too, looking down at my trapped elbow then up at her. "A little help maybe?"

She took a small step toward me, her fingers flexing, but again stopped in place. Her eyes were wide and dark. Her chest rose and fell in rapid, shallow breaths.

"Why are you undressing?"

"Because I'm planning to seduce you and make vigorous love to you," I sneered. "Why do you think? I'm hot. Now if you don't mind?"

I nodded at my trapped arm.

"Well, I... I'm not sure I should."

"I was only kidding, in case you couldn't tell. I promise I'm not going to take it the wrong way if your fingers happen to graze my manly chest," I joked. "And considering I can hardly move without severe pain, your *virtue* is entirely safe from my advances."

"No—it's not that. I..." There she stopped, leaving the sentence hanging.

What could be so terrible about helping a guy take off his

shirt? It took me a second to process her expression and tone of reluctance. When I did, corrosive bitterness curdled in the pit of my stomach.

"Oh, I get it. You don't want to *soil* yourself by touching a disgusting human. Fine. Just keep your distance then. I'd hate to accidently hurt you when I dislocate my shoulder while getting this effing shirt off."

Her subtle rejection left me feeling strangely hurt. Here I was, drooling over her appearance, and she found me repulsive. It made me angry, which drove my internal temperature even higher. I jerked at my arm more forcefully, determined to get the shirt off even if my arm came with it.

Alessia dashed forward again, grasping the edge of my shirt and carefully peeling it down my arm until my elbow sprang free. I let out a breath of relief and collapsed back into the pillows then dragged the garment from my other shoulder and arm, tossing it to the floor.

I chuckled, breathing hard from my efforts. "There. That wasn't so hard now, was it? And your pristine Elven fingers didn't even brush my distasteful *human* skin."

Alessia had retreated to the other side of the room again, hovering near the fireplace chair. Her expression was wounded as if she was the one who'd been insulted.

"That is not why I hesitated to touch you," she said, her voice barely above a whisper. "I… didn't want to hurt you."

"I've already told you—you can't make me sick. My immune problems are limited to human germs. Other than the fact you hate me and want to get as far from here as possible, you're the perfect companion for me."

She did not laugh at my joke. Didn't even smile.

"I don't hate you. Other humans, yes. But not you. You've been kind to me. You are kind to your horses. I saw them—a pathetic lot, other than the stallion. They are worthless, but you care for them anyway." She paused then said, "*That* is why I saved you."

The moment of honesty surprised me. And it seemed deserving of an honest response. "Well, perhaps many would see them as worthless—on the outside. But they have loving souls, and their value to me is immeasurable. Believe me, those animals have done more for me than I've ever done for them. Many people wouldn't understand that, but I think you do."

The faraway look on her face told me she was not seeing the room around us but a scene from her past.

"Yes. I have always loved horses. They were my best friends throughout my childhood. Even now—" She stopped abruptly, and her cheeks colored as if she had surprised herself with what she was about to say.

I nodded, studying her face, my belly clenching at the unwilling vulnerability I saw there. "You must be eager to get back home. I'm sure your family and friends must be frantic and missing you."

She nodded quickly, biting her lip and looking at the bedroom door as if she'd like to make a dash for it.

"Yes," she said rather noncommittally.

"So what were you doing downstairs all this time? Not cooking, I hope."

Her eyes flew to mine, wide with offense, but when she saw my smile, her rigid posture relaxed.

"I was checking the weather forecast online. The meteorologists are baffled. They say the storm shows no sign of moving. There is a lot of flooding on the mainland coast now. They didn't mention the islands except to say ferry service is still suspended."

"Speaking of online, I need to get some work done. Would you mind bringing my laptop up here?"

"You are in no condition to work," Alessia said. "You need to rest."

"I'm feeling better, and I don't really have a choice. The emails will pile up if I don't start addressing them. You didn't... look at them did you? Those communications require a high security clearance. I could get in a lot of trouble if someone else sees them."

My concern was not actually about work emails. My fear was that Alessia would see the ones from my mother. I didn't want her to realize my family and "the witches" who'd sent her here were one and the same.

"I didn't look at your emails at all. You won't be in trouble."

"Well, I *will* be if I don't respond soon and get at least a little work done. Don't worry. I won't use it to call in the cavalry. The last thing I want is a horde of disease-carrying humans descending on this house."

"Nevertheless, you have been severely injured. And you're on heavy pain medication. You cannot work."

"If I get fired, I won't be able to buy food for the horses."

She examined me with an extended narrow-eyed glance, like she was dissecting my answer for ill intent or hidden clues. "Very well. I will bring it up—tomorrow. For now, I'll check on the horses and then *try* to make some food for us. Do you have any preferences or suggestions?"

"No. No one's cooked for me in years. Whatever you make will be fine."

She nodded, her expression blank. "You should try to get some rest. Then when you've eaten again, I will give you another dose of pain medication so you can sleep. Perhaps in the morning I'll allow you to do a little work."

She turned and went to the door, leaving me battling a serious case of shock. She wasn't planning to leave immediately. She intended to still be here bossing me around in the morning. A swell of delight battled with a chilling sense of foreboding. In spite of my ridiculous pleasure at her continued presence, there was no getting around it—she *shouldn't* stay. Not if she valued her life.

Even if she didn't, I did. She *wasn't* the uber-evil being my mother believed her to be. She wouldn't have stayed to help me if she was. I didn't know what my mother and grandmother had in store for Alessia, but chances were, it wasn't good. She didn't deserve that. She had saved my life, and I was going to return the favor.

"Alessia?"

"Yes?" She stopped in the doorway and looked back over her shoulder, her eyes wary.

"As soon as the storm lets up and the ferry is running, you should leave."

"What?" She turned fully toward me now, her face the picture of disbelief. "You've kept me locked away here for days, and *now* you want me to *leave*? How will you eat? You are like a baby—helpless. How will you survive on your own?"

"You could help me move downstairs. The witches will come as soon as the storm ends. You don't want to be here when they arrive."

"You are a strange man, you know that? I thought you worked for the witches. Will you not be punished if they arrive and I am gone?"

Probably. I shook my head. "It doesn't matter. You saved my life. I owe you. And I never should have kept you locked up in the first place. I'm sorry. It was a bad decision."

She recoiled in visible shock. Then she stared at me, her gaze appraising me like an interesting new species she'd discovered and wasn't quite sure what to make of.

"It was also a bad decision to chase after me in that weather on an inferior mount, warning me of the dangerous conditions and the unreliable horse. What were *you* thinking? You should have known better."

I felt a small grin bend my lips. "I'm just a 'stupid human,' remember?"

She cocked her head to the side in thought. "Perhaps not *all* humans are stupid. Some of these writers are fairly intelligent, I suppose."

She glanced over at the fireside chair, where a book lay on the cushion then back at me. "And, well... *you* may not be *entirely* stupid."

"Thank you, Alessia. I'm very moved," I dead-panned. "But you don't have to stay. I can take care of myself. I've been doing it for over two years now."

I pushed myself up to a sitting position, the coverlet pooling around my waist as I did so. "I'm a big boy, you know."

Alessia immediately averted her gaze from my bare chest and stomach, turning her profile to me as she answered. "You haven't had a broken leg for two years. Now stop spouting nonsense and get some rest."

She left the room in a hurry and closed the door hard behind her while a smile developed on my face, and my skin tingled all over, making me feel better than I had a right to. The ice queen apparently had a mushy spot. And I was more interested than ever in melting her.

16

ALESSIA

He was right. I couldn't stay here.

Not just because of the witches. Because of... him. The sight of him there, all masculine and shirtless and so large he made the king-sized bed look like a double, well... it didn't bear thinking about. Neither did those striking sapphire eyes.

Making a mental note to keep his room considerably *cooler* from now on, I charged downstairs to the back door. Then I draped his large mackintosh over myself and strolled down the hill to the stables. In this moment, I didn't even mind the rain. I needed to cool down as well.

The atmosphere in the stable was a welcome break from the house where everything was so unfamiliar and yet familiar at the same time—it smelled like Wes in there, and the place was furnished with all the things he considered most important. I'd found it hard not to lift and touch each item, wondering about its significance to him and what his daily human life was like.

Here, I was much more relaxed. Tension released from my neck and shoulders as I took a few deep breaths. The horsey sounds and smells were comforting, and their quiet presence calming. I pulled on a pair of gloves and set to work, taking care to approach each of them slowly, with a low, gentle voice.

"Hello there," I said to the roan mare in the first stall. "Are you rested up from your ride?" As I spoke, I added fresh hay from a pile in the corner to her feed bucket then moved to the next stall.

"Oh my, you're a wise old fellow, aren't you?" I asked the stocky highland pony. "I'll bet you could tell some tales."

He moved forward, offering me his neck for a hello rub. When I obliged, he lifted his nose and breathed in my face, a greeting and sign of trust. "Yes, you know a horse lover when you meet one, don't you?"

With another pat to his neck, I moved to the next stall where a big Clydesdale had extended a curious nose. When I offered him my empty palm, he lipped it in investigation.

"No, I'm sorry. No treats. I'll have to ask your daddy where he keeps them. Aren't you a good boy?" Walking over to retrieve a new batch of hay for him, I fed him some by hand then deposited the rest into his bucket.

At the end of the line of stalls was the stallion. I felt like we knew each other at this point, but I didn't know what to call him. Unlike the others, he lurked toward the rear of his enclosure.

"Don't play hard to get with me, you tease. I've spent more time close to *you* than any man in my life. Now come here and say hello."

To my delight, the big thoroughbred obeyed, walking to the front of his stall and dropping his head over the gate so I could rub his neck. "See? Trust has its rewards," I murmured to him. "Doesn't that feel nice?"

After a few minutes I moved away and came back with fresh hay for him, then my eyes went to the staircase. I walked over and looked up the flight of stairs to the room at the top. The door still stood open.

Only a few days ago I had awakened inside that room, terrified and alone and repulsed by my crude surroundings. Today I felt entirely different about this place. Now I was the one in control. I was no longer a prisoner—in fact, Wes had encouraged me to leave. I would. Soon. But not yet.

I left the stable and started back for the house, taking in the myriad ocean-facing windows, numerous chimney-stacks, and the wraparound porch. It was large and quite beautiful. It could not have been cheap. Neither was taking care of five horses. Wes must have a good job. But what could it be?

If I remembered correctly, the isle of Eigg was one of the Scottish small isles, part of the Hebrides. There was not much commerce on any of them and only a small population. I hadn't seen any sheep or other livestock apart from the horses, so I didn't think he was a farmer. That left some kind of outsourced remote career, like writing or perhaps a computer tech job.

And he never sees anyone.

Not his family, not his friends. If he lived here alone, worked alone, and never saw anyone else, did he even *have* any friends? It had to be lonely. Wes was connected to others through technology, but he was essentially alone in the world.

The thought made me feel an unwilling kinship with this isolated human. My heart thumped hard, though the climb toward the house was only mildly exerting.

Perhaps he had online relationships through social media or email chat rooms. Perhaps he had a long-distance girlfriend. That thought caused a *different* sensation to swell in my stomach. I tamped it back down. What foolishness.

I stepped into the house and removed the wet mack near

the door, kicking off my boots as well. Ugh. They were ruined. Oh well, I had hundreds of pairs of shoes at home—if the storm ever stopped long enough for me to leave this place.

Pulling on Wes's socks again, I moved to the office, where his laptop computer sat open. Eying the device, I went to the fireplace and fed a new log to the dwindling fire. Then I went to the kitchen and put the kettle on and dug around in the pantry until I found some teabags.

While the kettle heated I wandered back into the office. And glanced at the laptop again. *I really shouldn't.* Walking to the bookshelf, I read the spines of his vast collection and selected a new one for myself, but my gaze kept drifting back to the desk and that inviting black screen.

Finally giving in, I sat in the desk chair and tapped the space key on the computer, waking it, realizing belatedly I'd probably be able to see nothing. He must have a password. But the screen went immediately to his email inbox.

Right. No need for a password when you live alone and never leave your house.

At the top of the screen I saw his email moniker, WestonECDC. *Weston.* I would have thought his nickname was short for Wesley. *Hmmm.* ECDC. That one was confusing. Maybe he had multiple middle names? Some people did, especially if they were from sentimental families.

Ah—here was an email from someone simply called Mum. His mother. Had to be. I clicked it and read her complaints about the inn she was staying in with "Nanna." Apparently they were having a miserable getaway because of the incessant rain, and the accommodations were becoming a bit snug. *Try a stable room, Mum.*

I found I didn't like the woman much, based on her stern email to her son. She sounded accusatory when informing him she'd called several times in the past few hours and been unable to get through because phone lines were down.

As if it was his fault. I closed the email and clicked another. This one appeared to be professional in nature. It was from a colleague who also had the initials ECDC following his name. Oh, they weren't initials. They were an abbreviation. European Centers for Disease Control.

A little shock went through me. Wes's job had something to do with healthcare or medicine. There was an uncomfortable squeezing sensation in my chest. A man whose entire life was dictated by his poor health spent his days trying to protect the health of others. And this was one of the emails he didn't want me to see because of its classified nature.

I read it carefully, several times in fact. But still, I had little understanding of the technical jargon. I spoke and read English, but it was not my first language or even my second. And a scientist, I was not.

But apparently Wes was. I closed it and scanned his other recent emails, searching for anything else interesting—a woman's name for instance—but there was nothing. If he had an online girlfriend, he didn't use email to communicate with her.

A search of his browser history showed no social media accounts either. *Wow*. So he really was all about his work. One of the sites in his browser caught my interest. It was something to do with a map. I clicked on it, and all the air deserted my lungs.

It *was* a map—of South America—and there in the corner, just over the tiny gold mining town in Peru where I'd accidentally touched the fan pod girl and set into motion a world-ending plague, was a large bulls-eye. Radiating out from it were tiny red markers.

European Centers for Disease Control.

Wes and his colleagues were tracking the emerging cases of plague. That had to be what this map was about. I stood up and shuffled back from the desk as if *it* were diseased. Wes was trying to stop the outbreak by looking for the source of the contagion. He was looking for *me*.

My heart crashed against my breastbone. My stomach cartwheeled with panic. This was incredible. Was *this* why the witches had sent me here? So he could *study* me?

But he didn't seem to know anything about my terrible glamour. He'd even speculated it had something to do with animals, or even more ridiculous, with *healing* people.

They might know about me, but Wes didn't. And he could never know. It didn't matter that my triggering the Plague had been accidental. The result was still the same—the extermination of his friends, his family, the entire world as he knew it. He would hate me if he ever found out what I'd done.

I looked at the door. *I have to get out of here.* Why wouldn't this storm stop? It was almost as if the gods had devised the perfect punishment for me—trap me in purgatory with a man who was *guaranteed* to hate my guts because he was more qualified than almost anyone else on the planet to understand the consequence of my crimes.

If I could have taken back what I'd done, I would have. But I couldn't. What was done was done. In spite of Wes's best efforts, there was nothing he could do to stop the coming plague. There was nothing anyone could do.

Although… something Nic had said niggled at my brain. He'd said if I'd trust him and help him, there *was* a way to stop it before it got out of control. Had he only told me that in order to distract me and protect his girlfriend? But then, no—that wasn't possible. We'd been communicating mind-to-mind. It had to have been true.

Frustration made me slap the desktop and swear. I had

been *so close* to telling Nic where the virus had been activated. If the witches hadn't stopped me, or if they'd just waited a few *seconds* longer, maybe Nic could have intervened and done something to save humanity. Now I had no idea where he and the nymph were or how to find them.

Did I want to? Glancing at the staircase, I pictured Wes lying helpless and injured in his bed. He didn't deserve to die. What if there were other humans like him? Other horse lovers or those who, like Wes, spent their lives trying to help others? It was a reasonable assumption. He couldn't be the only good human in the world.

All of a sudden the magnitude of what I'd done hit me. I staggered back and fell into the desk chair again. I had to do something. I was still desperate to leave this island but for a whole new reason. I had to find Nic and Macy again. Not to kill them. To try to help them stop the Plague.

But what about Wes? I went to the kitchen to gather some ingredients and attempt to cook something for supper. I

couldn't leave him here alone. And there was no way to leave the island anyway until the storm subsided. As soon as it did, though, I would take his advice and flee before the witches could arrive.

I might deserve their punishment, but I couldn't stick around to face it. The fate of the world depended on me getting out of here.

17

MACY

Early the next morning I rose while it was still dark, dressed in one of the pixie dresses—this one in tones of deep blue and dark purple and black to blend with the night—and left Mae's house.

Thankfully, she was still sleeping. I hated to leave her without saying goodbye. She'd been so kind to me. But I didn't want to worry her, or implicate her in my escape—or give her the opportunity to stop me.

The gatekeeper's cottage was at the opposite end of the cavern from the palace, she'd said. It shouldn't be that hard to find. I'd follow the river and when I got to the portal, whatever that was, I'd figure it out.

The capital city was quiet, but the villages beyond it were bustling with early risers. I'd been hoping to avoid being seen altogether, but that proved impossible as the lanes filled with pedestrians, shopkeepers opening for business, children on their way to school.

To my great relief, no one seemed alarmed to see me or even surprised. Everyone who took notice of me smiled and offered a friendly greeting. Some even seemed to recognize me. Had I met them at the dinner last night? I couldn't remember.

"Fallon! Hello there, love," said a woman emerging from one of the shops. "It's good to have you back. Your mother must be overjoyed."

Oh. Now I got it. These villagers thought I was my mother. I gave her a quick "thank you" and a wave and scooted on down the path, not stopping to chat.

I hadn't asked what the population of Sidhe Innis was, but it must have been very small for so many people to have known Fallon. Either that or my mom was some kind of local celebrity.

Continuing to follow the path along the riverbanks for roughly a mile, I eventually reached the end of the canyon where the path ended and the wall of stone rose high and imposing before me. And stopped dead in my tracks.

I needn't have worried about recognizing the portal when I saw it. In the center of the rocky cavern wall was a huge circular opening. Through the bottom of it flowed a steady stream of crystal clear water, which dropped off from the circle's edge in a waterfall to the river below.

The ring-shaped portal was bordered by a sort of frame, thick stone engraved with nymph symbols like the ones I'd seen since arriving here and the one on my mother's letter. Its edges were partially grown over with moss and vines, making it look like it had been there a very, *very* long time.

The space above the water was not dark like a cave but occupied by a filmy, moving membrane that I supposed acted as a barrier to the outside world. As I got closer, I realized it was a thin sheet of water itself, stretching from the top to the bottom, like a blue, rippling mirror filling a frame.

There was a loud cry from the riverbank opposite me, and I turned in time to see a boy jumping from the embankment into the river at the base of the falls. Several other boys applauded and laughed and then jumped in themselves. Either they were playing hooky from school or going for a quick swim beforehand.

I kept going until I reached a single house standing alone at the end of the path, just inside the cavern walls below the portal. This had to be the gatekeeper's cottage. Nic could be just on the other side of those walls.

But how was I going to get inside? They were holding him for a reason, and I doubted Elven prisoners had visitation rights.

A guard rounded the corner of the house and halted in surprise at the sight of me. Like the other men I'd seen in the employ of the queen, he wore a jacket and kilt of deep midnight blue with a matching cloak.

"May I help you miss?" he asked, obviously taking me for a local.

"Yes. I'm here to see the prisoner. Queen's orders." I hoped I sounded confident and official. I also hoped he didn't have a phone or something like it that would let him quickly check the validity of my claim.

"And you are…" he said, waiting for an answer.

Oh crap. What do I do?

I decided to capitalize on the fact that so many people had mistaken me for my mother. She'd been high-born enough in Sidhe society that she'd been engaged to snooty Lord Hulder, so my hope was she outranked this gatekeeper. And that he'd fall for it.

"Fallon. I have returned. Now step aside and let me in." There. It was my best bluff. If he didn't buy it, no doubt I'd be on house arrest myself very soon.

"Oh, of course. I didn't recognize you at first—it's been so long. Forgive me." He opened the door and gestured inside. "Down the hall—last door on the left."

Well. That worked better than I'd expected. The guy

seemed nice, and I certainly didn't want him to get hurt, but I was relieved he seemed to be the only guard on the gatehouse premises. With his much greater size, Nic should have no trouble overcoming the man. We could tie him up or maybe lock him in a room until we could escape together.

I thanked him and entered the cottage, hurrying down the hallway. Reaching the last door on the right, I took a key from the hook just beside it, inserted it into the lock, and turned, but it seemed to have been unlocked already. My heart hammering, I pushed the door open.

Nic raised his head, looking up in a lazy glance. Then his eyes widened, and he jumped to his feet.

"Macy." He rushed to me and took me in his arms, nearly crushing me with the intensity of his hold. "How did you find me? How did you get in here? Are you okay?"

I nodded against his chest, wrapping my arms around his waist and breathing in the wonderful scent of him, somehow intoxicating and comforting at the same time.

"I'm okay. Are you? Did they hurt you?"

He loosened his grip but kept his hands on me, moving them from my waist to my arms to my cheeks. Cradling my face and looking down into my eyes, he gave me a watery smile, the skin over his cheekbones flushing.

"No. I'm not hurt. They're not exactly friendly, but so far they've left me alone. I've been going mad worrying about *you*. When the men came in during the night, and I got a look at them, I knew they were there to take you. They put something over my face that knocked me out. When I was losing consciousness, I was terrified they'd just kill me and take you, and you'd have no one to protect you."

I squeezed him hard around the waist again. "I was worried about the same thing—that they'd done something horrible to you. I woke up here in a boat with no idea where I was at first and no idea where you were."

He nodded. "I woke before we went through the portal. This place is something else, isn't it?"

"You have no idea. Farther down the river, there's a massive capital city and a palace. There was a huge ball there last night. Oh, and I met my mom's nanny, Mae, and lots of people remember her, and they say I look just like her. That's how I got in here just now—I pretended to be Fallon. I'll tell you the rest later. We should get out of here now while there's only one guard on duty. Come on."

I tugged at his hand, already starting toward the door. Nic's feet didn't move. When I turned back, the look on his face worried me. He shook his head.

"I've already tried escaping. It's no use."

"No, it's okay. The guard out there thinks I'm here on an errand from the queen. He thinks I'm my mother. I'll just bluff again and maybe we can walk out of here—or at least it'll give you the chance to overcome him, and we can lock him in here or something while we run."

"Macy. It's not going to work. I've had free run of the house since they brought me here. I've tried every window and door. I can't get out."

"So we'll unlock them."

He stepped close and placed his hands on my shoulders, looking me straight in the eye. "You're not understanding me. I *can't* leave. There's some kind of... spell or something on this cottage. I can open a window or open a door—but when I do, vines grow over it at lightning speed. I can't push through them. It must be some kind of nymph magic."

"Oh. Well, they *are* able to control the weather and natural elements—I guess plants are included. Maybe *I* could get through them. I don't know how to use my nymph abilities, but I *am* one. You could hold my hand, and maybe the plants won't interfere."

He gave me a hopeful glance. "Maybe. It's worth a try. I

173

can't say I'm eager to stick around. They don't exactly like me."

"It's your race. It seems the Elven history books were accurate—your people terrorized them."

"Yeah, I figured." He grimaced.

Hand in hand, we went to the front door. I prepared myself to face the guard outside, planning to tell him I had orders to escort Nic to the palace. If that didn't work, we'd have to jump the guy. We had to do whatever was necessary. Obviously Sidhe Innis was *not* a safe place for Nic to stay.

Nic opened the front door, and I went through first, still gripping his hand. Nothing happened. I strode forward, looking for the guard but stopped short, as if on a leash that had been jerked tight. Twisting back, I saw the vines had indeed grown over the doorway, forming a tightly woven barrier. As Nic and I were still holding hands, the vines had simply grown around his wrist. Only his hand was visible. The rest of him was trapped.

"Nic—are you okay?"

I could hear his muffled voice from behind the barrier of vegetation. "Yes. It doesn't hurt. But I'm stuck. Just let go of my hand and leave. I don't want you to get caught."

"No." I squeezed his fingers more tightly. "I'm not leaving you."

I stepped back toward the door, and the barricade of vines dissolved, freeing Nic's arm and allowing me back inside.

"Wow," I breathed.

He nodded. "Yeah. That's what I was afraid of. This may be an Elf-specific security system, or maybe it works on anyone who isn't a nymph. In any case—I'm not going anywhere until they're ready for me to."

"Nic." I clung to him, laying my head against his chest. "What are we going to do?"

"You said you went to the palace? Did you see the queen? Do you think you might get a chance to talk to her and plead our case?"

"They took me to see her immediately after I got here—but she didn't give me a chance to ask. She just asked me a bunch of questions and dismissed me. I was hoping to talk to her again, but when I found out they were holding you here—"

"Well, it sounds like you're going to get a second chance," he said, raising his brows and nodding toward the door.

"What do you mean?"

"Listen."

I went silent and attuned my attention to the cottage door. Then I heard it—the sound of marching feet approaching. A bunch of them. I guessed the gatekeeper made a phone call after all.

A guard in a highly embellished version of the blue uniform opened the door. "Please come with me."

When I didn't respond, he grabbed my upper arm.

"Hey—be careful," Nic warned, glowering at the man and straightening to his full height. "Or you'll be dealing with me."

The guard ignored him and began dragging me toward the opening where Nic could not follow.

"I'll be back for you," I promised. "I'll be back soon and get us both out of here."

"I love you, Macy," was all he said, and then the door closed behind us, blocking his face from my view.

* * *

"I UNDERSTAND you broke your curfew and left the city, abusing the gift of freedom I generously granted you."

Queen Ragan glared at me from her throne. Today she

wore a gold dress that appeared to be covered entirely with autumn leaves.

I lifted my chin, determined to stand my ground this time. "I went to see my fiancé."

"I am aware," she said in a droll tone. "*And* tried to help him escape."

"You shouldn't have him locked up. Nic would never hurt anyone, much less my family. He was trying to help me find them. He *loves* me."

"He's bonded to you." It was a statement, not a question. I had no idea how she knew. Maybe he'd told his captors. Though... he didn't speak the language.

"Yes."

"But you have not yet bonded with him. Why?"

And here we go. My answer was either going to lead to salvation for the human race—or a nice swift death for me and Nic. I clenched my fingers into fists to keep them from shaking.

"I... you know I don't know much about my racial heritage, but I was told... my blood could be used for healing."

Her face showed no reaction, but her hands curled slightly around the arms of her throne. "Go on."

"And that it might lose its healing power if I was... after I'd bonded with someone. I didn't want to take the chance because there's something terrible happening in the human world right now."

Her eyes rolled toward the rainbow glass ceiling. "There's *always* something terrible happening in the human world. Why do you care?"

"My human parents were—*are* very loving and good to me. My human sister is so lovely and sweet, and I have many good friends. I would do anything for them."

"Including sacrifice your own blood?"

"Yes. Absolutely. But what's happening out there right now is not like the ordinary troubles of the world. The humans really need help—that's why I was seeking you. A new plague has been unleashed—a super virus—and if nothing is done to stop it, the sickness will wipe out the entire human race."

The queen looked rather unconcerned about the whole thing. In fact, she stifled a yawn with the back of her hand. "And? My people do not need the human race to survive."

"There are many, many good humans like my adoptive family. They cared for me and kept me alive and well, even though I wasn't one of them, out of the goodness of their hearts. I've been accepted and well-treated by my human peers in all my travels around the world. There's bad, but there's so much more goodness. They don't deserve to be wiped out."

"Perhaps not. Or perhaps it was meant to be. They did, after all, create their own destruction with this… 'super virus,' did they not?"

"No, actually. They didn't. It was created by an Elven healer working for the Ancient Court. He was a horrible man who hated all humans."

Queen Ragan's expression turned murderous. "There is no end to their evil."

"Not all Elven people are like that—my fiancé Nic and his family for instance—they want to stop the Plague, too. And the Light Elves leave the humans alone altogether and mind their own business. Some in the Dark Court in America are very good people who want to do the right thing. But I agree with you about the Ancient Court."

I could tell from her disengaged posture and body language I was losing her. Appealing to her sympathy wasn't getting me anywhere. I had to try a different approach.

"I'm not sure if you've considered this, but if the humans

are wiped out, the Elven race will be unhindered in their agenda to rule the world."

A new alertness entered Queen Ragan's eyes. Encouraged, I continued. "Nymph blood can stop that from happening. There are thousands of us here, so no one would need to give much. Some friends of mine—healers from the Light Court —have already developed a formula for the cure using my blood. It works. There's just not enough of it. If I could save the world on my own, I'd do it. But I can't. I need *your* help."

The queen's expression told me I'd finally made her think twice. She was silent a few minutes, her lips rolling in and out and her fingers tented in front of her chin as she considered my words.

In a slow, deliberate motion, she spread her arms and placed her hands back on the throne's armrests. "Very well. I have no wish to see the Elven race have free reign over the world again. I will ask my people to assist in this cause. If any are willing, your healer friends may retrieve small amounts of their blood to use for this cure—and then their minds will be wiped of any memory of it and this place."

"Oh, thank you so much. I'm so grateful, I can't even tell you how—"

"Silence, girl. I am not finished."

I shut my mouth instantly and waited for her to go on.

"I will help you, but you must do something for me in return."

"Anything."

She smiled, though the look wasn't what I'd call friendly. "Stay."

"What? I don't understand."

"You will stay here in Sidhe Innis with your people. You will leave behind your human life, your human family and friends, and live here... for the rest of your days."

Shock reverberated through me, vibrating my bones,

shaking me to the core. It was so unexpected. It was so harsh. But how could I say "no" to her bargain? If I didn't take it, there would *be* no more family and friends left anyway. The whole world would die.

"Why?" I asked in misery. "Why would you even want me here? You don't know me. You never even knew I existed before a few days ago."

The smile evaporated, replaced with the serene mask she usually wore. "I know now. And we want *all* of our people here in our sanctuary where I know they are safe from the evil of the outside world."

"There *is* evil out there, but there's also a lot of good. If you only knew the humans..."

"The choice is up to you," she said flatly, knowing I *had* no choice.

I sighed, my eyes filling with tears as the faces of all the people I loved, the beauty of all the places I'd visited flashed before them as if I was falling from a great height to the hard ground and certain death below.

"I accept."

The queen smiled again. Her voice was utterly pleasant. "Very good. There's just one more thing... you must give up the Elf."

Excruciating pain snapped my heart in a jagged vice, like I'd just fallen headfirst into a bear trap.

"No." I shook my head, clasping my hands in front of me. "Please not that. Please don't separate us. We've been through so much to be together. We love each other. And you know he's bonded to me. He can't take another mate. He'll be alone for eternity. That's cruel. He's done nothing wrong—nothing but care for me and protect me and help me every day since he's met me."

"Be that as it may, there is no place for him here. You should be with your people and family. He should be with his. He will be released, unharmed. An Elf will never be welcome—or happy—in Sidhe Innis. There is too much bad blood between our races."

Tears streamed down my face as I tried to get my throat to work, tried to maintain enough control to say words I hated, to accept a bargain I'd resent every day for the rest of my eternal life. I had no choice.

"I agree to your terms."

18

ALESSIA

Two more days passed, and still the storm roared. I had never seen weather like it in my life, but maybe that was what the Scottish isles were like.

I took Wes his meals, checked his injury, and tried to spend as little time in his room as possible. I needed to stay focused on getting out of here. Wes was in an equally restless mood. When I brought in his lunch tray, he fairly slammed his laptop closed and pushed it to the side, an uncharacteristic surly note in his voice.

"I can't spend one more minute looking at this today."

"Why do you have no television in your bedroom?" I asked, setting the tray on his now-empty lap and placing his coffee cup on the table beside his bed. "You could watch movies to pass the time."

He reached up and rubbed the bristle on his jaw. With a few days growth he was beginning to look a bit less like a superhero, and a bit more like a villain, dark and dangerous and unbearably sexy.

"Because it's a *bed*room," he growled. "I was meant to

sleep here, not live my entire life surrounded by these four walls. I've never spent this much time indoors in my life."

I tried to keep my tone bright, feeling eager—for some reason—to cheer him. "Would you like me to bring you a book? I know you've read them all, but maybe you have a favorite?"

He shot a grumpy look over at the chair near the fireplace. "What were you reading?"

"Oh. I forget the title. It's good, though. Want me to bring it to you?"

"Read it to me," he demanded.

"What? No. I'll bring it to you." I hurried to the chair and grabbed the book.

"I want *you* to read it. My eyes are tired. I can't get up. I can't ride. From my office I can sometimes see orca and dolphins leaping in the sound. I can't see *anything* out the window now but storm clouds and rain. I stink. I can't even get to the loo on my own for God's sake. My leg aches. I'm going to go insane. Ah, screw it, I'm getting out of this effing bed."

He made a move to get up, and I immediately gave in.

"Very well. I'll read to you. Just… stay put."

The last thing I wanted was to have to re-set the bone. I needed for him to continue to recover so I could leave as soon as the storm abated. Settling into the fireside chair, I opened the book to the page I'd folded earlier and began to read.

Wes settled back onto his pillows with a satisfied sound. He folded his arms across his chest and closed his eyes.

For a while, everything was fine. But as the book approached its midpoint, something dawned on me. This was a *romance* novel. I'd never read one before. Though I was still enjoying the story as much as ever, I began to feel a bit…

uncomfortable about reading aloud from it. Especially to a man. Especially to *this* man.

The fictional couple, who'd been at cross purposes up until now, had found some common ground. Each of them had just confessed deep, dark secrets from their pasts, and now they were wrapped in each others' arms, kissing passionately.

Though, for myself, I was desperate to turn the page and see what came next, I was not at *all* sure I wanted to narrate the progression of passionate events for Wes.

I stopped reading and glanced up at the bed. Maybe he'd fallen asleep.

"Go on," he said without opening his eyes. "I'm enjoying it."

I stood, closing the book. "I think that's enough for now. You must be getting hungry."

"No. That lunch was filling. I want to hear the story." He cracked an eyelid, and the corner of his mouth lifted. "What's the matter? Why are you squeamish about a little skin-to-skin contact?"

I nearly choked. He had no idea. I stood motionless for a second, indecisive. Taking in his overly interested expression, I opened the book again and sat back down.

"I'm not. I'll read to the end of the chapter. Then I must go and prepare dinner."

Forcing myself to continue, I read the next paragraph. The hero and heroine were doing much more than kissing. My face grew red, and my insides heated with a warmth that had nothing to do with the fireplace nearby. There was *no way* I was reading any more of this out loud.

I attempted to edit as I read, skipping over large sections of choreography and description. Basically anything to do with mouths and hands—I left out. The end of the chapter came very quickly. I slammed the covers closed and rose from the chair.

"There you go."

"Well, that was rather abrupt," Wes said. His low voice held a note of amusement, and his eyes—which were now wide open—gleamed with mischief.

"You know. I could have *sworn* there was a love scene in that book at right about that point," he said, stroking his chin. "It certainly seems like two people who've opened up to each other about their intimate thoughts and feelings would be ready for the next step."

"If you know the whole book by heart, why'd you ask me to read it to you?" I threw the paperback at him.

Wes laughed. "I like your voice. And… I like to watch you squirm."

"Well, now you can watch me *leave*." I turned on my heel and stomped out the door.

"Hurry back," Wes called after me, laughing. "I seem to have found my appetite. In fact, I'm *ravenous* now."

Infuriating man. I had half a mind to leave him alone for a couple days with a loaf of bread and a stick of butter.

* * *

OF COURSE I WOULDN'T. I fled downstairs to the kitchen and rummaged for something to prepare for our dinners.

He'd be eating it alone tonight, though. If he wanted to make suggestive remarks and use that teasing tone, he could talk to *himself*. Maybe some solitary confinement would make him think twice before playing a trick like that on me again.

Thirty minutes later, I was in deep concentration, reading a cookbook I'd found on one of Wes's many shelves. Preparations were going well. I hadn't burned the pasta or blown up the microwave when melting butter for the broccoli. Now all I had to do was heat the sauce, sprinkle on some cheese, and we'd have an actual edible meal.

Checking the kitchen window for the hundredth time first, I breathed a sigh of relief to see the rain and wind still doing their thing then opened a cabinet and took out a plate. Which I promptly dropped when a loud crash shook the ceiling above my head.

I took the stairs two at a time, heading for Wes's room. Only one thing could have caused that kind of impact. He'd fallen out of bed. Had he dozed off and rolled over in his sleep? He'd seemed so alert when I'd left him.

When I opened the door, I saw I'd been right—he was no longer in the bed. But he wasn't on the floor near the bed either. I checked both sides just to be sure.

Where could he have gone?

That's when I noticed the door to the bathroom standing open and the light on inside. *Idiot. Stubborn mule.*

I ran to the bathroom and jolted to a stop just outside the door. Inside, Wes was lying on the tile floor wearing nothing but a towel and a smile.

My breath seized in my throat, my heart stopping. His body was magnificent, long and lean and aggressively muscled. The towel wrapped around his waist barely covered his thighs and rode low on his hips, revealing a set of abdominal muscles that bunched and segmented and made my mouth water.

"Wha—what do you think you're doing?" I demanded.

His grin widened. "Examining the grout. It could use a bit of bleach, I think," he joked.

Not the least bit amused, I barked, "Why are you out of bed?"

Then I noticed the steam in the room. Marching over to the shower, I opened its glass door and looked inside. Beads of water trickled down the walls. The scents of shampoo and soap still perfumed the air.

With one hand on my hip, I turned around again to glare down at Wes's unrepentant smile.

"I wanted to freshen up," he explained as if it made perfect sense. "And it had uh... been a while since I'd visited the loo."

"Oh. Right."

I felt bad for not thinking of it sooner. Of course he had to use the bathroom. The poor man had probably been suffering in silence while I had run out of the room like a nervous tween.

"I would have brought you a bedpan, you know."

"Yes. I know." He smirked and faked a shudder. "And that's why I moved hell and earth to make my way in here on my own."

Glancing back at the bed and the wide-open expanse between it and the bathroom door, I asked, "How did you even get in here?"

"It wasn't all that hard. I pushed myself to the end of the bed and then held onto the bedpost and stood. I took a few very uncomfortable hops over to the hearth and retrieved that handy dandy cane right there." He pointed at a fireplace poker lying near the shower stall. "And voila—here I am all clean and shiny."

"And lying on the floor where you obviously *fell*. You're lucky you don't have a broken hip to go with your broken leg."

"You make me sound as if I'm a feeble old geezer. I'm twenty-two years old, for God's sake, I work out every day, and I can go to the effin toilet without asking anyone's permission."

I blanched. "Well of course you don't need my permission, but you could have asked for my *help*."

"And what would you have done? A big *No thanks* on the

bedpan. And I've got to learn to do this on my own eventually. You're leaving, and I'm not going to sit there and stew in my own sweat for days on end. Besides, you're grossed out by touching me."

"That's not true. I've already told you—"

"I know, I know—you were afraid of hurting me. You weren't afraid of that when you re-set my leg with no anesthesia."

"That was different. It was a matter of life and death."

"Well, I have some news for you. I'm not an eighty-five year old geezer, and I'm not made of glass either. You can touch me without hurting me."

He was so wrong about that, but I certainly didn't want to discuss the truth of my glamour curse with him. I didn't want to discuss anything with him in his almost-naked condition. What I wanted was to get away from him as quickly as possible, but of course I couldn't leave him lying there on the tile.

"Fine," I snapped. "Would you like some help getting back to bed... or would you prefer to sleep here?"

His sarcastic attitude disappeared. "Actually, yes—I would appreciate a hand. I'd argue that I'm too large for you to lift, but you got me up the stairs and into the bed somehow, so I'm guessing you can handle it."

"Well, you *were* quite heavy. And like I said... life and death. I don't think I could pick you up under less dire circumstances. I'll help you to stand on your good foot, and you can lean on me and sort of shuffle back to the bed."

"Sounds like a plan."

He lifted a hand toward me, clearly ready to begin the process right then and there. I, on the other hand, was *not* ready. Not until he was covered.

"Here." I grabbed a thick, navy bathrobe from a hook on the wall and tossed it to him. "Put this on. I'll be right back."

I retreated from the bathroom, giving him a few minutes of privacy and going down to the kitchen to retrieve something I'd need. The bathrobe was for his health, of course. Minimizing skin-to-skin contact was just smart.

But the image of his powerful nearly-bare body assaulted me and made me feel weak as if *he* was the one with glamour and I was the unwary human.

"Are you decent?" I called out when I returned.

His answer was laced with humor. "As much as I ever am. Come and sweep me off my feet."

Peeking into the bathroom first to make sure he was fully covered, I eased in and offered him my hand. It was encased in a rubber glove I'd found under the sink in the kitchen.

Wes glanced at it oddly. "Were you washing dishes?"

"No, I *was* making your supper. Which is no doubt burned black at this point thanks to your stunt-work here. I thought the gloves would be prudent considering what you told me about your health."

His expression clouded, his thick brows drawing together. "You *don't* have to worry about that—I told you it's only human germs that are a problem for me."

I shrugged, acting more casual about it than I felt. "Better safe than sorry. Come on now. Up with you."

Wes gripped my offered hand and pulled himself to a standing position. He was even taller than I'd realized. Once upright, he towered over me. His scruffy chin pressed against my temple as he draped a heavy arm over my shoulders and leaned against me. I braced my legs to help support his considerable weight.

"You all right?" he asked, the gritty tone of his voice belying the pain he was in.

"Yes, I'm good. Are you?"

"Just dandy. Okay, let's go."

Wrapping my arm around his robe-clad waist, I began

moving slowly toward the bathroom doorway. Wes smelled of soap and clean, warm skin. A ruffle of sensation went through my lower belly as the recent image of all that skin came back to me.

Stop it, Alessia. It's pointless. I bit down hard, working to suppress the feelings his nearness was stirring.

When we reached the door, he gripped the frame for extra support. "Sorry about this," he ground out. "I know I'm leaning on you hard."

"I said I'm fine. Just keep going—you're almost there. A little bit more and you can rest." *And I can escape.*

The last few steps were the hardest, as it always seemed to happen in life. By the time we made it to the bedside, Wes's freshly showered face was covered in beads of clean sweat.

He slid his arm from my shoulder, but still gripped it with his hand, using me for support while he hopped in a circle to put his back to the mattress. Then he toppled backward onto it.

It was surprisingly sudden. As my fingers still gripped the back of his robe, and his hand was still clamped on my shoulder, when he went down, so did I. I ended up on top of him, chest to chest and face to face.

"Oh," I said in breathless surprise.

"Sorry." He sounded just as breathless. But instead of releasing me so I could scramble back away from him and end our mutual embarrassment, Wes's palm flattened on my lower back, preventing me from moving.

"Your leg," I protested weakly, struggling to lift myself.

His hand pressed harder, trapping me against him. "What leg?" he growled.

And then before I could respond, he lifted his head, and his mouth met mine.

Oh no.

A flare of blind panic allowed me to access strength I

didn't realize I had. I pushed against his shoulders and broke his hold on me, leaping back from the bed in astonished fury and overheated confusion.

"What was *that*?"

He raised his eyebrows, turned his jaw to the side and chuckled. "If memory serves, it was a kiss. I don't know, though. It's been so long, it's possible I've forgotten."

My fingertips came to my lips. A kiss. *He kissed me.* It hadn't been a long time since *I'd* been kissed. It was the *first* time I'd been kissed. Ever.

The facetious smack I'd planted on Nic's lips when I'd encountered him in the palace hallway in Corsica didn't count. He'd been avoiding me, and I was making a point—he knew I intended the gesture to make him ill instead of seduce him. But *he'd* never kissed *me*. No one had. Until now.

"Why did you do that?" I asked, truly bewildered.

"Why? Because you're beautiful, and sexy, and desirable, and I wanted to kiss you." His tone made it seem like the answer was obvious. And the things he was saying about me made my face flush and my heart rate pick up even more frantic beats.

"You... shouldn't have done that."

"Maybe not. It was probably way out of line. But I have to say..." He lifted a hand to stroke his own mouth—not like he was wiping away the kiss but as if he was rubbing it deeper into his lips. "... now that I've done it—I'm not sorry."

The extra beats doubled. Tripled. My pulse had never raced like this before. My mind had never felt so chaotic. It was hard to find enough breath to respond.

"Well... you're *going* to be."

"Why?" He smirked. "Are you going to slap me for my 'impertinence'? Or make me eat burned food?"

His tone was so blasé, and the amusement on his face was obvious. He had no idea what he'd done. Here I'd been working so hard to save his life, and he might have undone it all in an instant. The thought that I might have killed him with a kiss brought a rush of moisture to my eyes and made my nose sting.

I whirled away from him, pinching the bridge of my nose and swallowing hard, fighting to regain control of my unruly emotions. I *did not* cry—or at least I hadn't since early childhood. What was the matter with me?

"Alessia?" Wes said. "Hey, I'm sorry. I was only kidding about your cooking. It's not *that* bad."

"It's not that," I managed to choke out through a throat that felt swollen nearly shut.

"What is it then? The kiss? Are you engaged or something? Or *married*? I didn't see a ring."

"No. I have been engaged—twice. But I am not now. And not married."

"So then, you just aren't that into me. I get it. There's no need to cry." He paused. "By the way, I *can* do better than that. Like I said, I really *am* out of practice."

Feeling a bit more in control, I turned back to Wes and his contrite expression. I needed to make him understand something like that could *never* happen again. No matter how much I might have liked it.

"No. That's not it, either. You did a... very good job. It's just... *that* is not a part of my life. With anyone. I can't... be close to people."

His brow furrowed. "Are we talking, like, emotional damage or something? Childhood abuse?"

"No, nothing like that. It's my glamour. You asked if perhaps I had healing glamour. It's quite the opposite, actually. I make people sick—literally. Anyone in close proximity to me begins to feel ill. So you see... *kissing* is not something I do."

Rather than appearing afraid or even sorry for me, Wes

looked… pleased. A grin sneaked across his face as he nodded slowly. "So you *did* like it."

"Oh! You are impossible. I just told you I make people ill, and *you* have a compromised immune system. What is the matter with you?"

He shook his head, still wearing a smile. "I've been close to you several times now—when you were unconscious and I carried you, when you brought me up here, when you helped me with my shirt. I'm totally fine."

I gave his leg a pointed glance and raised one brow.

"Other than a broken leg, I'm fine. I'm not sick, Alessia."

"If I spent any more time near you, I'm sure you would be."

Shrugging, he tossed his head to one side, his lips pursing momentarily. "I'll take my chances."

He lifted one hand and curled the fingers in an invitation for me to come closer. Did he actually want to kiss me again?

I back-stepped away from the bed, incredulous. "No—you won't. You really *are* a stupid human if you can't understand the risk. Do I need to wear a label with a skull and crossbones? I'm *poisonous*. I'm bad for you—for everyone. *I'm* the one who should be living alone on an island."

If he knew what I'd done, that I'd activated the deadly epidemic he was working to contain, this would not even be an issue. The conversation would be over. But somehow I couldn't bring myself to tell him that part.

The sexy come-hither expression on Wes's face morphed into one of concern and then sadness.

"Who sold you on that story—that you're *bad*—that you're 'poison'? Was it your parents? Your teachers?"

He shook his head in disgust. "As I said before, no one is all good or all bad. How we grow up and how we think of ourselves depends on which part of us is fed and nurtured.

And somebody taught you to hate yourself." He paused and shook his head before adding, "You poor thing."

During his entire speech, I'd stayed stock still, wearing a blank mask while inside, a firestorm of emotion raged. As soon as I heard his pitying last words, though, the flames erupted.

"I do *not* need your pity. And for your information, I *didn't* like the kiss. I don't want you that way."

He laughed, unconvinced. "Okay princess, whatever you say."

Infuriated, I whirled and went to the door, slamming it behind me and intending to leave him alone for a *long* time to think about what I'd said and get it through his thick skull. And I would wait until he was asleep to deliver his food tray. I had no intention of facing him again tonight.

I'd never been so affected by a man's words—or the look in his eyes. Just picturing the knowing look on Wes's face made my insides feel hot and shaky. God, I was so weak. What had those witches done to me?

I'd actually started believing for a minute that he wanted me, though I knew very well he had to be lying, or desperate for female companionship—or maybe just plain ignorant. No one could really be attracted to *this*—not knowing the truth about my glamour.

I could no longer lie to myself about my attraction to him, though. *I* was the stupid one. Those feelings had no place in my life. I couldn't do anything with them.

The only thing I could think to do was avoid Wes as much as possible for the remainder of my entrapment here with him. What was the alternative? Give in to the pull I felt toward him—and kill him?

WES

I woke, smelling food and still turned on. Not by the pasta and marinara but by the memory of Alessia's mouth and body on mine.

Sometime after she'd fled the room in obvious terror, I'd drifted off to sleep. But the nap had done little to calm my craving for her.

The way she looked at me.

When she'd stopped in the bathroom doorway, her eyes had roamed over my towel-clad body, hungrily devouring the sight. My body had instantly reacted to *her* over-the-top reaction. And now I knew why she'd been so affected.

If kissing was not "a thing" in her life, then spending time in small, enclosed spaces with nearly naked men couldn't possibly be on her playlist either. That pleased me probably far more than it should have.

And after feeling her slight weight and soft curves on top of me, I'd never be able to look at her again without thinking about it—without wanting to repeat the experience. I laughed. I shouldn't be able to even *think* about things like that after sustaining the injury I had. Whatever she'd given me had *really* worked.

Because thinking about it, I was. More specifically, I was thinking about how to get her to kiss me again. I wanted to prove to her she couldn't hurt me—or wouldn't—with her nearness. But I had a feeling she was going to keep her distance from now on. Case in point, she'd waited until I was sleeping to bring in my dinner.

It was a dilemma. I couldn't exactly chase her down and sweep her off her feet. I'd have to be clever about this.

Though I was hungry, I did not eat my dinner right away. Instead, I set the plate aside. Then I removed the bathrobe I was still wearing and pulled the sheets and coverlet over the lower half of my body. I knew the sight of me shirtless affected her, and asking her to bring me a t-shirt and some boxers from my drawer would get her close to me again.

That was pretty much where my scheme ended. I'd just have to wing it after that. But first... I had to get her back in here.

The sound of my falling had brought her running before, but I wasn't willing to go that far. I might actually re-injure my leg, and *that* would put a considerable damper on my seduction plans.

Giving the plate of fragrant food a last, longing glance, I raised my arm and brought it down hard, swiping the heavy porcelain plate from the bedside table onto the floor. A minute later, I heard the sound of Alessia's footsteps trampling up the stairs.

"What have you done now?" she demanded from the hallway, her voice growing louder as she approached. "You better not have gotten out of bed again."

Great. She was coming, but she was angry. She'd be even more annoyed when she saw I'd ruined my dinner just to get her back up here. I had to come up with a story—something she'd believe—and fast. And then I smiled.

Got it.

As the door to my room opened, I lay back on my pillows and tried to appear delirious.

"I swear I will leave you lying there this ti—" Her rant stopped in mid-stream as she spotted the food on the floor and my feverish-looking sprawl.

"What happened? What is the matter with you?" Her tone rose in panic as she rushed toward me, stopping just at the edge of my mattress. "Where is your robe? How did your plate fall on the floor?"

"Hot," I whispered in a ragged voice. "Tried to pick it up, but I feel…"

"Oh no," she breathed. "I knew it. You're ill." She twisted one way then the other, looking around the room, though I wasn't sure what for. Then she moved toward the door.

"I have to get some help. I will ride to the village. Which way is it?"

"No," I commanded in a stronger voice. "The germs. I won't survive them."

Turning back to me, her tone rising, she argued, "But you're sick already. What should I do?"

"You need to… check me for fever."

"How?"

"Put your hand on me—my forehead or my chest."

Instead of moving toward me, she backed away another step. "I can't do that. If you feel hot, then I'm sure you *are* feverish. What do you need? Ibuprofen? Acetaminophen? I saw them both in your medicine cabinet. I'll get them and refill your water glass."

She rushed away toward my bathroom. *Well, that backfired.* I had to find a way to bring her closer. I smiled as an idea occurred to me.

When she came back, I obediently swallowed the medicine. "Thank you. I think we should try something else —something that will bring the fever down faster."

"What?"

"Run the cold water. Soak a washcloth in it."

Without a word, she hurried to the bathroom again. I heard the closet open and close then the sound of running water in the sink. Alessia came back into the room holding up both hands, water dripping from her arms to the wooden floor.

"I brought two."

"Good. Fold one and lay it on my forehead." After she'd followed those instructions, I gave her a new set. "Use the other to wipe down my body."

Her hand froze in mid-motion. "What?"

"Just my neck and chest—maybe my shoulders and arms, too. I'm *not* trying to make a move on you," I lied.

Apparently the feigned weakness in my voice convinced her because she complied. Very cautiously, she laid the wet washcloth on my chest and began to rub.

My plan had been to show her that her nearness wasn't dangerous to me, but I'd be lying if I said I wasn't getting something out of it. Her gentle touch made me glad the comforter was substantial and bunched around my waist and thighs.

"Is this good?" she asked in a small voice.

Oh yes, I groaned internally. Out loud I said, "Yes. Keep at it. I think I'm starting to cool down."

Actually, I was starting to heat up—for real this time. Everything inside me demanded I take action—grab her wrists and pull her down to me, but I resisted. That was the surest way to scare her off. I needed to be smart about this, take advantage of the opportunity I had here to convince her. I felt a little bad about my ploy, but it *was* working. I'd let her off the hook and confess as soon as I'd made my point.

"I'm feeling a little better," I said, to show her that her presence was *good* for me instead of bad.

"I'll stop then," she said and popped up from the edge of the mattress where she'd been sitting.

"No, I mean, it's working. But you should continue—at least until the medication kicks in."

She eyed me suspiciously but put the washcloth back on my body, moving it over my shoulder and down one arm.

"Do you believe me now?" she asked in a sullen tone. "You doubted what I told you about my glamour earlier, didn't you?"

"No. I believed you, and I still do. But... I *don't* think it's as bad as you say."

"What? You think I exaggerated? How can you say that? Look at yourself. I hurt you."

"I'm not doubting your glamour—I'm just saying I think you can *control* your power. I think you have the ability to pull it back when you want to."

"No." She shook her head. "I cannot. Dr. Schmitt said I could increase the effect on others but not decrease it."

"I see. And this Dr. Schmitt... was he a *trustworthy* person?"

Her hand stopped moving momentarily then resumed its ministrations. Reading her unguarded reaction to my question, I could see she wasn't certain about the answer. It hadn't occurred to her that the man might have been misleading her.

"Maybe he told you that for his own selfish reasons," I continued. "It doesn't make scientific sense that you could turn something up without being able to turn it down as well."

She stopped moving the cloth again and looked directly

into my eyes, unconsciously kneading her lips together, drawing the full bottom one inside her mouth and then releasing it.

"Try it," I encouraged. "Touch me—without the washcloth —and focus on dialing back your glamour."

"No." She drew her hand up to the base of her throat. "It's too dangerous to experiment on you. Besides... I don't *like* touching people—or being touched."

"That's not true."

"How do you know? You've known me less than a week."

"I know because the night I found you and carried you into my house, you responded to my touch in a very... *positive* way."

She stood abruptly. "What do you mean?"

I held up a hand in a reassuring gesture. "I only touched your hands and arms. You were freezing. I was trying to head off frostbite by massaging your skin to get your blood flowing." I paused before adding, "You liked it. Very much."

Her face flushed instantly, going deep red.

"You shouldn't be embarrassed. It's a basic need— everyone needs to be touched."

"Not me."

"*Especially* you. In fact, if you ask me, you need connection and physical intimacy more than anyone I've ever met. Now come on, give it a try. I promise you won't hurt me."

Competing emotions warred across her features. Her eyes revealed a ferocious longing, but the stubborn set of her mouth told me mere words were not enough to convince her.

"I can't." Then her tone hardened along with the set of her jaw. "I don't *want* to. You're a human. I find you... repulsive. There's nothing about you that appeals to me. I have *no* desire to touch you any more than absolutely necessary, and... and... it disgusts me to think about you touching me."

"That's not how it seemed when you squirmed and moaned in pleasure a few nights ago."

Eyes widening in fury, Alessia leaned down and slapped my face. It was exactly what I'd wanted.

I grabbed her wrist and pulled her off balance, causing her to topple onto me. Clamping an arm around her waist, I held her body to me and slid my other hand around the back of her head. Then I kissed her, communicating with my lips and tongue all the pent-up longing and frustration I'd felt since she'd first dropped into my life.

At first Alessia resisted, but her pushing quickly transformed into clutching, and her squirms of protest into a subtle, rhythmic rocking that caused my entire body to tense and my temperature to skyrocket for real.

Releasing my restraining hold on her, I used my hands to instead explore the extraordinary figure I'd only been able to admire at a distance. Everything about Alessia felt incredible —her soft skin, her lean, powerful limbs, her silky hair falling against my cheeks and ears. She smelled delicious, like fresh pears and Madagascar vanilla.

And the sounds she made in response to my touch, the gasps and sighs and soft moans—wow—I was getting *way* too excited, which wasn't ideal if this was to be her first time with a man, which I suspected it was. Experience told me it would be best for her if I took things slow, drew out each stage of this until she was begging me to move on to the next, to go faster, to do *more*.

All *I* wanted to do was roll full-steam ahead. It had been a *long* time, and I'd never been with a woman I found so attractive and intriguing.

In spite of the distinct possibility of embarrassing myself, I would not stop touching and kissing her for the world.

Couldn't stop. I needed to explore every part of her with my hands and mouth. I wanted to devour this woman. I was immensely grateful for that ill-advised shower and for the fact I hadn't had the opportunity to re-dress myself afterward.

Now to get her *undressed.*

I moved my hands slowly over her hips and down to the bottom hem of the oversized sweater she wore, sliding it up, up...

Alessia sucked in a breath and leapt off of me, landing on the floor beside the bed like a startled cat. Her hair was mussed, her eyes wild and dark. Her lips, which had been beautiful before, looked even more tempting now, red and slightly swollen from my kisses.

"You... you idiot," she cried. "Why did you do that? You have just killed yourself."

"Worth it," I said, hoping to show her how unconcerned I was. But she was in no mood for glib remarks and flirtation. Tears swam in her eyes, which clawed at my gut. I stretched a hand toward her.

"Alessia. Nothing happened, love. Nothing bad anyway. Look—I'm fine. I didn't even have a fever in the first place—I made it up to get you close to me. Now... calm down and come back to bed."

But there was no calming her. "You are a fool," she spat, tears running down her cheeks. "You tricked me, and now you will pay with your life, you idiotic human."

Breaking into sobs, she turned and ran from the room.

20

ALESSIA

I charged down the staircase, swiping at my face with one sleeve.

I had cried more since meeting Wes than I had since early childhood. What was it about him that reached right down into my core and drew out every emotion I'd been trying not to feel?

Obviously the answer at the moment was his incredible physical allure—and his skill at kissing. Now I understood what everyone carried on about. The pleasure was... shocking. I hadn't thought myself capable of such sensations. Apparently they'd been there all along, lying dormant in my untouched body.

Even now, as I chastised myself for allowing it, I couldn't help but relive those moments of scorching forbidden intimacy. Blazing heat traveled from my head to my toes, lingering in the middle. Wes had made me feel alive in a way I never had before. He'd made me feel like a woman.

He'd also made me a murderer. At least I would be if I didn't get some medical help for him. He may have lied about being feverish earlier, but that lie would soon be the truth—I was convinced of it.

In spite of his baseless beliefs, I could not control my glamour. I was toxic. Deadly. My own parents had been afraid to get too close to me. I had to get away from here—I couldn't seem to resist getting close to Wes, and it was possibly too late for him already. There was no way he could have been exposed to me that directly without suffering severe consequences. I had to get him some help.

In an instant of wild panic, I wished for one more moment with the nymph—Macy. I'd apologize for my horrid treatment of her and beg her to give him a little of her blood. But that was foolish. I had no idea where to find her, and even if I did, she'd never help me after what I'd done. I had to do *something* though.

Glancing at the ocean-view windows, it came to me. I'd make my way to the mainland—sway a boat captain if I had to in order to make him sail in the storm. *Yes.* That would work. Then I'd sway a doctor—no, a team of doctors—and force them to go to the island, warning them first about Wes's condition so they'd take proper precautions concerning germs.

Reaching the kitchen, I looked through the cabinets until I located a large bowl. I loaded it with fruit and bread, crackers , hard cheese, and other non-perishable items. I filled a large jug with fresh water then lugged all the provisions up the stairs, stopping just outside his bedroom.

I hoped he was sleeping. I didn't want him to know what I was doing. He'd try to talk me out of it, and I just couldn't face another emotional scene with him tonight. Setting the jug on the floor, I eased the door open and peered inside. Good. He was out.

As quietly as possible, I crossed the floor to his bed,

placing the bowl of food and water jug on the table beside it. Then I tiptoed toward the door again. Before I reached it, something lying on the fireside chair caught my eye—the book I'd been reading. I was overcome by the urge to take it with me—a small souvenir of my time here with Wes.

I picked it up, tucked it under my arm, and glanced back one last time at him. He looked comfortable. He looked *beautiful*, his powerful body sprawled across the bed with the covers draped over his midsection, one long leg protruding.

He didn't look sick, but it was coming. A lifetime of experience had taught me there was no way our kissing had left him unaffected.

Wes smiled in his sleep, dreaming about something pleasant. Lifting my hand to my cheek, I blinked furiously and wiped another tear. It seemed I'd sprung a permanent leak.

My throat tightened in a painful vise. I couldn't imagine never seeing that smile again—or those blue eyes. But I had to go. I had to get help for him, and I had to keep going, find Nic and Macy, and help them stop the Plague. Even if Wes actually *was* the only good human on the planet, he was worth the effort to save it.

Would he miss me? The thought produced a twinge of pain in my chest. I moved toward the door again. He wouldn't be *around* to miss me if I didn't get help for him. And all the people he loved would die if I didn't find a way to stop the Plague. It was time to go.

As I opened the bedroom door, the cover of the book bumped it, making a noise. Wes began to stir. I hurried through it, rushing into the hall before he could catch a glimpse of me. I heard his voice as my foot reached the top stair.

"Alessia." Louder, he called, "Alessia. Don't go. Please."

I didn't answer, just ran down the stairs and toward the back door.

"I'm sorry. Forgive me. Don't leave me."

His voice followed me, and the leak opened up to a full flood, the tears running down my face mixing with rain as I stepped out into the storm.

21

WES

Damn it! The sound of Alessia's weeping ripped my heart out. And the sound of the back door closing smashed it flat.

She was leaving me. I shouldn't have kissed her—or touched her like that. Don't get me wrong—it had been the most sensual, enjoyable experience of my life. But I'd scared her. I'd forced her to leave.

She was so afraid of her own glamour and its potential to hurt me she'd chosen to go out in this horrific storm, with nowhere else to stay, no money, no way off the island, instead of staying in this house with me any longer.

Oh God. She wasn't going to try to *force* her way off the island tonight on a fishing boat or something, was she? Knowing her stubbornness, the answer was yes. She was.

I had to stop her. The sound between Eigg and the mainland would be churning due to the gale force winds. The swells had been known to drive small vessels into piers and large rocks, and that was during storms far less vicious than this one. I'd been taught Elves were immortal—but their lives could be ended by violence or accident. I couldn't let Alessia die because of my mistakes.

My first one had been agreeing to do my family's bidding and keep her prisoner here. My second had been falling head over heels and pushing for too much too soon.

Dragging myself to the edge of the bed, I got to my feet—foot—and used the bed, then the dresser as props to make my way to the window. Rain lashed the glass. Beyond it, only darkness. Where was she?

As if in answer, a flash of blinding light streaked across the sky, illuminating the grounds. There. She was running down the hill toward the stable. She meant to take one of the horses into the village—Sebastian, probably, since she'd ridden him before and knew his strength. I didn't have much time. He was a pain in the ass to saddle, but she hadn't bothered with a saddle last time, riding him bareback.

Hopping to the fireplace, I retrieved my poker/cane and used it to hobble to the dresser where I retrieved a shirt and a pair of loose shorts I could get over my splinted leg. It didn't feel fantastic, but it really was better, much less painful than it had been even earlier today when I'd made the trip to the shower.

I quickly dressed then limped to the bedroom door and out of it to the top of the staircase. *Oh boy.* This was going to be a challenge. I'd run up and down this expanse hundreds of times over the past two years—maybe thousands. Today, the set of wooden steps looked like an impassable mountain range. No, not impassable. Difficult. Possibly painful. But I could do this.

Gripping the railing with one hand and stretching the poker to the step below me with the other, I shuffled my good foot to the edge of the top step and then over it, landing with a thump.

"Okay. One down... seventeen to go."

By the time I reached the first floor—still in one piece, thank God—I was shaking and sweating, the muscles in my arms and shoulders strained almost to the point of failure. My broken leg was pulsating with a painful heartbeat of its own, making my head pound in commiseration and my stomach nauseous.

I hopped the short distance to the sofa and sank into it, needing to rest a minute before tackling the hillside. God, how was I going to manage it? There was no handrail out there, and my makeshift cane would sink right into the saturated earth. Not to mention the unevenness of the rocky terrain.

No doubt Alessia was already mounted by now. It had taken me far too long to get down the stairs. Now, even *if* I could make it to the stable and get on a horse, she'd be gone, and I'd be too far behind her to catch up.

My head dropped to the sofa cushion behind me as my chest constricted and hot tears stung the backs of my eyelids. I felt defeated... and utterly alone. I'd been alone for years now and gotten used to it, but tonight—the future seemed to stretch ahead of me like a long, dark highway with no exits and no ending.

I was trapped—by my leg, by my illness. My life would continue in an endless cycle of loneliness. Having Alessia here these past few days had only served to highlight that fact for me. I wished I'd never met her. I wished—

The back door opened, the wind blowing it against the wall with a noisy bang and bringing in a whirl of salt-tinged cold air. I opened my eyes to see Alessia step through it. She was bedraggled, sopping wet—and the most beautiful thing I'd ever seen.

"You were right," she announced, pushing a heavy lock of wet hair from her face. Her cheeks and nose were red with cold. Her eyes were puffy. She'd been crying, too.

Managing to find my voice, I said, "About what?"

"I *am* a porcupine. Even the horses hate me. I tried every

one of them. They wouldn't leave the estate. They just kept turning around and going back to the stable. Sebastian even reared on me."

I wasn't sure how such a fast emotional turn-around was possible, but I actually wanted to laugh. She was so adorably miserable. And I was so happy.

"They don't hate you, love. They just didn't want you—or themselves—to die trying to ride in this godforsaken storm. Either that... or *I'm* the one with a glamour for animal communication, and I told them not to let you leave. They knew I needed—*wanted* you to stay."

Her eyes locked with mine for a long moment, sparking with hope, searching for any deception or doubt on my part. And then she blinked, and her expression changed to one of alarm.

"Wait—how did you get down the stairs?" She rushed toward me. "Did you re-injure your leg?"

When she got close, she stopped short, her eyes wide with fear. "And you're... crying. You're sick, aren't you? For real this time."

I shook my head slowly and reached out for her hand. "No. I'm not. You didn't want to hurt me earlier—and you *didn't*. I told you... I believe you can control it. That doctor, whoever he was, was either incompetent... or he lied to you."

She shrank away from me, pulling her hand back until it was just out of my reach. "Then why were you crying?"

I gave her a small smile. "I was sad. It's a human emotion. Perhaps you're familiar with it?"

"Sad? Why?"

"Because I missed you. Because I knew I'd miss you for the rest of my life." Leaning forward, I captured the shy little hand and pulled her toward me. "Because the girl I love was leaving me."

Alessia snatched her fingers back again. "You can't love

me. I'm a bad person. I've done terrible things. And I'm dangerous to you."

"No—you're not. Your cooking maybe, but not you."

I chuckled and then got serious. More serious than I'd ever been about anything in my life. I needed her to believe me. I needed her to understand I accepted her and wanted her, flaws and all.

"You are perfect for me, Alessia. You're smart, and funny, and beautiful, and so sexy it almost hurts to look at you. You make me feel *better*, not worse. I'm *not* sick. And whatever it is you've done you think is *so* unforgivable... we've all made mistakes. I forgive you. There. That's done. Now come here and kiss me—before I have to stand up and chase you down on one foot."

She shook her head, tears trickling down her cheeks. "You say that because you don't understand. If you knew what I'd done..."

"Well tell me then. Just spit it out and let me prove it to you. There is nothing you could tell me that will change the way I feel about you."

"You're wrong."

"*You're* stalling." I went quiet and just waited, watching as she chewed her lip and stared at the floor between us. Finally, her eyes came up to meet mine.

"I saw your work—on the computer," she said, in an apparent attempt to change the subject.

"I don't want to talk about my work right now. I want to talk about us."

"I *am* your work. *I* am the cause of the disease outbreak you're tracking—the infection? That started in Peru? It happened because Dr. Schmitt injected a girl with a virus he engineered. There are many girls like her, all over the world. They carry the virus, just waiting for it to be activated and begin a new plague that will wipe out the human population of the world. But doctor Schmitt's plan needed a catalyst—something that would trigger the latent virus at the right time. He needed *me*."

She swallowed hard and continued. "I went to that village. The girl touched me. And now she is sick. The sickness is spreading. Eventually it will spread everywhere—even here. If my nearness does not kill you, the Plague will eventually. There is no stopping it. There is no cure."

Now her eyes came back up to meet mine, shining with the reflection of the fireplace. "So you see... I am not worthy of your love. I don't deserve your forgiveness. And now you hate me."

For long moments I sat looking at her, breathing in and out, letting my mind process what she'd told me. It was shocking, to be sure. But she was obviously consumed by remorse. And I was right about that so-called doctor—he'd *used* her, turned her glamour into a weapon.

No wonder she thought she was unlovable. Had her parents also let her believe she was destined to do nothing but hurt others, that she was born to be bad? It made me angry—I wanted to strike out at all of them. But this moment didn't call for more strife or for violence. It called for gentleness.

"You're right, that *is* a lot to take in," I admitted. "It certainly explains a lot about this disease cluster we've been tracking. And the prospect of a new plague is damned scary. It'll take a lot to stop something like that. But it's not unforgiveable. Alessia—when you get right down to it, none of us really *deserves* love and forgiveness. But if you ask for it, sometimes you get it anyway."

My heart broke as tears streamed down her face. Each of the shattered pieces had her name written on them.

"The person who's suffered the most harm as a result of your glamour... is you," I told her. "So it's not my forgiveness you need. I don't hate you. I *love* you. And you need to love yourself enough to say, 'I made a mistake. I didn't mean it, but I messed up. And now I'm going to do my best to fix it.' I'll do everything in my power to help you."

She shook her head in protest. "There's nothing anyone can do."

"Well, let's not give up until we've tried, okay? With the inside information you have about the Plague, my colleagues and I can start putting together an action plan. Who knows, maybe you have some small piece of critical information that could help us snap together the puzzle we've already started constructing? It's worth a try, isn't it?"

She nodded, a new light coming into her eyes. "I might know of someone else who could help us."

"Who?"

"My former fiancé, Nicolo. He said there might be a way. At the time I wasn't sure whether to trust him, but I think now we have no choice."

Feeling an unreasonable stab of jealousy, I asked, "Do you have his number?"

She shook her head. "I don't think he's carrying a cell phone anymore. And he's been changing locations frequently. I was... tracking him before—him and his new fiancée. It's a long story."

"Okay." I let out a breath. "Well, give me whatever information you have about him—and her—and I can tap into my resources at the government. Maybe they'll be able to pick up his trail."

She nodded, started to speak then stopped.

"What is it?"

"Do you really... forgive me?"

I smiled. "I do. And before you can ask... I really do love you as well."

Now it was her turn to smile. "I love you, too, Wes. That's why I left. I was so afraid I'd sentenced you to death. I was going to get some help for you whether you wanted it or not."

My smile had turned into a goofy, full-mouth beaming. "All I want—is you. Come here, princess."

She walked into my open arms and sank down to the couch with me. I pulled her across my lap, kissing her hard, then soft, then hard again. She responded with so much enthusiasm I felt my body preparing for a repeat of the scene that played out in my bedroom earlier. This wasn't the right time, though. We had a lot to talk about first.

When we pulled apart, I stared into her beautiful topaz eyes. "There's something I'm curious about. Are you really a princess?"

She nodded, wearing a small grin. "I am. I'm also a recording artist."

"Wow. You are just *full* of secrets."

Now she shook her head in vigorous denial. "Not anymore. I don't want there to be any more secrets between us. Ever again. Promise me that, okay?"

A wave of guilt crashed over me. She had confessed *her* Big Bad Secret. I still hadn't told her mine. When she found out the witches who'd teleported her here into captivity were actually my—

"Wes?" A familiar female voice rang through the house from the front entry hall. "Wes dear, are you home?"

My heart dropped to the bottom of my stomach and then rebounded into my throat.

Alessia's face whipped toward mine. "Who is that? I thought you said you lived alone. Do you have a... do you have a *wife*?"

"No," I answered her in a quiet, clipped voice. "That's not my wife. I mean—I don't have one."

Heels clicked through the tile foyer and across the wooden floor of the formal living room, headed this way.

"Well who is it then?" Alessia demanded.

My eyes pleaded with hers for understanding. "I *was* going to tell you."

The two of us were still twisted together on the sofa in a tangle of limbs when my mother stepped into the room, followed closely by Nanna.

"Oh, there you are," Mum said. Then she sucked in a huge gasp as her eyes landed on Alessia, who sported my sweater along with a nicely developing beard burn on one cheek.

Mum's eyes came back to me, narrowing on me like the laser scope of an assault rifle. "Weston William Rowan... what have you been doing, *son?*"

22

ALESSIA

Son? *Son?*

The word seemed to ricochet through the room like a gunshot in a narrow canyon. I recognized that woman. The older one, too. They were the witches who'd attacked me and sent me here.

The look of guilt on Wes's face told me everything else I needed to know. He hadn't been manipulated into working for the witches. He was *one* of them. That ricocheting emotional bullet pierced my heart.

I leapt away from him, off the sofa and toward the back door, intent on escaping in my bare feet and bare legs. The storm was no longer my greatest concern.

"Stop right there, Elven she-devil," the older woman commanded. "Unless you want another dose of what we gave you in Bristol. If I recall, you didn't care for it over-much."

I froze in place. It wasn't an empty threat. Whatever they'd done to me that day, it had been the most painful thing I'd ever felt.

"Nanna, no," Wes said. Gripping the sofa back he rose

from the cushions to stand on his good leg. "She's not who you think she is."

It was the younger woman who answered him in a smug tone, sauntering toward him while pulling off her gloves. "And just who do *you* think she is—some sweet little innocent sent here by mistake? I thought you were smarter than that. She's gotten into your head, son—and from the looks of things, into your *bed* as well."

"You're wrong. I *know* her, and I won't stand by and let you hurt her," Wes said.

As the woman rounded the corner of the sofa, her eyes fell to his splinted leg. "It seems you can barely stand at all. What did this Elven tramp do to you?"

She wheeled around to face me. "First my daughter, now my son? You will pay for attacking my children—*after* you've given us what we want."

So it was true. "Son" hadn't just been a term of endearment. This frightening woman was Wes's *mother*. That was why she had sent me here for him to guard. He was *in* on whatever scheme they had cooked up. And I had trusted him. *Fool.*

All the happiness that had filled my heart only minutes earlier crystalized, encasing my emotions in ice. Well, I wasn't going to give them *anything.*

I whirled and darted for the door, even managed to get it open before the pain knocked me to my knees. I grabbed my head with both hands. My brain was being stabbed by a hundred rusty knives. My ears were exploding from the piercing blast of noise. Screaming in agony, I writhed on the floor, trying futilely to escape the barrage.

* * *

CONSCIOUSNESS RETURNED GRADUALLY. I heard faint snatches

of conversation as if from a great distance. One of the voices was Wes's. He sounded angry.

"... come in here to my house and..."

"... why you're getting so upset... only trying to protect you."

My head still rang with the echoes of pain, my stomach nauseous. This time I had no saol water to counteract the effects of the spell—I'd given it all to Wes.

"Hush. She's waking up," the female said.

Both voices fell silent. There was only the sound of Wes's uneven gate, a painful shuffle crossing the floor toward me. But where was I? Oh, on the sofa. I was in a reclining position, but I wasn't exactly comfortable. My hands and feet were bound. As my eyelids peeled up, I saw the hazy form of Wes's mother following him into the room.

"Keep your seat—you shouldn't be moving around, son," she said. "I will check on her."

"Stay away from her," he growled. "You've done enough damage already."

The sofa cushion depressed under his weight beside me, and I felt the light stroke of his fingers on my jaw. "Alessia? Can you hear me? Are you okay?"

I jerked my chin away from his traitorous touch. "Leave me alone."

"I'm sorry. I was planning to tell you. But I was worried about... this—that you'd be angry with me—that you'd hate me because of who I am."

"And you were right. It was bad enough when I thought you were only human. I can't *believe* you're a witch, too."

"I'm not. The Earth-wives are all female. The power is only passed down to girl children. Something about the Y chromosome stops it from developing."

"Whatever. You're a liar. You've done nothing but lie to me."

217

"That's not true. I meant everything I said to you... about how I feel. Please believe me." I reached toward her bound hands, intending to release them.

Alessia jerked them away. "Why should I?"

"Just let her be, Weston," the woman said. "You see her true, spiteful nature now, don't you? Now that she's awake we can question her, and then we'll take her out of here and leave you in peace to recover."

Wes stood up and turned to face his mother, towering over her. "No. No one's taking her anywhere."

"What has gotten into you?" The woman asked, clearly perturbed. "Mother, come here and look at Weston. Do you think something's happened to the ward?"

"What ward?" Wes asked.

The older woman marched over and grasped Wes's chin, holding his face still so she could peer into his eyes. "No—it's still in place. He's fully protected."

So *that* was why I'd been able to be close to Wes without making him sick. The witches had put some kind of protection spell on him. He had been honest about not being affected by my glamour.

"*What* ward?" Wes repeated, this time more emphatically.

His mother sniffed in impatience. "We warded you and Olivia against Elven glamour—perhaps you don't remember. You were young. I thought perhaps this girl had managed to undo it—it would explain why you're being so unreasonable."

"I thought that protected against Sway," Wes said.

"Yes, that, but also whatever *other* tricks they may have up their sleeves. And it's a good thing, too, or we never would have been able to send *her* here. It would have been too risky with your health condition." She paused and smiled sweetly. "But then of course, I'm sure while she was persuading you of her 'innocence' and 'sweetness' this one didn't *happen* to mention what her glamour 'gift' is, did she? It's a doozy."

"As a matter of fact, she did," he said. "And I don't care. I love her."

Both women reeled back in obvious shock.

"That's ridiculous," his mother said. "You've only known her a few days. More importantly, she's *Elven*. You're descended from Earth-wives. Love between you is impossible."

"Apparently not," he countered. "And she's staying right here with me. If there's something you need from her, you can ask nicely. If you can't do that—*you* can leave."

"Well, I never," said his grandmother. "If it weren't for our ward, you never would have even been able to get close to this poisonous tart. In fact... I have a mind to remove it. We'll see how much you *love* her when you can't even touch her without getting deathly ill."

"I think that's a fine idea," his mom chimed in.

"You'd take away the one happiness I've found in years? Sentence me to a solitary life forever?"

"Better than letting you waste it on this piece of Elven trash," the one he'd called Nanna said.

His hands clenched into fists, and I swore I could hear a low growl. "Fine then. Go ahead. It won't matter. I'll *still* want to be with her. I fell in love with her before we ever touched. I'll be happy if all I ever have is the chance to be in the same room with her, talking and laughing. Or riding horses together. Your threat is wasted on me—because it's not her body or her beauty I love most, but what's inside her."

Shock broke over me in waves. I couldn't believe he was defending me—that he still loved me—after all I'd done. After I'd accused him of being a liar.

For a long moment their stare-off continued. Finally, Wes's mother backed down, her demeanor becoming docile.

"Very well, dear. I understand. You males are the weaker

of the species, at the mercy of your... drives and lesser natures." She turned to me. "Do you want your freedom?"

Was this a trick question? "Of course."

"I'm sure you have no more desire to stay on this island than I have for you to remain here with my son. Therefore... I have a proposal for you. All we want is the nymph. Her blood could heal Wes, give him his freedom. You found her before, and we believe you can do it again. Leave with us—right now—and help us find the nymph. Do this, and you can have your freedom."

"Don't do it, Alessia. You can't trust them," Wes warned.

My glance bounced between the three of them—the two witches with their smug expectation and Wes's beseeching gaze. If I stayed, denied their request, the witches would remove his protection spell. My nearness *would* make him violently ill, possibly even kill him. We'd be together but eternally kept apart by my glamour and his immune deficiency.

If I left, I'd have a chance to find Macy and Nic. Once I'd located them, I'd beg Macy to heal Wes. He could live a normal life, mixing with people of his own kind, traveling and working, living the life he truly wanted.

And I'd have the chance to possibly stop the horrible disaster I'd set into motion and make up for a little of the wrong I'd done. It was what I'd wanted. It was the only choice I could make.

"I accept."

"Alessia, no," Wes pleaded. "Don't go."

"It's all I've wanted all along," I told the women.

I needed to convince them I had no intention of returning here to "corrupt" their precious son and grandson. Of course, I *would* come back to him— after I'd found Macy. I would not turn her over to the witches but bring her—or at least a tiny bit of her blood—back here myself to cure him.

Maybe if all went well and the powers of Alfheim were on our side... I could stay.

Turning back to Wes, I fervently wished I could communicate with him in the Elven way, mind to mind. I could have told him my plan and prevented the wounded look that shaded his blue eyes.

"Goodbye, Wes. I wish you well."

He just shook his head, saying nothing, his jaw rock hard.

"Very good," his mother said. "Let's do be off then. No time to waste. We've a nymph to find."

23

MACY

The boat ride to the gatehouse went too quickly.

With every bend in the river, my heart grew heavier. I craved seeing Nic's face again but not under these circumstances. This was a moment I would have put off forever if I'd been given a real choice.

When I entered the cottage, he was in the living area, dozing in a chair. His eyes opened, and he sprang up, reaching me in two long strides and sweeping me up onto my tiptoes with his embrace.

"You're back. I was so afraid I'd never see you again. I wasn't sure what was going to happen after they marched you away from here."

"I'm fine."

I did my best to give him a smile. I didn't want his last impression of me to be a red-faced, blubbering mess. I had a few minutes left with Nic, and the memories we made today would have to last the rest of my life. Would he remember me? He would forget the location of this place, but I hoped the Skye water would leave him at least some memory of our time together.

I would remember *everything*—every moment with him. Missing him was going to drive me insane. My only hope would be to escape my sorrows temporarily in the intoxicating food and water. I was going to be the only resident of Sidhe Innis to weigh five hundred pounds. It didn't matter. Nothing would matter once Nic and all my family and friends were out of my life for good.

"Macy, what's wrong?" Nic asked, obviously reading my expression. I'd always had a useless poker face. "Didn't you see the queen?"

I nodded. "I did. She agreed to help the humans. She'll direct her people to donate blood and work with the healers from Altum."

His face contracted in surprise, and then he smiled. "Well, that's great news. You don't seem happy, though. Was she mean to you?"

I couldn't keep up the brave front any longer. My throat began closing up, and my eyes swam with tears.

"Nic, I… I have to say… goodbye."

His body froze, his brows lowering and pulling together. "What are you talking about? To the queen? Are you sad about leaving this place after all, about leaving your people?"

I shook my head. I had to get this out. "I have to say goodbye… to you. I have to give you up. That's the deal. Queen Ragan said it's the only way she'll help the humans survive the Plague. You have to leave… and I have to stay here."

"I'll come back for you," he vowed angrily. "After the Plague's been cured, I'll come back and get you. She can't keep me away. She can't stop me."

"Nic. Be realistic. She's stopped you from even being able to leave this cottage. She created a monster storm to keep the witches from following us here. Don't you think if she wants to keep you off the island and out of Sidhe Innis she can do it?

He shook his head, his face reddening with anger. "It doesn't matter. I'll find a way. I'm *not* saying goodbye to you —and I don't want you to say goodbye to me."

My heart melted and dripped down to my toes. "What should I say then?"

"Say you love me." He took me in his arms again and rested his forehead against mine, staring into my eyes. "Say you always will, and that you'll never forget me."

It was all true—more than he'd ever know—and though it hurt, I did as he asked.

"I love you, Nic. I'll never forget you... no matter what happens. No matter who I—" My vows stopped abruptly.

Queen Ragan had dropped one more bit of news on me before dismissing me from the throne room. Apparently Lord Hulder had taken a liking to me last night.

He'd informed the queen he would consider himself duly *refunded* for the loss of his runaway bride if he were allowed to have me, her daughter, as a replacement. The queen said it was fair in her eyes, and here in Sidhe Innis, her eyes were the only ones that mattered.

Nic's gaze sharpened as he picked up on the intent of my fragmented sentence. "No matter who you *what*? What were you going to say, Macy?"

"Queen Ragan has offered me to a nobleman here. As his... mate."

With a growl, Nic spun and punched the nearest wall. "No. I won't allow it. You're *mine*. We can't let this happen. I'll kill him. I'll kill them all."

"The only ones we'll be killing are the humans if we don't agree to this... this... devil's bargain. There's no choice, Nic. You know it's true as well as I do. I'm so sorry."

Nic came back and seized me, dragging me into his arms.

We both broke down sobbing. Emotion flowed between us. Grief and anger mixed with helplessness as the reality sank in.

"I'm sorry, too. I should never have agreed to this search," Nic finally said. "I should have kept you safely in the human world. She's worse than any of the rulers in the Ancient court—with her hatred of our entire race, her sweeping judgments on all of us based on what's happened in the past. And she's worse than the Earth-wives with their jealousies and fears making them attack first and ask questions later. Evil witch. I'll make her pay for this. We never even got to be together, and she's going to force you to bond with some old, rich man."

I nodded against his neck, hating the cruelty of fate, the cruelty of the nymph queen as his sad words repeated in my head.

We never even got to be together. My heart raced as something occurred to me.

I lifted my head so our tear-stained gazes met. "There's still time. We *can* be together... right *now*."

His gaze intensified. "Now? Are you sure you want to do that?"

I nodded. "I'm sure. It's our last chance. You're bonded to me already. I want to be bonded to you. I already am in my heart. It doesn't matter anymore if my blood loses its healing power. And I don't know exactly how it works with nymphs, but if I'm unable to produce an heir for Lord Hulder or something because I've already bonded with someone else, well then... *good*. If he's angry to discover on his wedding night his 'bride' isn't *pure*, even better. It serves him right. I love you. I want *you*, Nic."

My breath hitched. "Do you want me?"

He tilted his head to one side, giving me a narrow eyed glance brimming with heat and passionate intention. One corner of his mouth lifted. His voice was roughened and soft.

"I've wanted you since the minute I laid eyes on you climbing the courtyard wall in your underwear. Wanting you has been my chief occupation since then. I'm going to want you every day for the rest of my life."

Nic clamped his arm around my lower back, drawing me tightly against his strong body. His breath was hot and delicious on my lips. "But if this is the only chance I'll ever get… I'm going to make it count."

His mouth covered mine. For a moment we both froze, absorbing the feel of our bodies molded against one another and the knowledge of what was about to happen. *At last.*

All the fine hairs on my arms rose in unison. Everything from my neck down went warm and weak. And then it all combusted, and we were both consumed in a firestorm of need.

Nic kissed me with ferocious yearning, seeming ravenous as his mouth moved over mine with lush, sensuous strokes. Fierce pleasure seared my nerves, and I surged against him, gripping his back and shoulders and going up onto my tiptoes in my desperation to get closer.

Groaning into my mouth, he swept his arm under my legs and lifted me. As he carried me down the hall to the small bedroom, I clung to him, shivering with desire. Now that I was allowed to have all of him, I felt starved for the touch of his fingers on my skin, his mouth everywhere, and the solid weight of his large, muscular body over mine.

Nic's hunger had been unleashed as well, and he nearly threw me onto the bed, lowering over me and pinning me to the mattress while his lips coasted from my face to my neck and lower still. As he worked his way down, he pulled and tore at the pixie dress. Ripping noises filled the quiet space, accompanied by Nic's ragged breathing and my own pleading whimpers.

I'd never felt like this. I'd never seen *him* like this—wild, nearly desperate. He was on the verge of losing any semblance of control. And that was fine with me.

My urgency matched his as touch for touch, kiss for kiss, we moved together toward an inevitable culmination. I was ready for it, and I grappled at the fastenings of his clothing, my eager fingers trembling with impatience and excitement.

Nic pushed up and stood at the bedside, quickly stripping off his clothes and revealing the ribbed muscles and smooth, satiny, tan skin I'd been longing to freely explore for so long. I wanted to look at him forever, every day for the rest of my existence. But all we would ever have was tonight.

He stared down at me with dark flames lighting the depths of his brown eyes. "You are beautiful, Macy. I've never wanted or needed anything so much in my life."

"Then take me," I whispered, trembling from head to toe and feeling almost frenzied with love and desire for him. "I'm yours."

Nic didn't wait to hear any more. He came back to me, crawling over me until his powerful form hovered just above me, close but not touching. "And I am yours, piccola, until the sun no longer rises and sets. I love you."

And then words dissolved into movement and touch, emotion into physical expression as an act as old as time became new again, joining two lives and two people into one.

* * *

WHAT WE'D DONE TOGETHER, as wonderful as it was, only made it harder to say goodbye. And I had to say goodbye.

The knowledge wrapped my heart in a painful

tourniquet. The pressing ache was in my throat as well, keeping me quiet as my pulse gradually slowed and my breathing evened out. No words could make things better, anyway.

Nic and I lay together for a long time, each collecting and storing away the exquisite, life-altering sensations and memories for the long, divergent futures that lay ahead of us. When I heard a formation of Queensguard approaching the cottage, I slid from the bed and hurriedly dressed in what was left of my tattered clothes.

"How do I look?" I asked Nic.

His eyes roamed over me, shining with tears. "You're the most ravishing thing I've ever seen, piccola. I will keep this vision of you in my mind and treasure what we just shared in my heart for all eternity."

A loud knock at the door signaled the end of our time together. One of the Queensguard spoke in Nymphian as she entered the house.

"It's time."

I opened Nic's bedroom door and stepped into the hallway. The guard's eyes dropped to my torn dress and traveled up to my disheveled hair. One of her brows lifted, and the corner of her mouth quirked. Okay, so Nic had obviously lied—I must have looked a mess.

"What happens now?" I asked her.

"Soldiers will take the Elf through the portal and put him on a boat for the mainland. He'll be forced to drink the Water of Skye so he does not remember the journey or the location of our sanctuary. I will escort you to the top of the Sgurr so you can call the Elven healers."

"Okay. Just give us a minute."

She nodded and stepped outside. Nic walked me to the cottage door, holding my hand so tightly my circulation was cut off.

"I'll find Alessia," he whispered to me. "She'll tell me where the Plague was triggered, and I'll help the Light Elves distribute the cure we already have on hand. And I'll call your family and tell them where we hid their cure doses—just in case."

"Thank you," I said, turning to him before bursting into an uncontrollable sob.

Nic and Alessia were going to end up married. I could see that future as clearly as I could see his beautiful brown eyes in front of me. They'd never be able to bond, but he said she didn't have any interest in that. And she'd get to see him every day for the rest of forever. I would be mated with smarmy Lord Hulder for eternity. At least I had this precious memory of Nic to sustain me. It would have to be enough.

"I love you. Always. No matter what," I promised through tears.

He took my face in his hands. "I love you. And no matter what they do to me, I'll *never* forget you. How could I? You are my heart."

My guard stood just outside the open door. She cleared her throat and gestured for me to come outside. Nic stepped through the door after me, without a single vine obstructing his progress. Guards surrounded him and began marching him down the path toward the waterfall portal.

As I was escorted to a boat that would take me in the opposite direction, toward the city, I looked back over my shoulder in time to see Nic and his attendants step through the shimmering water-wall of the portal, back to the real world and out of my life for good. A lance of raw pain pierced my chest as the back of his head disappeared from view.

Swiping at my face to dry my tears, I jerked my head back around, staring straight ahead. "How do we get to the summit to make the phone call?"

"There is a tower that reaches to the top of the enclosure, just under the floor of the summit. You will see," the guard said.

As we had when I'd first arrived, we entered the city and took a lift. This time it didn't stop until we'd reached the pinnacle of the city. The elevator doors opened up to a soaring platform, enclosed on all four sides by a wall. Just above us, the strange transparent membrane that covered Sidhe Innis showed the faint impression of stone overhead. Looking through that, I saw dark clouds and heavy rain.

"The storm is still going strong. How will I get a cell signal in *that*?" And then something worse occurred to me. "How will Nic's boat be able to cross the sound? This weather is too dangerous. The seas will be too rough."

"Have faith in our queen," the guard instructed.

Behind us the elevator doors opened up, and Queen Ragan herself appeared. A dark feeling I'd rarely experienced seeped through my veins. Hatred. She looked so serene and confident, so pleased with herself and her victory. My feelings didn't matter to her at all.

The guard stretched her arm up and tapped the tip of her spear on the barrier above us. As the queen reached us, the platform beneath us begin to move, lifting us higher and higher toward the stony ceiling. I was about to duck when the queen raised both arms straight up over her head. The solid stone above us seemed to vanish.

As we surfaced, fresh air filled my lungs and a few drops of rain sprinkled my bare skin. Then the rain stopped abruptly as if someone had turned off a garden spigot.

The dark clouds that were hanging just above the Sgurr lifted, moving higher and higher until they were out of sight. The sun came out, shining on the summit of the rocky mountain as well as the island stretching out below us in a panorama of green grass and black rock.

In the distance, moving slowly away from the shoreline, was a small boat. I couldn't see who was aboard, but as it was departing at the exact moment the terrible storm abated, I could make a safe guess. It was Nic and his escorts.

"You've done the right thing," the queen assured in a tone of unmistakable satisfaction.

I didn't respond, and I looked away from the retreating boat, trying not to think of it. There was no point in torturing myself by watching until he disappeared from sight. I'd made my choice, and now it was time to set the rest of the plan into motion.

Ragan handed me a cell phone. "Make the call. Summon the Elven healers."

"How will I explain where we are?"

"I'll take care of that," she said. "Just make contact."

I couldn't call Lad and the Light Court healers directly. I wasn't even sure Light Elves used phones. But Nox would know how to get in touch with them, and I'd called his number enough times in the past to remember it. I was a bit concerned he wouldn't pick up a call from an unfamiliar phone, but he answered right away.

"Hello. Nox?"

"Macy? Is that you? We haven't heard from you in so long."

"Hi. Yes, it's me."

He gave a short, joyful laugh. "I almost didn't answer. How the hell are you? How's Nic?"

"Um… a lot has happened since we've last talked. Nic is safe, and I'm… okay. You know we went searching for my birth family to ask for help in saving the humans?"

"Yes…"

"Well, we found them, and they agreed."

"That's great news. Wow, you weren't kidding. A lot *has* happened."

"Yeah. I need you to get in touch with Lad and have him send Asher and Wickthorne here to collect the blood donations, so they can produce enough antidote for everyone."

"Okay." He dragged the word out, his tone now sounding cautious. "What are you not telling me? There's a catch, am I right?"

"Yeah." I had to pause before continuing, swallowing a lump in my throat and fighting to keep it together. "I'll be staying here. And Nic won't."

"What? You guys broke up?"

"The decision was... made for us. It's a condition of the deal I struck with the nymph queen."

"Well that bi—"

At that, the queen took the phone from my hand and put it to her own ear. "This is Queen Ragan. If you share this girl's concern for the human world, you will follow my instructions without fail or deviation."

She spoke in perfect English. Her subjects might not have learned human languages, but she had.

"In addition to your healers, I require one of your leaders —you, if you wish—to travel here to our sanctuary where you will be held as collateral until the collection procedure is complete. I have no wish for the Ancient Court to reign unfettered over this planet and no ill will toward the human population in general. But the safety of my own people is my primary concern."

She paused before adding, "When I am assured no harm comes to them and the Elven healers leave this place, then the Elven ruler will be released. But if anything should go wrong—I *will* kill him. Those are my terms."

I could hear Nox's low, determined voice. "I'll be there. Just tell me when and where."

"You should leave immediately. Your destination is the

Isle of Eigg, Scotland. You'll reach it by ferry from Mallaig. The weather will be ideal for your travel. My scouts will be on the lookout for you. And your emissaries will come alone —no guards, no soldiers, no weapons of any sort."

She provided directions to the portal and handed the phone back to me.

"Nox? It's me."

"Nice lady," he sneered.

"Yes. She's got a bit of a trust issue."

"Well, don't worry. I'll put in the call to my pilots as soon as I hang up with you. We'll be there as soon as possible. And when we leave, we're taking you with us."

A rush of unexpected yearning caused my breath to catch. "No. It's already done. Nic is gone. I can't back out of this. I've been... promised... to someone here."

"Oh, Macy." He paused, letting out a long sigh. "We're on our way. Don't give up hope."

"Goodbye Nox. I'll see you soon."

I hit the end-call button, knowing there *was* no hope to hang onto, and handed the phone back to Queen Ragan, who wore a brilliant smile.

"There. Your precious humans will be saved, and you can begin your new life with your own people. Now, let us get back home. Lord Hulder is very eager to get on with your formal courtship. It begins tonight. He will make you a very good match, and you will be happier this way. You'll see."

"I won't," I told her with complete assurance. "I made you a promise, and I won't break it. My body *will* be here. But as long as Nic is somewhere else... I'll spend the rest of my eternity without a heart."

She gave me an arrested glance. "You look—and sound— so much like your mother right now..." Shaking her head, she turned away and made a signal to the guard.

The platform lowered, and the shield closed over our

heads, blocking out the wind and all sound from the outside world, but not the sunlight. My heart sank as well. And for the first time in my life, I felt truly related to my birth mother, Fallon.

This must have been how she felt, being forced to marry someone she did not love while letting go of the man she did. Knowing that her future would not be her own, but owned and controlled by someone else. Forever.

Unlike my mother, I couldn't run away. The fate of the human world depended on me sticking to the deal I had made. And no matter how dreadful the rest of my life looked, I would do it.

24

ALESSIA

The Earth-wives and I emerged from the house together, and I was shocked to find the air dry, the sky clear, as if there had never been a storm at all.

Astounded, I looked at the mother-daughter duo. "Did you do this?"

They simply shrugged and got into the front seat of the car in the drive, indicating I should get into the back. Wes had told me there were no cars allowed on the ferry, but they'd managed to get a hold of one somehow, and we drove into the village, boarded the boat, and headed for the mainland town of Mallaig.

The woman Wes called Nanna turned to look at me. "You've made a very good decision. My grandson is much better off, and you will have your freedom. That is if you don't try to escape us."

I settled back, crossing my arms over my chest and looking out my window at the passing scenery. The water of the sound was smooth as glass. "No. As I said, I'm getting what I've wanted all along—to get off the island and back to my home."

"Very good. Now tell us, how did you find the nymph before? You tracked her to our house in Bristol?" A covetous gleam lit the old woman's eyes.

"I didn't, but I have a tracker who works for me. He can help me locate the nymph again. I just need a cell phone or landline that actually works so I can call him."

"Cell phones won't work out here on the sound," Wes's mother said. "When we reach land, you can make the call. And don't try any funny business. We'll be listening in. Remember... Wes's health is hanging in the balance."

"Of course. I remember. I am curious... if you were able to ward him against Elven glamour, why couldn't you just ward him against human diseases?"

Nanna lay a finger across her chin and adopted a sarcastic tone. "Oh gee, Ciarra, why didn't we think of that?"

Then her tone became surly again as her disdainful eyes met mine once more. "It's not possible. Magic works against magic far more effectively than against the powers of the mortal world. When Wes was young, we were able to heal him repeatedly of his frequent illnesses, but our efforts became less and less effective until we could no longer preserve his life, and he had to retreat into a solitary existence."

"But you think the nymph's blood will work for him?"

"Yes. The Earth-wives' archives speak of it—nymph blood used to be the basis of many of our healing elixirs. If you'll remember your own history, that was the root of the rift between our factions—the Ancient Court used to share the nymphs with us. Then they got greedy and wanted their blood all for themselves. Of course, the Elven scrolls may tell it differently."

"It's not just legend," Ciarra interjected. "We've seen it. My daughter Olivia's blood has been completely cleared of the Plague virus that your *people* in the Ancient Court *infected* her with. She said the nymph—Macy—administered an antidote. It had to have been derived from her blood."

I nodded, remembering Nic's words about a possible solution to the Plague. He'd been telling the truth. "Yes. That makes sense. Dr. Schmitt was afraid of it. That's why he sent me—and others—to hunt the girl down."

Nanna became more animated now, practically rubbing her hands together in anticipation. "When I think of all we could accomplish with just the blood of that one little nymph—"

"Mother," Ciara cut her off with a sharp admonition.

That did it. I was certain now there *was* a way to stop the pandemic. It was even more imperative I reach Nic and Macy as soon as possible. But I'd have to lose my two tails first. I was beginning to suspect that if I led the Earth-wives to her, they might drain the girl and hoard all her blood for themselves and their spells. I couldn't allow that for a whole host of reasons.

When we reached the mainland and disembarked, Ciarra handed me her phone along with a warning. "Don't try to run. You *know* we can stop you."

My head still ached from the last attack, my belly still fragile enough I hadn't eaten all day and didn't want to. "I won't."

Leonardo answered immediately. "Your Highness. Are you well? Everyone's been worried. No one's heard from you."

Conscious of Ciarra and Nanna standing nearby listening to my every word, I chose them carefully. "I'm fine. Are you at the palace?"

"Yes, I returned as soon as I was released on bail from the Las Vegas county jail. Thank you for arranging it."

"Of course. There's something I need for you to do, Leonardo."

"Anything."

"I need you to go back to the States. Find the nymph again. It's more important now than ever that we apprehend her."

"Already done. Actually, as soon as I was released, I resumed my mission. I thought you'd want a status report when you checked back in."

"Oh. Yes. Well…. Good job." *That was easy.* "And… you know where she is?"

"Not exactly."

"What does that mean?"

"She is no longer in the States. She's not in Italy with the prince, either. But I believe she's in Europe. I tracked them to Scotland."

"Scotland?" I was stunned. I was standing on Scottish soil at that very moment. What would Nic and Macy be doing here? Were they trying to find *me*? And if so, for what purpose?

"*Where* in Scotland?"

"A harbor village on the west coast. It's a popular ferry port for travelers to and from the Hebredian isles. It's called—"

"Mallaig," I said before he could.

"Yes. That's right. You know your Scottish towns, Highness." He sounded surprised. "But that is where the trail went cold. They were there and then… not. They seem to have disappeared without a trace."

Merda. That wasn't good. If my tracker didn't know where to look next, how was *I* supposed to figure it out? Just then, a man moving through the crowd at the docks caught my eye. He was tall and handsome with bright green eyes and curling dark blond hair—obviously Elven. But there was more. He was a Light Elf.

The humans around us probably couldn't have detected

the difference, but I could. Seeing him here was more than strange. Light Elves didn't mix with humans as a rule. They preferred to keep to the old ways and live their lives separate from human concerns and settlements.

He had two companions, an older man, a Light Elf as well, and a young dark-headed guy who appeared to be half human-half Elven.

My heart thrummed with excitement. What were they doing here? It was too coincidental the unconventional group of travelers would *happen* to be in this small Scottish town at the same time as Nic and Macy. I kept my expression clear, not wanting to tip off the witches to anything unusual. But I followed the men with my eyes, watching as they boarded the ferry. Ah—they were going to one of the islands.

"Leonardo... didn't you once tell me there was something that could throw off your tracking glamour?"

"Yes, your Highness. Large bodies of water."

I had been almost sure of the answer already but hesitated to ask for confirmation directly with listening ears so close by. Turning to survey the view over the sound, I detected the hazy shapes of several islands on the other side, one of them Eigg, with its distinctive mile-long rock ridge.

"Do you believe they sailed from there?" Leonardo asked.

"I do," I said, smiling. "But not very far."

As soon as I ended the call, the witches assailed me with questions.

"Do you know where she is? Did your tracker find her? Did you say something about Scotland?"

"Yes. In fact, he said he'd tracked them here—to Mallaig."

"What?" Nanna said.

"How odd. You'd better not be lying to us," warned her daughter.

"I'm not—you were listening. He lost track of them here, but the village can't be that large. There must be people here who have seen them and could lead us to them. I propose we split up and begin asking around at the shops and restaurants."

Nanna narrowed her gaze on me. "This wouldn't be some sort of trick now, would it?"

"I want to find them at least as much as you do," I said truthfully. "I want Wes to be cured."

Ciarra smiled. "Good. Well, keep in mind, if you are trying to pull something, going back to Wes is not an option —if anything goes *wrong*, we'll hop right back on the ferry and remove his ward against Elven glamour. The next time he sees you... will literally be the death of him."

Shuddering at the thought, I said, "I understand."

Of course if things went *right*, the next time Wes saw me, I'd be delivering the permanent cure for his lifelong health problems—Macy's blood. I couldn't return to him without it.

"Well, we should hurry," Nanna said. "We don't want to give them a chance to leave the village before we pick up their trail."

"Right. I'll ask around at the harbor," I said.

Ciarra analyzed me with one last suspicious look before saying, "I'll ask at the pubs near here. And mother, you can check in with the shopkeepers."

The two women scurried away toward the town. I walked up to several people, saying hello and asking for the time, pretending to question them about Nic and Macy. As soon as the witch pair was out of sight, I hurried over to a fisherman who'd apparently just pulled in to the docks.

"Excuse me sir, I need to hire your boat."

He stood and faced me, a frown wrinkling his wind-chapped skin. "I've just come ashore, lassie. I'll not be going back out again today. If you're needing passage to the islands, the ferry's just pulling out, but there'll be another in an hour.

And if you canna wait, there's a private boat service a short walk away."

I smiled at him and turned my Sway up to its highest strength. "No thank you. I believe your boat will better serve my needs. Now let's get aboard and follow that ferry."

Having no choice, the man obeyed, dropping whatever he was doing and re-boarding his boat. I glanced around to make sure the witches had not returned then followed him aboard, ducking into the standing shelter so as not to be seen.

After we were away from shore and a short distance behind the ferry, I asked the man, "Where does the ferry stop?"

"First at Eigg. Then after about a half hour, it'll depart for Muck."

"Not the Isle of Skye?"

I'd once seen a picture of some gorgeous waterfalls emptying into a magical blue pool. The photo was taken on Skye, and the place was called the fairy pools. If the nymphs were likely to be anywhere in this area, that seemed like a good bet.

"No lassie, that'll be a different ferry altogether. But I do have enough fuel if that is where ye wish to go."

"No. Just stay with the ferry. I'll let you know."

As he'd said, the ferry boat docked at Eigg. We stayed in the harbor while I watched the passengers debark. I began to think the Light Elves would stay aboard, but then I saw them. All three walked down the boarding ramp onto the dock and looked around.

"Pull in here," I ordered the fisherman. "I'm getting out."

"As you wish."

He motored to the dock, idling and offering me his hand as I stepped onto the dock myself. I turned back to him. "Thank you. You can go now."

He nodded then blinked several times and looked around. From the look on his face, it was clear he wondered why on earth he was in Eigg's harbor instead of Mallaig's. He'd forgotten me already, which was just how I wanted it.

Turning toward the village, I spotted the three extremely tall visitors and set off on foot after them. Were Nic and Macy staying in Galmisdale then?

How bizarre that I might have been right in the same town with them earlier today and boarded a boat away from them instead.

But the Elves didn't stay in the town. They began walking. Within minutes, they'd left the village limits and then left the road itself, cutting across the countryside and toward An Sgurr, the huge rocky outcropping that rose from the landscape like a headless sphinx and overshadowed the whole island. Odd. *Were* they just here for some hiking after all?

It didn't seem likely. There was purpose in their long strides, and they didn't joke and chat with one another as men out for a day of recreation would. I followed them as they trekked across the rocky land and then turned, not uphill toward the bluff, but down toward the sea.

What on earth? They went directly to the edge of the island where the patches of grass and heather turned into a small bluff then began picking their way down the uneven rocks to the narrow beach at the bottom. I waited a minute then followed, watching as they traversed the narrow strip of sand between the ocean and the cliff.

They stopped at an opening in the rock wall then ducked inside. *A cave.* My pulse whirred in my ears. This was big. This was *something*.

When I reached the entrance myself, I read the signs posted there. They declared the cave CLOSED TO VISITORS and DANGEROUS.

Okay then. Clearly these guys knew something I didn't about this island. I wasn't sure where the mysterious chasm in the cliff led. But I was about to find out. Ducking my head to fit through the low opening, I slipped inside. It took a moment for my eyes to adjust to the change in lighting.

There wasn't much in here, but I followed the voices of the three Light Elves as they moved through the passage, deeper and deeper into the cliff side. A faint glow from up ahead helped me keep my bearings. I assumed at least one of them had brought along some of the phosphorescent mineral rocks used for lighting in Altum, their subterranean home.

The Light Elves had a clear advantage as they were accustomed to traveling and living underground. I myself shrank away from the cold, wet walls and tried to make sure I didn't make too much noise or fall too far behind and get left in the dark while trying not to draw too close either. As we moved into the cave, it opened up, becoming roomier and airier, though still dark and bare as far as I could tell.

What could they want in here? Was it another Light Elven stronghold? I was certainly not aware of any Elven tribes living on Eigg.

All at once the low murmur of male voices ceased, replaced by a loud, rushing noise. Was it wind? No, it sounded more like... water. I rounded a bend in the rocky passageway, and there in front of me was a large waterfall. And nothing else.

I twisted side to side. This was where the path ended. Where had the Light Elves gone? There were no passageways in or out of this chamber except the one I'd just taken to get here. Had the men somehow doubled back and slipped past me without my realizing it?

Impossible. The passage was too narrow. I moved forward and stretched a hand out toward the falling water. Cool mist rose and covered my skin.

It smelled earthy and fresh in this room, the running water re-oxygenating the air around me. There was also the faintest hint of... flowers? How was that possible? No flower could possibly grow down here. Unless...

Perhaps there *was* another way out of this chamber. Preparing for a fully-clothed cold shower, I pushed my hand into the flow of the waterfall, finding myself able to get my entire arm through it, up to the shoulder without touching rock on the other side.

Then I took a deep breath, ducked my head under, and stepped through.

25

MACY

The Light Elves arrived in late afternoon.

The guards who'd been waiting for them at the portal brought them to the palace gate where Queen Ragan had commanded me to be with her, acting as a liaison. I was surprised she'd even agreed to meet with the Elves herself. I'd thought she might assign some underling to handle the matter.

The other surprise was the Elven ruler who'd accompanied Asher and Wickthorne, the other healer from Altum. It wasn't Nox, as I'd expected. As the group approached on the path, I caught sight of golden hair and the most intense green eyes I'd ever seen. They could belong to only one person. Lad.

"Your Highness," I said to him, performing a quick bow when they reached us. "I wasn't expecting you to be here."

He smiled warmly. "It's not the ideal time to have left my bond-mate, but I couldn't send my people into hostile territory while I stayed tucked away safely at home. Besides... I persuaded Nox my glamour might be more useful in this situation than his."

It made perfect sense. I'd been told the Light King had leadership glamour, that his mere presence inspired trust and cooperation. We could certainly use more of each around here.

"And I *do* have a vested interest in the survival of the human race," he added. "Especially now. I'm here to help however possible."

"Thank you so much for coming—all of you."

I shook Asher's hand and then Wickthorne's. Turning to the queen, I identified each of the visitors for her.

Queen Ragan did not smile at the party, but her greeting was at least civil.

"Welcome. You ambassadors of Altum are the first Elven men to ever set foot in Sidhe Innis—except for Macy's former betrothed, but he never made it past the guardhouse. I trust we will have a peaceful exchange. All measures will be taken to ensure your work is successful. And quick."

She spun and went through the palace gates without another word.

As soon as she was out of earshot, Asher muttered, "In other words… 'hurry up, get it done, and get the hell out of our home.'"

The other two men snickered at his perceptive comment as the rest of us fell into step behind her, flanked by the guards, naturally.

"Speaking of exchanges, Nox said you're essentially selling yourself into slavery in exchange for the cure," Lad said.

His expression was tense with concern. I'd heard his own marriage was a love match rather than the traditional arrangement found in Elven society. Well, not all of us were lucky enough to end up with the person we loved for eternity.

"Slavery might be too harsh a word for it. But yes, I did

agree to stay here and marry a nobleman chosen by the queen. I don't see any other way."

He nodded gravely. "I'm so sorry. That was a brave decision—a selfless choice. Thank you."

I nodded, pressing my lips together and turning away. I couldn't let my thoughts turn back to Nic right now. I had to be able to function. We proceeded through the halls of the palace toward a room where the blood donation volunteers had been assembled.

The royal residence was a busy place today, teeming with servants and visitors. Except for the guards, who remained straight-faced, every nymph we passed stared openly at the tall, handsome visitors. Most of them had never seen a human, much less an Elf.

Based on their storybooks and histories, they'd probably expected terrifying fanged creatures with claws and horns or maybe that these guys would turn and attack them any second. They didn't know the Light Elves were some of the most peace-loving beings on the planet. They were the original practitioners of the *live and let live* philosophy—very different from the Dark Elves of the Ancient Court.

Considering the way the people here scurried away and whispered among themselves, I doubted we'd find many volunteers gathered in the donation room.

"How many pints do you think it'll take to treat the entire world population?" I asked Asher, since Wickthorne only communicated in the traditional Elven way, mind to mind.

"Well, that would be about seven and a half billion people," he said. "Even if ten thousand nymphs donated blood, and we divided each pint into a million parts—which would be challenging to say the least—that still wouldn't be enough to dose every single human. Also, the logistics of trying to reach them all would be a nightmare. There aren't enough Light Elves to carry it out."

"Oh." I felt my hopes sinking. "Is this not going to work then?"

"We'll need to use some strategy, so we won't *have* to treat literally every person in the world. We've already gotten to a good number of the fan pod girls who are carriers. Estelle and Anders are still working on that, along with my father. But there's still the active infection to deal with. If we can locate the hotspot where it started and treat everyone in that region before it spreads too far, we'll be able to stop the pandemic right there. The rest of the world won't need to be treated."

"*If* you can locate it? You still don't know where Alessia triggered the virus?"

"No. And by the time it makes the news, it really might be too late to contain it. With the way people travel these days, the Plague could easily escape the original region and go international at any point. That's why we need to find Alessia."

"She's not going to be exactly helpful," I warned him. "No one in the Ancient Court will be."

Asher shook his head. "I know. My bond-mate could get the truth out of Alessia, but the Italian princess seems to have disappeared."

"Nox told me he's put out feelers all over the European Dark Court," Lad interjected. "No one has seen or heard from the Italian princess in nearly a week."

"Maybe Nic can find her," I said, though my hopes were waning. What if the witches really had "disappeared" her? What if they hadn't just transported her elsewhere but had zapped her into total nothingness? Were they capable of such a spell?

"We'll have to hope so," Lad said.

We entered the grand hall where the residents of Sidhe Innis who were willing to donate blood had been instructed to report. I was stunned by the number of them—there were at least three thousand—fully half of the population of Sidhe Innis.

Actually, "stunned" was the wrong word. I was *moved*. Hope made a resurgence, expanding inside me like a marshmallow in a microwave.

I'd always had great admiration for anyone with the compassion and courage to show up and volunteer to give their own blood for people they didn't know, people they'd likely never even meet. But the volunteers here were acting to save people who were not even their own species.

And then it occurred to me—maybe the queen had "volunteered" them against their will. I hoped not.

I still wasn't sure why she had agreed to this. Yes, I understood she didn't want to see the Ancient Court take over the world, but still, something about it didn't add up. In any case, the nymphs in this room were all heroes in my book, and I planned to thank each and every one of them for saving my human family and friends.

Asher and Wickthorne looked out over the crowd then at each other and smiled simultaneously.

"I think this will cover it nicely," the younger healer said. "We've found even the tiniest amount of nymph blood to be highly effective."

"Well, I guess we should get to work then before the queen changes her mind. Tell me what you need for me to do," I said.

"Let's get people organized into groups and split up, so we can move them through as quickly as possible. Think you can handle doing some draws?" Asher asked me.

"I think so—once you get things set up for me. I've been on the other side of this enough times I should be an expert by now."

Though Queen Ragan did not volunteer to donate blood

herself, she stayed close by, monitoring activities in the makeshift blood donation center and guarding the well-being of her people. Working under her watchful gaze was a bit like trying to take an exam with your meanest teacher hovering over your shoulder.

Following Asher's instructions, I got things situated at my station, then looked up to call forward the first donor in my line. It was Mae.

When she reached me, we hugged. The maternal hold caused a sweet pain to envelope me. I pulled back to look into her eyes. "You didn't have to do this. Wait—*did* you have to do this? Were you forced?"

She smiled and patted my hand. "Not at all, love. After what you told me about your human family, how kind they are and what good care they took of you, I wanted to be sure to do my part. I went around the village, too, encouraging my neighbors. Some of them were scared, you know? It's a strange request, to be sure. But I assured them it was the right thing to do and that you're a sweet girl with a good heart, just like your mother. I told them you wouldn't have asked had it not been of vital importance. The queen's *encouragement* might have helped as well."

Looking around at all the other donors, it occurred to me the vast majority of them were young—my age or younger. Too young to be mated. It seemed to be in keeping with what the Elven healers believed about the power of nymph blood. But Mae was old, and she was here.

"Mae... how are you able to donate? Is it not true that only..." I whispered the next word. "... *virgins* are able to heal with their blood?"

She smiled at me kindly. "No, it's true. I never married. I was too busy taking care of other people's children to ever have any of my own. And now I have the opportunity to save potentially millions of children in the human world."

My eyes moistened, and I hugged her again. "Thank you, Mae. I'll bet my mother loved you dearly."

We worked long into the night, all of us ready to drop by the time the last donation was collected.

"We are finished, your Highness," I told her.

"Let us withdraw to the throne room," she said and swept out of the room, leaving her guards to escort the rest of us.

"What's going on?" Asher asked under his breath. "Are we in trouble?"

"I don't think so," Lad said. "She'll likely want assurances now—and to brainwash us all so we can't possibly return."

"How do you think it went?" I asked Asher as we made our way through the corridors. "Did you get enough?"

"It went well. I can't imagine a better turnout. As long as Queen Friendly lets us leave here alive, we're in good shape," he added in a whisper. "We've got enough blood to make the vaccine and antidote to treat a few million people. Now our only concern will be finding ground zero for the virus's activation so we can start administering it in the right place and not waste it."

My belly knotted with anxiety. After all Nic and I had been through to get here—and after what we'd sacrificed—there was still a chance this plan could fail.

"Maybe Olly could help," I suggested, casting about for solutions. "I was basically passed out at the time, but Nic said her mother and grandmother were the Earth-wives who zapped Alessia to... wherever they sent her. Olly might know where to look for her. Or if she doesn't, maybe she could find out and feed me the information somehow. I'd have to get the queen's permission to go see her or at least to call her."

"Call whom?" Queen Ragan asked from up ahead, obviously overhearing the tail end of our conversation, if not every word of it. She stopped at the doors to the throne room and turned to face us, waiting for us to catch up.

"Olly. She's a girl I know. She might have information we need about where to begin treatment of the infected humans. Her family are… they're Earth-wives."

"Absolutely not," said the queen. "I will not have you in contact with them for any reason. Young or old, they are too dangerous. Why do you think I created a storm to keep them off our island? Elves are bad enough. There will be *no* contact with the Earth-wives."

"I understand, my queen. But there is an Elf we need to find. It's imperative."

"*Another* Elf?" She sounded like someone who'd been offered a cancerous tumor, but there was a bemused turn to her mouth, and her pale silver eyes gleamed with comprehension.

"Yes, your Majesty. But this one's not a friend. She's the one who triggered the virus we're trying to stop. We must talk to her. She has information we need. And the young girl might be our only chance at locating her."

With a wicked grin, the queen said, "Perhaps not the *only* chance." She turned and pushed the doors open and strode into the throne room.

There, standing between two fierce nymph guards, was *Alessia*. A surge of electricity shocked my senses.

"Would *this* happen to be the Elf you're looking for?" Queen Ragan asked.

Asher, Wickthorne, Lad, and I all stopped in our tracks. The three guys turned to look at me, and I realized I was the only one of our group who'd ever met Alessia.

"What… how…" I took a few steps forward, just to assure myself it really was her. "How did you find her? How did you get her here?"

"She got *herself* here, apparently," the queen said. Her tone turned harsher, more threatening. "Unless these three are double-dealing and brought her along."

Now Lad stepped forward. "No, your Majesty. We did not. I've never even seen this woman. None of us have."

"I followed them," Alessia blurted. Her eyes were wild with fear, her usually immaculate appearance drastically altered. She was makeup free. Her hair was a mass of wild curls, and she was wearing… what was that? Men's clothing?

"I followed them from the mainland to the island and then into a cave and through the waterfall. The guards grabbed me just as I stumbled through."

I whirled around to look at the queen. "You knew she was here all this time—while we were doing the collection? Why didn't you tell us?"

"I wanted to see your reactions. I wasn't sure what to make of her. She's been talking non-stop since her capture, telling stories of witches and Plague… and wanting to help save the humans as well. I wasn't sure if she was with your friends or if there was some trickery afoot. As I told you… if *anything* goes wrong, I *will* keep your Light King as forfeit."

"No," I said. "You can't do that. His people need him. He has a bond-mate. And it's not his fault if she followed him. If anyone's to blame here, it's me. I'm the one she hates. I'm the one she's been pursuing."

"I don't hate you, Macy," Alessia pleaded. "That's not why I'm here. I'm sorry for my past actions. I do want to help. I'll tell you anything you want to know about the virus, about Dr. Schmitt's plans. I'll do anything you want. The reason I followed them, the reason I've been searching for *you*, is because *I* need *your* help."

I spat a humorless laugh. "Yeah, right."

"It's true. I came to beg for your help for someone—a human man. He is very ill, and there is no human cure for his condition. I thought maybe you could give him your blood."

"You—want to help a sick human." I snorted. "You actually expect me to believe this?"

"It's completely true. And he's here on the Isle of Eigg. You wouldn't have to go far."

"You brought him with you?"

"No. He was already here." She stopped and shook her head, waving her hands in front of her in frustration. "It's a long story. If you'll just come with me, I can show you—"

"We don't really have time for long stories right now," Asher said. "Or Ancient Court tricks and lies. Thanks to you, we've got a plague to stop. *No* thanks to you, we have a cure for it. The only thing any of us wants to hear coming out of your mouth is the location of the girl you touched. Where was the virus triggered?"

"You have a cure?" Her expression and tone brightened. "But this is wonderful. And Wes can help you distribute it— Wes is the man I was telling you about. That's his job. He's a scientist. He works for the European Centers for Disease Control. He's been tracking the Plague, and he knows people who could get the cure to the right people quickly."

Asher tossed his head and huffed a skeptical laugh. "Great. So tell us where to go."

Alessia opened her mouth as if to answer, but then shut it again. She looked around the room, studying our eyes.

"You don't believe me."

"Not really," Asher said. "But if you cough up that location, it'll go a long way toward establishing trust. Where did you trigger the virus, Alessia?"

Again, she looked around the room. When she did answer, all she said was, "No."

"I knew it. She was bluffing," I said.

"I'm not bluffing. But I don't trust you."

"You don't trust *us*?" I laughed. "That's rich."

"I *will* tell you where to go—and I will help you in any way I can. But first you must heal Wes."

"Why don't you give us that promise in the Elven way?" Lad challenged.

All the Elves were silent for a few moments, though their expressions showed they were indeed communicating. Finally, Lad broke eye contact with Alessia and turned to me.

"She's telling the truth. The man exists. He is sick, and he does work to track world health threats. He's been following this one. She was also honest about her intention to help us in return for you healing him."

"Well, wonders never cease, I guess," I said. Then I turned to Alessia. "Tell us what we want to know, and I'll give him my blood."

She narrowed her eyes at me. "Give him your blood, and *then* I'll tell you what you want to know."

"Enough of this," said the queen. "You may go to the human, heal him, and get the information you need."

"You're going to let me leave?" I asked, stunned.

"Certainly. You and the young healer, and the female Elf. The Light King and the older healer will stay here—as will *all* the blood you've collected from my people. If you do not return, these men will never leave this place—and neither will your *cure*. The Light Kingdom will be without a ruler, and the humans you love will all die."

I looked between the two women who'd manipulated me into this tight spot. I couldn't admit to either of them that my blood might no longer be useful for healing now that Nic and I had bonded.

"I'll be back," I promised.

Queen Ragan clapped her hands together in two sharp cracks. "Very good. Go then. My guards will escort you to the portal and wait for your return. I'll make sure our Elven *guests* are comfortable until then."

Understanding that the queen's definition of

"comfortable" was "held under lock and key," I promised to make the trip a quick one.

Asher, Alessia, and I left the palace and started down the path to the river.

"I'm not buying the whole miraculous change of heart, by the way. This had better not be some kind of trick," I warned her.

"It's not. I don't want the humans to die either. I don't love all of them… but I do love one. And he is reason enough for me." She was quiet for a moment before adding, "Perhaps that, in itself, *is* a miracle."

26

WES

I sat on my sofa in front of the fire, injured leg stretched out on the cushions as I worked on my laptop deep into the wee hours of morning.

The virus cluster was growing. If what Alessia had told me was true, it would continue to grow until it had engulfed the entire planet in a new plague.

For my own sake, it didn't really matter. What did I have to live for? I was doomed to be alone for the rest of my days. My heart was broken. Alessia had only been pretending she cared about me and had abandoned me and this island the first chance she'd gotten.

But I *had* to care about the rest of the planet. Not only was it my job to track down and stop epidemics, I knew what the rest of my baffled co-workers at the ECDC did not—this one wasn't any ordinary epidemic. If I didn't do something to stop it, everyone I knew would die.

But what could I do? Unfortunately, Alessia had left without telling me anything that might help battle this unknown virus.

She *did* say there was a nymph—I hadn't even known there was such a thing—who might be able to help. Of course, now I had reason to suspect every word Alessia had said to me was a lie.

I shook my head and forced the rising pain in my chest back down, struggling to stop seeing her face. The look in her eyes just before she'd left with Mum and Nanna had made me believe for a few minutes she was actually sad to leave me, that her indifferent remarks were just for show, and that after finding the nymph for them, she'd find a way to return to me.

What a fool.

She'd given my mother and grandmother the slip only minutes after reaching the mainland. They'd been livid, but as for me... I was... broken. Just as everyone had warned, the Elven girl was only interested in herself.

She was long gone, and I was left to pick up the pieces—of this spreading epidemic... and my heart.

Movement outside the dark window caught the corner of my eye, and I jerked in surprise. My first thought was that one of the horses was out. But then I heard the sound of the back doorknob turning.

Could it be a lost hiker? Someone from the village?

"Hold on a minute," I called out, searching around me desperately for something to hold over my nose and mouth as an antiviral face mask. It wouldn't be very effective of course. I'd have to tell whoever it was to go away.

And then the unannounced visitor entered the room.

Alessia.

I lost my breath, and my pulse instantly kicked into a new, hurtling rhythm.

She came back.

And she wasn't alone. Two more people entered the room —a tiny girl—looked to be a teenager—and an extremely tall guy with jet black hair and turquoise eyes. Another Elf. Had to be.

Grabbing the edge of my blanket, I pulled it up to cover the lower half of my face.

"Stay back," I warned.

Alessia stepped toward me, wearing a look of such warmth and adoration it caused my heart to squeeze nearly flat.

"Don't worry, Wes." She smiled. "They can't make you sick. Both of them are Fae, like me. This is Asher—he's an Elven healer. And this is Macy, the nymph I was telling you about."

The blanket dropped from my slack grip, more out of shock than anything else. "The nymph," I repeated, almost robotically. She *had* been telling the truth after all.

Alessia's face burst into bright sunshine. "Yes. I told you. She wants to help us—and the humans. There is a cure for the Plague. But they need *your* help. They need to know exactly where to distribute the antidote and vaccine. I thought your organization could help with that. And that's not all the good news."

She came forward another few steps, obviously intending to come to me and embrace me.

"I said 'stay away.'" My voice was louder this time, my command more urgent.

Alessia stopped immediately. Her eyes clouded. "Wes. What's wrong? I'm sorry I left so abruptly. I was only pretending to be happy to leave you. I meant to come back all along with a cure for you. And see? I have."

I kept my arm extended between us with my hand up like a stop sign. "I see that. And of course I will help. I'll make a call right away and get a ground team mobilized. But Alessia…"

This next part was so hard to say I could hardly get my mouth to function.

"*You* can't come near me. My mother and grandmother removed the ward. They were furious at you for ditching them, and they were convinced you'd come back to me. They returned to the island and removed all my protection against Elven glamour. I kept telling them it was unnecessary—that you'd left for good and would never come back here."

Alessia's eyes brimmed with tears. "How could you think that? How could I *not* come back? I told you I love you. Do you... not love me anymore?"

A noise from upstairs caused us all to look up at the ceiling.

"You have to go," I said to them all in a harsh whisper. "You're not safe. Mum and Nanna are here. If they were to catch you—"

"Weston? Weston dear? Who are you talking to? I thought the phone lines were still down." Mum was no longer sleeping. She stood at the top of the stairs if I was correctly judging the location of her sleep-muddled voice.

I gestured frantically to the three visitors, pointing them toward the back door where they'd come in. I didn't want Alessia—or her friends—to get hurt.

"Sorry Mum," I called out. "I was watching You Tube videos. Didn't mean to disturb you. I'll turn down the volume."

Alessia did not move, holding her ground with tears in her eyes. "I'm not leaving you. Not until you're healed. Your mother will see that I've brought Macy to help you, and—"

Both Elves dropped to the floor, screaming and clutching their heads.

Twisting to see the staircase, I spotted my worst fear come true—Mum and Nanna standing together in their high-necked ruffled nightgowns, holding hands and staring at Alessia. They chanted in unison, the volume of their voices growing, keeping pace with the intensifying howls of pain that echoed through the room. My heart rate bolted to full-speed.

"Stop it," I demanded. "Stop it right now. They've come to help."

Instead of ceasing, the chanting increased. Alessia and the male Elf now writhed on the floor in obvious agony. I pushed myself up to my good foot, hopping toward them while holding onto the sofa back.

"Mum! Nanna! Stop this now."

They continued to ignore me. Alessia continued to suffer. Her wails shredded my insides. I did the only thing I could do.

Throwing myself to the floor in her direction, I gritted my teeth against the shock of pain to my leg and crawled the rest of the way. I covered her body with mine, pulling her in close to me and wrapping my arms around her twisting, struggling limbs.

"I've got you," I murmured into her hair. "I'm here with you now."

The chanting stopped, replaced by shrieks of alarm from my mother and grandmother. "Wes—no. Get away," Mum commanded. "What are you doing? You'll make yourself ill."

I clung to Alessia all the tighter, feeling the pained tension ebb from her body in spasms as the affliction spell began to wear off. When the last seizure ended, she looked up at my face, only inches from her own, and blinked in confusion.

"Wes? Wes, what are you doing? I thought you couldn't be near me."

I smiled into her beautiful jewel-blue eyes. "Being near you is worth *everything* to me. Never doubt..." I had to stop and breathe as a wave of pain hit me. "... that I loved you."

My hold on her loosened, and I fell back to the floor as

the full misery set in. The Elven glamour that would have made a normal person sick hit me exponentially harder.

I had never felt so ill in my life, struck simultaneously with fever, chills, nausea, muscle cramps, and a headache that felt like it would shatter my head into individual brain cells.

"Wes?" Alessia scooted away from me, belatedly realizing what was happening. Her glamour was killing me.

Now the room reverberated with a new kind of cry—not of pain—of panic. My mother rushed to my side.

"Weston!"

Asher got to his feet. "What's going on? What's happening to him?"

"He's sick," Macy explained. "It's Alessia's glamour. That's what it does."

Mum and Nanna hovered over me as Alessia withdrew to a corner, obviously shell-shocked. The tortured expression on her face hurt me almost more than the physical effects of her glamour.

"Forgive me, Wes," she whispered, breaking down into sobs.

Nanna turned to yell at her. "Look what you've done, you evil, wretched girl. You're far beyond forgiveness. You're nothing but a plague upon the earth yourself. Why were you even born?"

I shook my head, fighting to speak. A hoarse whisper was all I could manage. "No. No."

I couldn't get the rest of it out—the life was draining from me like rainwater sinking into dry earth. Alessia's glamour really was as powerful as she'd said. But she hadn't meant to hurt me. I knew that. She'd been out of her mind with pain and unaware I was even next to her—until it was too late.

I didn't want her to feel guilty, though I knew she would. I wanted to tell her she *was* forgiven—in fact, there was nothing to forgive as far as I was concerned. I wanted to tell her she was worthy of living and of love.

It was my life's greatest regret that I wouldn't be around to give it to her.

27

ALESSIA

Wes's eyes closed, and his body went limp.

"You've killed him," his mother screeched.

"No," I wailed. My thoughts and emotions swirled. I felt like I was being pulled into a sucking hole in the floor. "No. It can't be. I was trying to bring him a cure."

I scrambled to my feet and turned to Macy, pleading. "Maybe it's not too late. Maybe you can do something. Asher —can you help him? See if he still has a pulse."

Turning my full Sway on the stunned Earth-wives, I said, "You will not interfere—let this healer try to help Wes."

I wasn't sure if they were warded against Sway or not, but both of them backed away and didn't try to stop Asher as he knelt beside Wes and put two fingers to his neck.

"He's still alive, but he's weak. He won't last long."

"Give him your blood," Wes's mom begged Macy.

"Please," I said, holding out my hands to her in a beseeching gesture. "I know I don't deserve your help or your sympathy, but Wes has done nothing wrong. He is a good person. All he's ever wanted is to help people. And the world needs him. I need him. We can't let him die."

Macy didn't move toward him. Instead, she stayed in place, wearing a look of profound sorrow and shaking her head.

"I'm so sorry," she croaked. "I can't. I'd love to help him, but I can't. I've lost my... ability to heal. Nic and I... last night..."

She didn't have to explain further. I knew what she was saying. She and Nic had bonded. Her blood would not save Wes. And that meant nothing could. It was over.

An icy hand gripped my heart and crushed it. The witches were right about me. My parents had been right. Dr. Schmitt had been right—I was toxic. No one could be around me without suffering. Wes was dying because he'd dared to love me.

And now I was going to watch as the only man I'd ever loved, the only man who'd ever loved *me*, died in front of me.

"Macy—go back to your people," Asher said, moving toward Wes again and putting both hands on his chest. "Run —as quickly as you can. Retrieve some blood for him from the donations we collected. Hurry."

Macy spun around and flew out the door.

"Do you think she can make it in time?" My heart flickered to life again.

Asher looked up at me, his face grim. "No. But if Wes pulls through, he'll need it later."

"If he pulls through? Is there something you can do? Can you save him?" Hope exploded inside me like fireworks all around my chest.

Asher shook his head. "I can't. Not alone. But maybe the two of us working together can."

My head jerked back, and I looked at him like he'd lost his mind. "What do you mean? How can *I* help? I hurt people— not heal them." It was the hateful truth of my life. I had just proven it beyond doubt.

"Alessia…" Asher let out a breath of exasperation. "You're the most powerful healer I've *ever* encountered, far more powerful than Wickthorne or my father. How can you be unaware of that?"

Was this a cruel joke? Was he tormenting me *now*, of all times? But his expression was deadly serious. He waited for my answer.

"My touch… it's always been poisonous. And Dr. Schmitt said…"

Wes's words suddenly came back to me. *Maybe he told you that for his own selfish reasons. I think you can control your power.*

Could he have been right? *Had* Dr. Schmitt lied to me? Had my parents been wrong all this time?

"You saw a healer as a child?" Asher asked, incredulous. "And he *didn't* tell you about your healing glamour?"

"No. I never saw a healer as a child *because* of my glamour. My parents didn't want anyone to know. They kept it a secret."

Asher shook his head, his eyes growing wider. "This is unbelievable. If they *had* taken you to a healer and been upfront about it, you would have been taught that healing glamour is a two-sided coin. The power can be used to either extreme—to do great harm *or* to give life. You should have been learning from early childhood to control the darker side of your power. You could have been healing people all along instead of hurting them."

The room seemed devoid of air. I could barely get enough oxygen to speak. "I thought… that I was born… bad."

"*No one* is born bad. You were only allowed to think so for some ignorant reason. Now get over here and help me save your boyfriend."

I moved forward but stopped again, muscles stiff with fear. It was so hard to overcome the image of myself I'd held my entire life, hard to believe my glamour could possibly be a *good* thing. That *I* could be good. I was terrified my touch would kill Wes instantly.

"I'm afraid," I admitted.

"I get it," Asher said. "I do. But are you going to let your fear stop you from doing everything you can to save the life of the guy you love? Are you going to let ignorance win?"

I drew in a deep breath and moved toward Wes, dropping to my knees beside him. "No. I'll do whatever it takes to bring him back. Tell me what to do."

"You've only been told about the dark side to your glamour," Asher said. "But there is a light inside of you. Close your eyes and search for it. That's where your healing power emanates from. Focus on your love for Wes. Love is the pathway to the light."

I followed his instructions, closing my eyes and focusing on Wes, his smile, his laugh, his incredible blue eyes, his love for books and for those beat-up, rejected horses—and for me. I thought about his kindness toward me, his willingness to forgive me for the wrongs I'd done, to dig deeper and understand *why* I was the way I was and to love me in spite of it.

As I turned my focus entirely to that love, I began to feel warm, as if the sun had emerged from behind dark clouds—not outside—but inside of me. And I saw it. A light, far in the distance, as if I was viewing the exit of a long, dark highway tunnel.

"I see it," I said, my voice shaking with excitement.

"Good. Chase it, Alessia. Catch it. Don't let it get away. That's what's going to help you save Wes. You can do this."

"Yes." As I ran toward the light in my mind, seeing it grow larger and brighter, I repeated it. "Yes! I'm standing in it now. It's beautiful."

"Now reach out," Asher instructed. "Touch Wes. Transfer the light into him. Keep focusing on it, on your love."

I opened my eyes, seeing Wes's still form on the floor in front of me but also still seeing the light somehow. I spread my hands, laying one on his head and one over his heart. Asher touched Wes as well, placing his hands on his shoulders.

Nothing in my life had ever felt like the sensations coursing through my body. The sunshine warmth that had filled me seemed to flow from my heart and mind through my shoulders, arms, and fingertips and out of me, into Wes.

"That's good. Keep it up. Don't stop," Asher said. "He's getting stronger."

"Yes, I feel him coming back." I focused even harder, concentrated on pouring my strength into Wes, giving him everything I had. If I could manage to save him, nothing else would matter.

"Okay now, start pulling back—that's a little *too* much," Asher said.

I opened my eyes. "Can I hurt him this way?"

"No. But you can deplete yourself. You have to reserve at least a bit of energy so you can recover from the procedure. Wickthorne cautioned me it's possible to give so much you can't come back from it."

Reassured I wasn't somehow overdosing Wes, I shook off Asher's warning, closing my eyes again and turning up my newfound healing power to its highest level. I was going to heal this man completely, if possible.

He would never again have to hide from the world. He'd be able to live a full life, go anywhere he wanted, do anything he wanted. I was going to *fix* him—no matter what it cost me.

Asher put a hand on my shoulder. "Alessia…"

"No." I shook my head stubbornly, refusing to stop, though I was beginning to feel weak and dizzy. "It doesn't matter if I recover. I owe it to him. I have to make up for the harm I caused. I have to—"

"You have to be there... for the rest of my life."

The quiet words hadn't come from Asher. Wes had spoken. I looked down at his face. His eyes were open, and his hand lifted to cover the one I'd placed over his heart. He patted gently.

"That's enough, princess. Stop now." His smile was weak but divine nonetheless. "Save your strength."

"Wes?" I began crying. "Are you really okay?"

He nodded and then cringed as if the motion had pained him.

"You're not okay. Hold on—I'm going to make it better." I felt very light-headed now, but I closed my eyes again, seeking the light, intending to direct the rest of my energies into him.

He squeezed my hand. "You've already given me everything I need just by coming back through that door. And I have no interest in recovering if you're not going to be there to share my life. It's okay. You've done it sweetheart. I'm going to be fine."

Opening my eyes again, I finally relaxed my glamour output. Wes smiled at me. He was alive. I'd done it. I smiled back but then slumped to the floor beside him, completely drained.

"Alessia—are you okay?" Concern colored his voice. He sat up and leaned over me, looking into my eyes.

"Yeah." I nodded. "It's just... this 'being good' thing is exhausting."

His laugh was joined by Asher's then mine.

The back door opened again, and Macy raced through it. "Am I too late?"

She stopped, taking in the sight of the two distraught witches and the three people on the floor in a fit of giggles.

"Well, I guess you don't need *this* anymore." She held up a tiny vial of nymph blood.

Mum and Nanna spoke simultaneously.

"I'll take it."

"Give it to me."

I stretched out my hand. "Thank you so much for getting back so quickly. I'll take it. Wes has recovered from my glamour sickness, but he still has his genetic immunodeficiency problem."

Macy handed me the tiny vial of nymph blood, and I pressed it into Wes's hand. "Are you ready to have a life again—a *real* life this time—with no restrictions?"

He took my offering and leaned in for a quick kiss. "As long as you're willing to share it with me... the answer is *hell yes*."

MACY

Asher injected Wes with the donated blood I'd retrieved from Sidhe Innis then he and the new couple got to work, contacting the ECDC and the American CDC and sharing information about the Plague, making plans to get a team on the ground in Peru where they'd begin administering the antidote and vaccinating people in surrounding areas.

Wes's mother and grandmother packed their bags and headed for the mainland, infuriated with him for befriending an "untrustworthy pack of Elves," in their words.

He'd made them promise to stop pursuing me and my people, but I didn't like the greedy way they'd looked at me before leaving. There was nothing to fear, really, though. Soon I'd be tucked away inside the Sgurr, far from the reach of human—and witch—hands.

And Lad and Wickthorne would soon be on their way back to Mississippi with the blood we'd collected to ensure supplies of the cure wouldn't run out. The queen had given her word she'd release them as soon as I returned.

I'd given *my* word to uphold my end of the bargain as sad

as the prospect of an eternity in Sidhe Innis without Nic made me.

"What will you do now?" Alessia asked as I prepared to leave. "Find Nic and tell him the good news?"

I shook my head, battling tears. "No. Could you do that part? I know he'll be relieved. He worked so hard for this day to come. I promised to return to the nymph sanctuary... and stay there."

"I wish there was a way for the two of you to be together —I truly do." She took Wes's hand, leaning her head against his shoulder. "I didn't understand before about love. Now I do. I want that for Nic. You, too."

I nodded, trying to work up a smile. "Me, too. It's just not meant to be, I guess."

Leaving the farmhouse, I headed in the direction of the portal, bidding farewell to the outside world. The sun was rising, turning the early spring landscape into a glowing canvas of pink and orange.

The cry of a seabird flying overhead and out to sea brought a wistful smile to my face. I wanted nothing more than to fly across that deep blue water myself. To Nic.

Instead, I swallowed my tears and slipped into the cave, feeling my heart shut down and go into hibernation as the darkness closed around me.

* * *

I WOKE LATER in the day in my room at Mae's house, sat up and stretched, inhaling the scents of brewing tea and baking bread.

Mae had not been at home when I'd returned, which was just as well. I didn't think I could have stood to talk about everything that had happened. I needed some time to wrap my mind around my new reality. Today I'd have to set about finding some sort of employment here and start looking for my own place to live. I had to start my new life.

When I went downstairs, Mae smiled at me brightly.

"Good morning, dear. Did you sleep well?"

I nodded, yawned, and sat at the kitchen table. "Yes, thank you. I was beat. How was your night?"

She crooked a cryptic smile. "Very interesting."

"Really?" I studied her more closely now. Her smile hadn't faded, and she was brimming with energy. "What did you do? Did you have a date?"

She laughed out loud. "Mercy, no. That'll be the day. I went... visiting." Her eyes skated over me. "Is that what you're going to wear?"

I glanced down at today's pixie dress selection, which was just as embarrassingly skimpy and sparkly as every other item in my closet. "Yeeees." I dragged the word out. "Why? Is there something wrong with the way I look?"

"Oh no. You look lovely. I just thought you might want to dress up a bit *more* for your audience with the queen."

"With the queen?"

What did she want now? She'd already secured my lifetime residency in this place and sold me off to her buddy, Lord Hulder.

I didn't really want to see her face today—or for a *long* time to come. In fact, I'd gone straight to Mae's house last night, sending word with one of the Queensguard I'd returned so Lad and Wickthorne could get on their way with the blood donations.

"Wait—she didn't change her mind and keep the Elves here, did she?" I asked Mae.

"Oh no, dear. They left early this morning. She wants to see you about something else."

My heart thumped a few anxious beats. "Wonderful. She

probably wants to tell me all about the *exciting* wedding plans."

"Well, you'll just have to go see her and find out, won't you?" Again, Mae's mood was exceptionally cheerful.

"What's going on? Do you know something?"

She smiled and shrugged. "I'm just a servant. What could I possibly know?"

When I finished eating—and changing into an even *more* sparkly ensemble—I trudged up the path to the palace. Guards escorted me from the main entrance to the throne room where the queen waited.

"Come forward, child," she said when they'd left the room.

Only the two of us were here now, which was... different. I crossed the room toward her, trying to read her expression. Normally, her face was unreadable, but *she* was also different today. The way she was looking at me had changed.

When I came to a stop just in front of her, she lifted something from her lap and offered it to me. It was a book, small with a brown leather cover and ties to hold it closed.

I took it, thoroughly confused. "What is this?"

"It's a diary, a journal. It belonged to your mother. I never knew of its existence until last night."

Untying the leather laces, I opened the book. A childish scrawl covered the first page. Turning pages, I found the writing changing, becoming smaller, neater. The last section of the book was filled with long entries and sketches of a handsome young man. He had to be Uric, the soldier Fallon had loved.

"Where did you get this?" And she'd said she hadn't known of its existence until last night. Why *should* she have known of its existence at all? Something wasn't adding up.

"Mae brought it to me. I stayed up most of the night reading it."

"Okay..." I waited for an explanation.

"Remember when you asked me about the symbol you saw on the book in the store window? The one Fallon drew on her letter to you?"

"Yes. The symbol for Sidhe Innis."

"The symbol does not represent our domain... it is a family crest." She paused. "The crest of the ruling family in Sidhe Innis. After exhausting all efforts to find Fallon, I placed that book with the woman who runs the book shop in Mallaig. She is a friend to our people. The book was displayed as a signal to Fallon that should she ever want to return to her home, she was welcome here. It never occurred to me the person who would receive the signal and respond to it would not be my daughter... but my granddaughter."

Her gaze on me stayed steady, expectant.

"Your... daughter." I could hardly breathe as her words sank in.

"Yes. You are my granddaughter, Macy. I never knew about you, obviously. But Fallon did." She gestured to the diary in my hands. "She loved you very much. She loved... your father, too."

I blinked. Blinked again. "Why are you telling me this now?"

"I was planning to tell you about your family line as soon as the Elves departed, and I knew your intentions toward your people were true. But the reason I'm telling you now about your mother is... I don't want to see you end up like her."

"You mean as a rebel? A runaway? You know I won't leave —I promised you—"

"No. I mean I don't want you to be unhappy like she was. Reading my child's words last night tore my heart apart. I miss her every day, but I felt the pain of her absence more last night than I have in years. Reading about her hopes and dreams… and disappointments… it was almost like having her here with me again."

She got up and paced in front of the huge glassed-in wall, the reflected colors of the blooms outside it moving over her like a slowly spinning color wheel.

"I thought I was doing the best thing for her, arranging the marriage to Lord Hulder. He's a wealthy man from a good family line. She would never have wanted for anything, and I believe Lord Hulder would have treated her well."

She paused and looked at me. "I never asked her what *she* wanted. I never asked what was in her heart because at the time I thought it didn't matter. I thought her feelings would change as they do for many fickle young girls. But reading her journal entries, I was able to see into her heart and mind, and I realized I was wrong to force her to leave the young man she loved—your father Uric."

Coming to stand just in front of me, the queen went on. "Unfortunately, that realization has come much too late. Chances are, I will never see my daughter again, never have the chance to apologize and tell her how much I love her, to get to know her as a woman and not just a child. She is not here. She may not even be living still."

She reached for my hand, pulling it in between her two palms.

"But you *are*. I want to know you, not as a subject, but as a young woman. As my granddaughter. I want to learn about your life and the person you've become and find out how you're like your mother—and how you're different. That won't happen if I force you to marry Lord Hulder. You might not run away, as Fallon did, but your heart would never be open to me as a grandmother… or a friend. I would only ever be the person who took you away from the man you love and from the family who raised you."

Her shocking change of heart had me reeling. It was hard to keep up. "What are you saying exactly?"

"I'm saying you are free to go... if that is what you wish. But it is my hope you will choose to return—to visit and get to know your people and family—not to live. We still cannot welcome an Elf into our midst, you understand. But I will not stop you from following your heart and going to him, making a life with him."

I didn't know what to say. I was stunned. I was overwhelmed. I was *happy*. It was like my spirit took flight, soaring out of my body and around the multi-colored dome.

"Thank you. I... I *do* want to know you. I want to know everything about my mother and her people and this place. But if it's okay, I want to go and find Nic first. I *will* come back. I promise."

Behind me I heard the tall, golden doors open, and my grandmother smiled.

"I look forward to your return."

* * *

THE FIRST THING I did when I reached the mainland was call my parents.

"Macy. Macy, where are you sweetheart?" Mom said. "We haven't heard from you in several days. We were beginning to think something was wrong."

"No. Nothing's wrong. In fact, everything is very, very good."

"Really?" She sounded super interested now. "What's happening? Did you love Nic's family?"

"Actually, I found *my* family—my biological one. Not my birth mother but some other family members."

"Oh my goodness, what a surprise," she said. "And how wonderful. What are they like?"

"I'll tell you all about it. But I want to hear about you guys. How are you? How's Lily?"

"Well… hold on a minute. I'll let her tell you. Lily… Lily honey. Come here. Macy's on the phone."

A minute later, I heard my sister's voice. "Macy, hi! How are you? Are you and Nic in Italy?"

"Not yet. Well, he's there, and I'm about to join him. How are *you* doing? That's the important question. Any more feeling in your legs?"

She giggled. "Not more. *All.* Macy… I'm walking."

"What? Are you kidding me?"

"No. Today I went all day with no wheelchair at all."

My heart swelled with relief and gratitude. The transfusion of my blood had worked. "That's fantastic, Lil. And as it turns out… very good timing."

"Why? What do you mean?"

"Well, I'm going to need someone to walk down the aisle in front of me very soon. As in Maid. Of. Honor."

Her squeal caused me to hold the phone away from my ear. "When? How soon?" she demanded.

"Very. Now put Mom back on the phone, okay? I'll be sending you all tickets to Tuscany for the wedding, but first… I need to borrow her credit card number so I can get *myself* there."

Mom and I exchanged a bit more information, then I arranged for a flight from Edinburgh, Scotland to Bologna, Italy as well as train and ferry tickets to take me the rest of the way to Corsica.

Before I left Mallaig, I made one last stop. The tinkling of the bell over the shop's door brought the stocky black-haired shopkeeper out from the back storeroom. She stopped, gaping in disbelief when she saw me.

"You?"

I smiled. "Yes. Me. Thank you for your... *assistance* in finding my family."

She continued to stare as I advanced into the shop. Reaching into my bag, I withdrew the book she'd sold me.

"I'd like to return this item," I told her, laying it on the counter. "But I don't need my money back. I'd just like to make a request."

She moved behind the register, still eying me cautiously. "And what would that be?"

"Put it back on display in the front window. Someone else might come along someday who needs to see it."

"Verra well."

She nodded slowly as I backed away from the counter and made my way to the exit. I opened the door but turned back before leaving.

"I appreciate it... and so does Queen Ragan."

And then I stepped outside to the pavement, nearly skipping as I headed for home.

NIC

One month later

The family winery in Chianti had always been my favorite place, but it had never looked so beautiful. Or hosted such a joyous occasion.

A glow of euphoria overtook me as I surveyed the scene. Wine crates were stacked and overflowing with red poppies. An array of white-clothed outdoor tables featured flowers arranged in old wine bottles.

Candle lanterns hung from all the trees around the house and the barns and even lined the long drive from the street up to the winery. The doors to the main wine cellar stood open, warm light pouring out in an invitation for guests to explore, and later, to dance there.

Romigi and Teo had outdone themselves with the food and decorations—although they'd had a bit of help in that last department from my twin, Estelle. She'd started planning the day Macy returned to the castle on Corsica and gave me my life back.

That—was hands down the happiest day of my life—so far at least. Only this one might outdo it.

I'd been sitting in Papà's office with him, discussing the phone call I'd had from Alessia, who'd shocked me by telling me she was working with the Light Court healers and a human man from the European Centers for Disease Control to distribute the Plague cure. One of the servants knocked at the door and spoke mind to mind to Papà.

A huge grin had spread across my father's face.

"This discussion will have to wait," he told me. "Something more important has come up."

I'd frowned in irritation. "I'm telling you about the salvation of the human race. *What* could be more important than that?"

He stood and went to the office door, apparently leaving. "Come with me and find out."

The two of us had stalked toward the castle's front entrance, him smiling, me fuming. Nothing could make me *happy* anymore, not after losing Macy, but at least the news I'd been sharing with him confirmed the sacrifice we'd made was not all for naught. I simply was not interested in whatever "surprise" he had for me.

We'd entered the foyer, where two guards stood, blocking the open front doors. Obviously we had a visitor. I stopped walking. There wasn't a single person I wanted to see. Papà stopped and turned back.

"Nicolo, are you not coming?"

And then I heard it. A small voice from outside.

"Nicolo? He's here? Nic, is that you?"

I ran toward the doors and nearly shoved the guards aside.

Macy.

There she stood, the most beautiful sight I'd ever seen in her jeans and sweater, her old backpack slung across one shoulder. She dropped it as I swept her off her feet and swung her around.

"Piccola! How are you here? How is this possible?"

She didn't get the chance to answer as I covered her mouth and face with kisses, my heart coming back to life and bursting with joy. Finally, she laughed.

"My grandmother had a change of heart."

"Your grandmother?"

"Queen Ragan."

My jaw dropped, and then I laughed as well. "You know what this means, of course."

Macy shook her head, her sea-green eyes dancing with happiness and love. "No, what?"

"We're going to have a royal wedding."

And I supposed, that's what today's event was, though we'd opted to keep the guest list intimate—a mere three hundred—and I'd insisted on marrying Macy here instead of at the castle.

Mama wasn't thrilled about the "rustic" location of the ceremony and celebration, but my parents were both here, as were all of Macy's family and a few of her friends from home and from her gymnastics team—of which she was now a member once more.

It was the balmiest April evening anyone could remember in Tuscany, something Macy *may* or may not have had something to do with.

I had not seen her yet today, in keeping with tradition, and though it was only around five o'clock, the day had felt unbearably long without her.

"I just saw the bride," Estelle whisper-squealed as she came to stand beside me. "You are going to pass *out* when you get a look at her in that dress."

"I might pass out before then from nerves," I muttered back to her.

The guests, including Anders, Nox, and their bandmates

from The Hidden, were already seated in rows of chairs that had been set up on the hilltop overlooking the vineyards below. It was the spot where I'd first kissed Macy. And now, it would be the location of our first kiss as husband and wife.

If the ceremony ever began. My foot tapped. My fingers fidgeted behind my back where I'd clasped my hands. I was antsy to see my bond-mate and make this thing official.

Estelle and I stood in front of a vine-covered, flower studded arbor across from Macy's little sister Lily, who hadn't stopped beaming since she'd emerged from her family's rental car a few days ago. She wiggled with excitement, going up on tiptoe every now and again to look the crowd over.

"There are *so* many famous people here," she whispered.

I winked at her, amused at her giddy reaction to the assortment of Dark Elves in attendance. Yes, they were here, too.

Though the Ancient Court wasn't in full agreement with my family's attitude toward the human race, they'd extended the olive branch to my father after their plan to obliterate the humans with a catastrophic plague had mysteriously failed.

We were back in alliance with the other leaders, and the Elves were back to an uneasy co-existence with the planet's most populous race, the humans, obliged to keep our true identities hidden.

I had no doubt they'd try again someday, but next time, I'd be ready for them. My glamour would let me know the deepest desires of the other leaders, and if they should veer toward world domination and human extinction in the future, I'd be in a position to do something about it.

As the music that signaled the approach of my bride began, I had no idea if the smiles on their faces were genuine or feigned... but it didn't matter. All that mattered to me was the small figure in white coming into view at the end of the aisle. My heart danced in my chest as my cheeks pulled tight with an insuppressible smile of my own.

Macy was too beautiful for words. Her long hair was pulled up, a few tendrils loose and curling around her pretty face. The dress Estelle had helped her find was perfect for her tiny, strong figure, floating elegantly around her as she moved down the aisle, her hand tucked inside her father's elbow. But my eyes were drawn to her face. It glowed with happiness, her cheeks flushed, her eyes bright and shining.

No doubt my eyes would have seemed on the shiny side as well, if anyone were capable of looking away from my bride to see them. Tears brimmed, and my throat ached with emotion. Unable to stop myself, I mouthed the words, "I love you," to Macy as she approached.

She laughed, smiling even wider and blinking hard to stem the tears from falling. When she reached me and her father took his seat, I grasped her shaking hand and squeezed it tightly.

This was it—the moment I'd longed for and at times, believed would never come. I was determined not to forget a moment of it, from the look in her eyes, to the words of the priest, to the most important vow I'd ever make... to love her and be with her until the sun no longer rose and set.

Of course when the time came and she kissed me, all those other things fell away. As the guests applauded and cheered, we pulled apart enough to look into each other's eyes.

"You know, your glamour is going to be wasted on me from now on," she said, keeping her voice low so none of the humans present could overhear.

I looked down into her mischievous light green eyes. "How so?"

"My greatest desire has just been fulfilled—for eternity."

I smiled and bent to kiss her once more. "So has mine, piccola. Because my eternity belongs to you."

THE END

AFTERWORD

Thank you so much for reading my books, especially Hidden Hero, Book 3 of the Ancient Court Trilogy (Hidden Saga, Book 9.) I really hope you enjoyed it. If you did, please consider leaving a review at the retailer where you purchased it, and if your fingers aren't too tired, at Goodreads, too. Just a few words is all it takes, and reviews help other readers find great books!

This is the conclusion of the Hidden Saga, but don't worry— there *will* be new stories from the Hidden world from time to time. I'm working on something that goes back to the original POV in the series (Ryann's) that I think you will love, and I have a few other side stories cooked up as well. Stay tuned!

To make sure you never miss a release from the Hidden world and you're the first to know of other Amy Patrick books, sign up for my newsletter. You'll only receive notifications when new titles are available and when my books go on super-sale. I will never share your contact information with others. You can also follow me on Bookbub to be notified of my new releases.

I love to chat with my readers! Follow me on Twitter @AmyPatrickBooks and visit my website at www.amypatrickbooks.com. I'm on Instagram at least once a day, and I have lots of fun pics from the Hidden world on Pinterest. You can also connect with me on Facebook, where I hang out the most.

If you haven't read the earlier books in the Hidden Saga, beginning with HIDDEN DEEP, they give you the chance to delve into the Hidden world in America, from the backwoods of rural Mississippi to the glittering cities of Los Angeles and New York. I think you'll enjoy them!

ACKNOWLEDGMENTS

This journey into the Hidden world has been one of the greatest in my life. Of course, I did not travel the path alone, and I am so grateful for those who've been with me and supported me along the way.

First, love and eternal thanks to my Hidden honeys, the best readers in the world. You make all the hours, days, weeks, months, and years of work worth every minute.

Thank you to my fantastic editor Judy Roth and to Cover Your Dreams for never failing me even once.

Thank you to my husband John, who always believes in me and expects the best, and to my incredible kids Jack and Sean, who make me laugh every day and would be the ultimate book boyfriends if they were fictional teens.

To my lifelong best friend Chelle, who loves me and has my back no matter what, to Margie for being a cheerleader and true friend, and to the Westmoreland Farmgirls, who are always ready to read and celebrate.

A big shout-out to Deb Sheehan, who advised me on life as a microbiologist and public health contract worker for this book. Any inaccuracy and artistic license is my own. I still owe you a pizza!

I would be exactly nowhere without my incredibly talented, generous, and kind critique partner McCall Hoyle. Love and thanks to the rest of the fabulous GH Dreamweavers for the friendship, loyalty, honesty, and support, and to my Lucky 13 and Savvy 7 sisters for getting me off to a running start, for all the good advice, and continuing support. Friends are everything in the writing business and in life!

I'll wrap this up by thanking my first family— my mom who always told me I could, my loving dad (who's quite a storyteller himself,) my funny and loyal brother Richard, and Bethany, the best sister anyone's ever had. Thank you to my precious in-laws for all the love and encouragement over the years and to the rest of my friends and family for just making life good. I love you, and I am blessed.

ABOUT THE AUTHOR

Amy Patrick grew up in Mississippi (with a few years in Texas thrown in for spicy flavor) and has lived in six states, including Rhode Island, where she now lives with her husband and two sons.

She's been a professional singer, a DJ, a voiceover artist, and a TV news anchor/reporter where she wrote about true crime, medical anomalies, and mayhem. Then she retired to make up her own stories full-time. Hers have a lot more kissing.

A note from Amy: I love to hear from my readers! Feel free to contact me on Instagram, Twitter, and my Facebook page (where I hang out the most and respond to every comment.) And be sure to sign up for my newsletter here and follow me on Bookbub so you'll be the first to hear the latest news from the Hidden world as well as other new books I have in the works!

www.amypatrickbooks.com
amypatrickbooks@yahoo.com